Fade to White

Also by Wendy Clinch

Double Black

Fade to White

Wendy Clinch

MINOTAUR BOOKS

A Thomas Dunne Book
New York

This is a work of fiction. All of the characters, organizations, and events portrayed in this novel are either products of the author's imagination or are used fictitiously.

A THOMAS DUNNE BOOK FOR MINOTAUR BOOKS.
An imprint of St. Martin's Publishing Group.

FADE TO WHITE. Copyright © 2010 by Wendy Clinch. All rights reserved. Printed in the United States of America. For information, address St. Martin's Press, 175 Fifth Avenue, New York, N.Y. 10010.

www.thomasdunnebooks.com
www.minotaurbooks.com

Library of Congress Cataloging-in-Publication Data

Clinch, Wendy.
Fade to white / Wendy Clinch.—1st ed.
p. cm.
ISBN 978-0-312-59327-8
1. Women skiers—Fiction. 2. Murder—Investigation—Fiction.
3. Vermont—Fiction. I. Title.
PS3603.L545F33 2011
813'.6—dc22

2010037496

First Edition: January 2011

10 9 8 7 6 5 4 3 2 1

For Jon and Emily

ACKNOWLEDGMENTS

So many people have helped me along the way that it's hard to single out a handful. All the same, this book wouldn't be complete without a million thanks to those without whom it wouldn't even be here.

To my wonderful husband, Jon Clinch, whose unfailing support and love I depend on every minute of every day.

To the fantastic women of TheSkiDiva.com, whose enthusiasm and joy make my own love for the sport seem almost halfhearted.

To the great team at Minotaur, who have brought both of the Ski Diva mysteries to fruition.

And to the lovely people of my little Vermont ski town, who have made this flatlander feel almost like a native.

Fade to White

ONE

Harper Stone was a whole lot smaller than he looked in the movies, but his ego made up for it. He was a whole lot older, too, but then again he'd made his best pictures a long while back. His trademark combination of lounge-lizard panache and off-hand gunplay had gone pretty well out of fashion, or else he wouldn't have been freezing his butt on this chairlift, praying for snow, showing off his famous square white teeth for a pickup camera crew out of Albany. Slumming on a Vermont ski slope in a lousy mouthwash commercial.

What a morning!

The sky was lake blue and well deep, without a cloud anywhere. New England didn't get these gorgeous bluebird days very often, and Stacey Curtis didn't want to waste a second of it. She didn't even stop at Judge Roy Beans for coffee, but went straight to the mountain to make sure she got on the very first chair.

A hand-lettered sign in the base lodge threw a monkey wrench into things, though. The sign said that the Northside chair, the one that accessed the very best trails at Spruce Peak, was closed until further notice. Just that. No explanation. It wasn't a short-term wind hold, that was for sure. Not with this glorious, calm, blue weather. So she figured it must be something mechanical. She shook her head and told herself that if Richie Paxton would take better care of the place these things wouldn't happen. With his wife locked up for murdering his brother, however, Richie was too busy chasing every woman in town to take care of the mountain his family owned. So much for preventive maintenance.

There was an upside, though. If nobody could ride the Northside chair, that meant nobody could ski the Northside—except whatever hardy souls felt like trekking a half-mile through the woods from the top of the main lift. A group that Stacey figured would probably include nobody but herself.

She booted up, stashed her bag under a table, and headed out the door. She'd left her skis over by the lift so as not to have to walk forever in her boots, and as she clomped toward them she lifted her goggles, threw her head back, and took in that bright cloudless sky. Yep: It was the color of a bluebird all right—if they had bluebirds around here, which she didn't know. Underneath that sky she felt small and happy and dizzy and just a little bit cold, but she knew she'd warm up once she got to the top of the lift and began skating through the woods and along the fire trails over to the Northside.

She caught the first chair and kept an eye out for Chip Walsh as she rode up. Still, she saw only one red Ski Patrol jacket, and that was on a boarder. Not one of the younger guys, by the look of him, but some older dude who'd probably shifted from skiing to riding later in life. Good for him. She caught sight of him at the top of the Blowdown glades, slipping under the rope to check out the run before they let in the paying customers. *Now that right there*, Stacey told herself, *is the only reason in the whole world to be on the Patrol.* All the first-aid drills and all the practice with the rescue toboggans and all the other nonsense that Chip complained about—including the reckless, smart-ass college kids up from Connecticut, only five or six years younger than Stacey and Chip themselves but a world apart—all of that might just be worth the chance to put down first tracks anywhere you wanted. And call it work.

She slid off the lift, put her mittens through the straps on her poles, and took off into the woods. She was puffing pretty hard before she'd made it halfway to the Northside, but it was all good. She had let Chip buy her dinner last night at Maison Maurice, the nicest place in town—or at least the one with the highest aspirations—and she figured that this was as good a way as any to work off a dessert that she hadn't entirely needed. She emerged from the tree line into an open slope and skidded down below the stopped lift to catch her breath for a minute. The sky looked even bluer up here, where there was nothing but white snow and green trees for contrast. An absolutely perfect day, no question about it. Until she got about halfway down, and discovered why the lift was stopped.

It was bad enough that all these people were shooting some kind of video on a run she'd claimed as her own personal territory, right in the middle of the most brilliant morning on record. It was worse that that horrible Richie Paxton was glad-handing around the periphery of the crowd with that redheaded girlfriend of his, acting like he owned the place when the better part of it still belonged to his father. It was worse yet that they had all kinds of lights and reflectors and God knew what else set up on poles and standards and booms as if this glorious morning needed any help. And it was even worse that some old gray-haired guy in a long black leather coat far too urban for this Vermont morning was stalking around hollering at everybody through a bullhorn like some kind of Hollywood big shot.

Stacey could have tolerated all that. She could have waved at the crowd and skied right on by, found her way down to the bottom of the main lift, and kept doing it all morning long if not for one thing—a thing that happened to be wearing a garish yellow Columbia shell with black patches on the shoulders, topped by a long fleece hat with multicolored dinosaur spikes running the length of its spine. The kind of ski gear that went out of fashion with disco, but that certain individuals might still consider cool in a kind of retro way. The way that young men at exclusive golf clubs still wore the madras jackets and grass-green pants favored by the older crowd, either mocking them or fitting right in with them or more likely not knowing exactly which attitude they meant to adopt. Usually whichever one did them the most good at the time. That kind of young men.

Brian Russell's kind.

Brian, her ex-fiancé.

Brian, who'd cheated on her back in Boston.

Brian, right here on her own personal ski slope, wearing that barf-yellow coat and that stupid dinosaur hat as though they were billboards advertising his crappy judgment.

He'd worn the same stuff on the four or five days she'd gotten him on a mountain, before their relationship had fallen apart. She didn't know where he'd gotten it. In his world, a garish yellow coat and a hat that made you look like Barney were probably the sort of thing you inherited from Father. Things you kept in mothballs in a trunk somewhere, along with the silver and the stock certificates and the keys to the Bentley.

Just the sight of him spoiled her rhythm. It was as if she had been skiing with some kind of smooth and swoopy music playing in her head—an old Beach Boys song, maybe, or something cool and swinging like Frank Sinatra or Tony Bennett—and the station had suddenly been switched not just to music she didn't like but to something much worse. Rush Limbaugh. Howard Stern. Or maybe an all-news station, just in time for a forecast of some very bad weather.

TWO

The ex-movie star fished in his pocket for a cigarette. He found one and jammed it between his teeth and held a match to it, squinting from the corner of his eye at the pretty girl who occupied the other side of the chair. She was pressed into the farthest corner with her head down, hugging herself against the cold. She coughed at the smell of smoke but he didn't care. He blew smoke, sniffed, and looked at the sky, then spoke to the cameraman, a little bearded guy who hovered at his elbow on a cherry picker stenciled with the words RUTLAND ELECTRIC. "I don't get it," he said. "Can't they add a little goddamned snow in post production?"

"Not on this budget they can't."

"Come on."

"Honest. And you know what the problem is? I think the problem is they spent everything they had on you." The cameraman rapped his knuckles on the big fiberglass bucket where he stood, making it echo. "You and this crane, maybe."

"That's no crane. That's a goddamned cherry picker on loan from the electric company."

"See what I mean?"

"I know a crane when I see one."

"I'll bet you do."

"I've worked around my share of cranes."

"I know."

"You should have seen the rig that Marty DeNovo used on *Murder Town*. For the rooftop scenes? Now *that* was a crane." Stone paused and examined the cigarette. "He had it custom built by the Ferrari brothers. I kid you not."

"I'll bet it was something."

The pretty girl stuck her nose farther into her jacket and squeezed her eyes shut.

"It was something, all right." Stone drew on the cigarette, gave it a disgusted look, and squashed it out on the safety bar.

"Now look what you've done," said the cameraman from his fiberglass bucket. "We're going to have to clean that up before we shoot."

"We might see the Second Coming before we shoot."

"Still." The cameraman looked through his eyepiece.

"Is it in the shot?"

"Of course it's in the shot."

"Damn," said Stone. He shifted his weight and rummaged around in the chair. "What happened to that mouthwash, anyhow?" He found the bottle stuck halfway under his leg, hoisted it like a prize, and said to anybody who was listening, "Who's got a rag?"

The cameraman produced one and Stone cracked open the mouthwash and soaked it. "There," he said, rubbing at the safety bar. "I figure that crap ought to be good for something." He tossed the rag into the fiberglass bucket—two points—and gave the cameraman a look that was supposed to pass for mischievous but was actually just kind of creepy. "Hey," he said, "I'm not union. So don't tell."

"I wouldn't dream of it."

• • •

"If I'd known the new guy was coming," said the creative director to her assistant, "I'd have skipped this junket altogether." She kicked at the snow and dug her hands deeper into her pockets. "I can think of about a million ways to get a week in Vermont without spending the whole time with *Brian*."

"I'd pay good money for it," said the assistant.

"People do."

The creative director was an old pro named Karen Pruitt, who'd come up through the ranks with a T-square in one hand and a Sharpie in the other. Her assistant, Evan Babcock, was a bright-eyed recruit fresh out of the Rhode Island School of Design. He had a lot to learn, starting with the basic principle that you didn't take any creative input from the sales side of the agency, not even if the sales guy in question had a high-toned title like Vice President/Account Supervisor. *Especially* if he had a high-toned title like Vice President/Account Supervisor. *Most* especially if he was an idiot like Brian Russell.

Brian didn't like the actress that Karen and Evan had cast to sit beside the ex-movie star on the chairlift, and he'd been vocal about getting her fired. He'd begun by complaining that since she was a pale blonde she'd blend right in with the snow, which everybody knew was ridiculous. Then he'd switched tactics and said that the client didn't like the idea of using a Nordic-looking girl in this setting—too clichéd—but that hadn't held water either. In the end he'd tried claiming that there was a line somewhere in Harper Stone's contract that gave him *approval* rights over any actor or actress who might appear in a shot with him and that Stone's people didn't like the girl, but even though there was plenty of strange stuff in the contract (dietary guidelines, SPF requirements for outdoor shoots, clauses regarding the use of his own personal stunt double, and a complete list of acceptable Pantone colors for use in clothing and props and other surfaces that might otherwise contrast poorly with his skin tone), there was nothing that gave Stone leverage over the hiring of any particular talent. Karen had figured that Brian was just bullshitting, testing the limits, throwing the weight of his title around, and she wasn't having any of it. Vice President/Account Supervisor or not, he was still the new guy, and the sooner a new guy learned his place, the better.

THREE

Darkness came early in the valley, and the sky was too full of stars to offer any promise of snow. Whatever warmth there was had vanished with the light, leaving the little mountain town exposed to what for all intents and purposes was the naked blackness of outer space. Cartwheeling stars, utter cold, and down here on the earth a steady wind to make it even worse. Stacey cracked open the rear door at the Broken Binding and looked out into the darkness. Back at the bar the après-ski crowd had dwindled to nothing and the suppertime crowd hadn't arrived yet, so the pressure was off for a little while. She shivered, shut the door, and went back down the hall to the walk-in cooler to grab a case of Magic Hat and warm up a little.

The restaurant was a long, low-slung place spread out along the main drag from Connecticut, just at the edge of town. Like every other ski-town eatery in the Green Mountain State, it had a past. It had gone up in the sixties with barnboard paneling everywhere and a moose head mounted over the fireplace, and it was called the Broken Binding until a group of German investors arrived and gutted it and jammed it with corny Bavarian décor and rechristened it the Edelweiss. That didn't last, and when the deutschmark went into a slump against the dollar for just a little bit too long the bikers moved in to destroy whatever progress the Prussians had made. The bloom, in other words, was off the Edelweiss. Locals who knew what they were talking about shortened the place's name to the 'Weiss and pronounced it with a V and stayed away, until one winter night when a snowplow finally took the sign down and nobody even noticed.

Now the old Binding was back, thanks to an infusion of cash and kindness from a retired investment banker named Pete Hardwick, the finest export that New York had sent to Vermont in a long time. The look of the place passed for retro these days although the barnboard paneling was new, and even the original moose head—discovered in an attic crawl space stinking of beer, cigarette smoke, and a pungent old hint of sauerbraten—had been restored to a place of honor above the mantel.

The Binding was Stacey's home away from home away from home. She'd started out life in Boston, and she might have stayed there forever if Brian hadn't cheated on her and either spoiled everything or just clarified it. She was beginning to think the latter. That was all right. She'd caught him in the act and headed for the mountains in her beat-up old Subaru, and that was the end of that. It was also the beginning.

To tell the truth, although she'd rented a decent room from Sheriff Guy Ramsey and his wife, Megan, and it was comfortable enough, it came with kitchen and laundry privileges and all that, right now she pretty much considered the mountain itself her home. Good old Spruce Peak. She spent every minute there that she could. Spruce was a nice family place that still had some size and challenge to it, nestled up against a little Green Mountain town that fit about halfway along the scale between picturesque and bedraggled. A few too many gas stations for its own good, and no place decent to buy groceries, but under a blanket of snow it looked like a regular winter wonderland.

Which was the problem right now. There wasn't any snow. At least there wasn't anything fresh.

It was only the last week of February, and the thermometer was stuck at the bottom of the deep freeze, so the season was anything but over. Yet the snowbanks were retreating inch by inch and the roads were filthy and the whole town just looked sad. Even the trails on the mountain were showing signs of having endured a couple of weeks without anything fresh. The snow guns and the groomers could do only so much. In the distance, beyond the town and up on the mountain that jutted black against the starry sky, Stacey could see the groomers churning their way over the ski runs. She wondered how closely their pattern tonight matched their patterns from the night before and the night before that—in other words, if they just went over and over the same ground in the same pattern, the way obsessives scoured the same mental territory without ever getting anywhere. The way that everybody in the bar for après-ski had chewed over the need for a good snowfall, and the way that the supper crowd would do the same thing.

She guessed it was kind of silly for everybody to be so obsessed, but winter didn't last forever. The ski season was short. She'd gotten in more days this year than ever before, thanks to having set aside just about everything else in her life, but if you'd come up here for a long weekend from New York or Connecticut or Massachusetts or wherever, you just didn't have that luxury.

Plus if you'd come up to shoot a mouthwash commercial with a nice New England snowfall happening in the background, your clock was seriously running. Nobody from the commercial crew had been into the Binding yet, not that she knew of, but there was plenty of talk about them just the same. A Hollywood presence like Harper Stone didn't pass through a little town like this without making an impression, even if he was a little too old to register all that much with Stacey.

Tina Montero—as much a fixture of the Broken Binding as that smelly moose head and every bit as hard to impress—blushed like a schoolgirl at the mention of the actor's name.

"Let's just say I've always carried a torch for that one," she said, raising her chardonnay. It was her second or third, and she was pretty much the only customer left in the bar after the après-ski rush had faded, but who was counting?

Jack the bartender was counting, that's who—but only for commercial reasons. "Harper Stone," he said, leaning back and crossing his arms and softly chuckling. "In his day, that guy was the best."

"*In his day*," Tina scoffed.

"Hey," said Jack, smoothing back his gray pompadour, "his day and my day pretty much coincided."

Tina puffed herself up like a chicken. "I, for one, think he's still got it."

"Oh," said Jack. "Like I don't. Like I don't still have it."

"All right, Jack. You win." She sniffed and drank.

He smiled, thinking. "You remember *Lights Out*? That elevator scene? With the cables?"

"I do."

"How they did that stuff I'll never know. That guy must have been made of iron. Incredible."

"And how about *Murder Town*?"

Stacey pushed open the kitchen door with her butt, and backed in carrying the case of Magic Hat.

"*Murder Town*?" Jack marveled. "Oh, my God. I must have seen that one a million times."

"Did *Murder Town* come before *Afraid of the Dark*, or after?"

Stacey slid the case onto the back bar.

"Before," said Jack. "I'm pretty sure it was before."

"That's right." Tina tapped her glass with a fingertip. "He was still married to Melissa Marlow then. What a mistake *that* was. Like oil and water, those two."

Stacey looked at Jack and Tina as if she'd just stumbled into a debate between a couple of half-nutty geriatrics in the rest home.

"What's the matter?" he said. "Have you no respect for Hollywood royalty?"

"Ahh," said Stacey. "I get it now. That Rock What's-His-Name guy."

"Stone."

"No. It's not Rock Stone. That'd be sillier than the name he's got."

Tina didn't even look over to see that Stacey was just kidding. She hung her head in frustration, and Jack filled up her glass again.

FOUR

Brian came in later on, wearing something other than that yellow coat—but even without the coat he was still Brian. There was no getting around that. He was always going to be Brian.

He and a handful of other people from the TV crew stamped their feet off in the doorway, hung their coats on the pegs in the foyer, and stepped down into the bar. Brian had the air of a person evaluating something that wasn't quite living up to his expectations. That was him all over. Stacey polished a couple of wineglasses and watched him, trying not to draw attention to herself. Wondering if he'd seen her car out front. Wondering if he'd come all this way just to see her. Wondering how on earth he'd gone from getting that law degree to working for an ad agency or a film crew or whatever this was. Wondering if she could play sick and ask for the night off and get out of there, pronto, before they got settled in.

Unfortunately, nobody was on tonight except Jack, and Pete Hardwick wouldn't be in to count the money and make up a deposit until closing time, so she was pretty well stuck. Besides, the TV crew had already slid three tables together and were craning their necks around looking for her. It was altogether too late. At least Brian had his back to her. That was some consolation.

She got a pad and went over. During the last couple of months she'd come to pride herself on being able to handle any party's order from memory, no matter how big and complicated it was, but she wasn't about to show off that little trick in front of her old fiancé. It might have been kind of silly, but she didn't want him getting the idea that she'd thrown herself all that completely into the business of being a waitress. At the last second, though, when she'd stopped behind Brian but a couple of chairs to one side, when she'd cleared her throat over the sound of the jukebox and announced that her name was Stacey, when Brian turned around in his seat with a look of surprise on his face that she couldn't say was fake or otherwise, at the very last second she decided to hell with him and whatever he might think of her current career choice. She slid the pad into the back pocket of her jeans, smiled broadly, and asked what everybody would have.

"Your mother told me where you were," said Brian, leaning over the bar as she filled the order.

"*My own mother.*" Stacey pulled at the Long Trail tap as if she meant to do it some serious harm.

"The thing you've got to remember," said Brian, "is that *she* still loves me."

"That's only because I never told her what you did to her daughter."

Brian leaned in. "And that's because *you* still love me, too."

"Guess again, buddy." Stacey let go of the tap and set the glass on one of the round trays she'd set out on the bar. Thanks to him she'd almost lost track of the order, and she wasn't about to let that happen. She ticked through it on her fingers, shooting looks over at the three merged tables to jog her memory.

Brian put his hand on the tray, which made her jump. "How about I carry this back for you?"

"Don't do me any favors." She kept counting, stopped short, began all over again. "I can take care of myself."

"So I see." He seemed to say it without any irony, but it was hard to be sure. He'd never given her credit for anything during their whole time together, and if he was starting now she thought she could get along just fine without it.

Over at the big table, people were glancing her way and cocking their heads and whispering among themselves. She could practically hear them. *Brian the ladies' man. Brian the operator. Brian the guy who thinks he's irresistible, and who by sheer force of his insistence and nerve quite often turns out to be.* What she didn't guess was that it was more like *Brian the creep; let's hope she shoots him down big-time and we all get to watch the aftermath.*

They walked back side by side, and Brian insisted on carrying one of the little round trays. Such chivalry, especially from a guy who under normal circumstances couldn't keep his business in his pants. One of the younger guys at the table—a kid who looked barely drinking age, the assistant art director Evan Babcock—spoke up first. "Good job, man. Nice to see an account guy who knows how to make himself useful."

The matronly woman alongside the kid smiled as if she'd taught him well. Karen Pruitt—his mentor in all things, as Brian had explained to Stacey. He looked so young next to her. It occurred to Stacey that she might have set him up with the line. The truth, on the other hand, was that poor judgment and childish humor came naturally to Evan. Agency life brought out that kind of thing in some people, especially the younger ones. Most particularly the younger ones with a creative bent, who half-figured they'd be in this stifling line of work only until their artistic ship came in.

Brian took the kid's joke as if he had an ounce of good nature in his body. He grinned and tilted his head toward Stacey and said, "Right. Then why don't you tell *her* I'm good for something. I've been trying to get that message across for years." He started distributing the drinks, getting every one of them wrong except his own.

"For *years*?" The words came from someone somewhere around the table. It was hard to say who.

Brian unbent himself from swapping the drinks around and said, "Friends, I'd like to introduce you to Stacey Curtis—my fiancée."

There they were: two boldfaced lies in one sentence. The *friend* part, followed by the *fiancée* part. That was probably some kind of a record, even for an account guy like Brian. Even for one who used to be a lawyer. Although what he'd said explained things well enough, it smelled wrong to everybody—so Stacey, having the most to lose, was the first to speak up.

"*Former* fiancée," she said. Then, clarifying that and providing a little additional distance, "In a former *life*."

"That's OK," the wiseguy Evan said. "We're not his friends, either. Not even former friends."

Karen Pruitt gave an approving nod. "Former fiancée? Then you've got both looks and brains. Not a bad combination."

Brian looked a little hurt, but let it go.

Stacey was making her way around the table, sliding coasters under the glasses that Brian had already put down and that the crew was still busy swapping around. She decided she liked these people well enough. She tended to like pretty much everybody well enough; everybody except Brian, but he was a special case. He'd shown his true colors a long time ago. For the most part, though, Stacey was the kind who tended to give people the benefit of the doubt. It made things go easier.

Her father had always been exactly that same way, and she'd seen how liking people from the start—actually *liking* them, and expecting them to like him in return—had smoothed plenty of roads for him. Her mother, not so much. Stacey was glad that she'd gotten this trait from the genetic stew that had brought her into this world. It certainly helped her make the transition when she'd thrown aside life in Boston and gone the way of the ski bum in this little mountain town. It also kind of explained why she was so at ease tending bar here at the Binding, in spite of the BA in Classics from Amherst (and the MA in Art History from Williams) that had cost her parents a fortune. Some things just come naturally to a person, whether or not she thinks she's going to have any use for them.

"Friends of yours?" Tina Montero asked when Stacey got back behind the bar.

"One friend," Stacey said, thinking numbers, not specifics. "Sort of."

Tina sipped her chardonnay and studied Brian over the rim. "He's pretty cute."

"You can have him."

Tina lifted an eyebrow.

"It's Brian. You know. *Brian*."

Tina nodded sagely and put down her glass and folded her hands around the base of it. "I still say he's cute."

"And I still say you can have him."

Brian was there when Stacey announced last call; and he was there when Jack closed out the cash register; and he was there when Pete Hardwick showed up bleary-eyed and yawning to make up the night's deposit. He was sitting at a little table over past the silent jukebox, as though he was waiting for somebody and didn't care if everyone in the whole world knew.

"Hey," Pete said, sizing up the tape. "You had a good night."

"One good table is what we had," said Jack. He took the tape, ran it through his fingers, and found one transaction, twenty or thirty times the usual.

"That's all it takes."

"Definitely an expense account situation."

Pete looped the tape around itself and pressed it flat. "Nice."

Jack picked up a spray bottle and worked on scrubbing the bar, moving in close to where Jack stood. He tilted his head ever so slightly in Brian's direction. "That's the last of them right there," he said. "The TV people."

"Huh?"

"You know, the TV people. That commercial they're making over at the mountain."

Pete forgot all about the money. "The one with Harper Stone?"

"If they're making more than the one commercial, that's the first I've heard of it."

"Come on, man. Harper Stone was in here and you didn't tell me? You didn't call?"

"You said no calls unless the place burns down." He kept working the spray bottle, moving along the bar. The bottle quacked like a duck when he squeezed the trigger. He breathed in the sharp smell of disinfectant. "That's your rule. No calls to your house, unless I call the fire department first."

Pete looked aghast. "I don't believe it. You didn't—"

"Take it easy, boss. Take it easy. There weren't any movie stars in here tonight." He pointed with the spray bottle at Brian, who was distracted for the moment by the bottom of his empty glass. "That guy right there's as close as we came. He's the one signed the slip."

"My new best friend," said Pete, his face softening. "Movie star or no."

"I thought you'd see it that way."

Stacey came out from the back where she'd been putting the

vacuum in the storage closet. She stopped short to see Brian there still, then she turned around and went back for her coat.

"Hey," Brian called before she could disappear. "I could use a lift back to the condo, if you don't mind."

Jack and Pete exchanged a look.

FIVE

They had to sit side by side in the freezing car for a while, their breath blowing thin clouds of smoke, until the engine warmed up and the windows cleared. Stacey pushed the gas pedal to hurry things up and the Subaru coughed and hesitated and steadied itself. Brian shivered and turned the thumbwheel to switch on the heated seat, but nothing happened.

"Doesn't the heater work," he asked, "or is the light just broken?"

"That heater hasn't worked in five years," Stacey said. "If you'd ever lowered yourself to ride in my car, you'd have known."

"Sorry."

"That's all right."

"I'll try to do it more often from now on."

"Oh no, you won't." Stacey threw the transmission into gear and hit the gas. If there had been any snow on the ground it would have been a risky move, but even in the Binding's ill-maintained parking lot there wasn't much of anything on the ground but gravel and frozen dirt.

They were quiet as they drove through town, and the streets were quiet, too. No lights anywhere except the big arc lamp on the front of the library and the yellowing overhead fluorescents at the gas station. Bud's Suds was closed up tight, along with the pizza joint next door to it and the grocery store down the block. All of the other restaurants and bars were shuttered and dark, too.

She asked him why he was here shooting a television commercial instead of doing research or whatever for the family law firm. He said that he'd been made an offer he couldn't refuse by an old college classmate of his father's who sat on the board of an international conglomerate that owned the consumer products company that owned the pharmaceutical company that owned the mouthwash company that employed the agency that was spending a fortune on this new campaign with the old defunct has-been of a former movie star. He was there to keep an eye on things. He said that last as if it were possible that he could keep an eye on anything. Loser.

When they reached the far edge of town—it didn't take long— Stacey turned up the access road. Brian hadn't said exactly where he was staying, and there were quite a few possibilities, but most of the nicer condos were more or less together.

"We're all at the Trail's End," he said.

"Nice place," she said. It wasn't a question.

"It's all right. They've got underground parking."

"That'd be an advantage, if you had a car."

"Oh, I've got my car," Brian said. "I just didn't feel like bringing it out. What if we got snow?"

Pure Brian. Both eyes on his BMW, and none on the Weather Channel. She slammed on the brakes. "In that case," she said, "you can walk from here."

"Stace."

"Don't 'Stace' me."

"Come on."

She reached across him and pulled at the door latch. "Out."

"Come on."

"A little walk will do you good. Out of the car."

"You're kidding."

"Try me." She waited a beat, looking straight ahead, up the hill. Then she turned to give him a look that would have propelled any sane man out the door.

"All right," he said. "I'm going." He opened the door and the light popped on. "But if I slip and fall in these loafers, it's on your head."

Oh, God. There they were, in the glow of the dome light. A pair of useless Gucci loafers, tassels and all, in a pale and highly vulnerable color that Stacey could only describe as looking like undercooked veal. What on earth was he thinking?

"Go on and shut the door," she said, starting up the hill while he was still off balance. "I can't leave a helpless creature to die out here."

She didn't sleep all that well. Between Brian's arrival and the lack of snow, things were going downhill around here fast, and her dreams were oppressive. Nothing but misery and melt. Come morning she squeezed her eyes shut against the light and lay in bed listening while Megan Ramsey made coffee in the kitchen, and when everything was quiet again she pulled on her robe and went out to wait for the first cup. She leaned against the doorsill with her bare feet cold on the linoleum. Beyond the kitchen window the Rutland *Herald* lay in the gravel drive, wrapped in thin blue plastic. She thought about going out to get it just to check on the weather forecast, but decided that it probably wasn't worth the trouble. When it felt like snowing again it would snow. Besides, the weather around here varied so dramatically from one valley to the next that the official forecast never counted for much.

Guy came down the stairs while she was stirring a little sugar into her coffee. He turned the corner from the foyer into the kitchen and snugged up the belt of his white terry cloth bathrobe at the sight of her. He never seemed to get used to the idea of finding a boarder in the kitchen. "Hey," he said.

"Hey," she said right back.

"Solve any good murders lately?"

"Not lately. You?"

"It's been a little slow in the murder department."

"That's good."

"I guess." He measured half a cup of oatmeal into a pot, added some salt and a cup of water, and set it on the stove. He fired up the gas burner and turned it down a little from full. Then he cut up a banana into a shallow bowl and went to the refrigerator for orange juice, which he poured over it like milk over cereal. Such was his breakfast, seven days a week, summer and winter. He sat at the table and addressed the bowl with a tablespoon, keeping an eye on the pot. "So," he said from a mouthful of banana, "you seen any of those movie people around?"

"It's a commercial. A TV commercial."

Guy waved his hand dismissively. "Movies, TV . . ."

"What's the difference, right?"

"Right. What's the difference." He sipped some OJ from his spoon. He was due upstairs to brush his teeth before the oatmeal was ready, but something was on his mind. "So you've seen them," he said.

"They were in the Binding last night."

"Tell me," Guy said, putting down his spoon. "How's the old man holding up?"

For half a second Stacey thought he was asking about Brian, and for the next half a second she hated herself for thinking it. The idea that her old fiancé was somehow that present in her brain freaked her out entirely. "Oh," she said, "that guy Stone. The actor."

Guy had lost all interest in his breakfast now—which wasn't a huge problem, since the banana would never get any soggier than it already was, and the pot on the stove hadn't yet started to steam. "I'll bet you're too young to remember him very well, but I loved his movies."

"I'm not *that* young."

"Oh, yes you are." Guy did some calculations in his head. Stacey wasn't that much older than his own kids; seven or eight years, give or take. That wasn't enough to have made any difference in her appreciation of Harper Stone's career. "And television doesn't count," he said. "You had to see them on the big screen."

"My dad took me to see *Devil May Care* when I was in junior high."

"Sorry. Stone didn't have much more than a walk-on in that, if he could have walked. Wasn't that around the time he had the knee surgery they kept so quiet?"

Stacey shook her head and sipped her coffee and shuffled toward her room.

"So was he there or what? At the Binding?"

"Sad to say, no. There were a couple of old men with canes, but they were from the retirement home in Woodstock."

"You never know," said Guy, getting up to stir his oatmeal.

"You never know."

"Keep your eyes open."

"I will."

What she didn't expect was to run into Harper Stone himself on her way to the mountain.

Under ordinary circumstances it never would have happened. But under ordinary circumstances she wouldn't have been stopping at the Slippery Slope. The place was a riddle wrapped in a mystery inside an enigma, the biggest ski shop in town but also the emptiest. Biggest as in the most square footage and the widest selection of gear. Emptiest as in *no customers, ever*. It was weird, is what it was. As many times as Stacey had driven by the place since she'd first come to town, there was hardly ever more than a single car in the parking lot. As often as she'd stop in to check out the merchandise, there was never more than a couple of customers in the place. Not like the crowds that always jammed MountainWerks or the Sitzmark: frustrated parents up from Connecticut, outfitting whiny kids with stuff they'd forgotten at home; high rollers up from New York, bagging the latest and greatest of everything whether they needed it or not; locals trolling the sale racks. Nope. For all the activity at the Slippery Slope, the whole property may as well have had yellow police tape strung around it.

It wasn't until she actually went in a few days back to shop for a pair of skis—Heads, a brand nobody else in town carried, sad to say—that she figured it out. The guy who ran the place was a piece of work. Surly, arrogant, irritable, lazy, cantankerous, mean, distracted, ill-tempered—there weren't enough adjectives in the English language to describe his attitude problem. But if she was going to get those skis she had her eye on, she hadn't had much choice but to do business with him.

His nametag read BUDDY FROMMER, and she knew within ten seconds of trying to distract him from whatever he was looking at on his laptop screen that whoever had first called him that must have meant it as a joke. *Buddy*. Sure thing. He snarled at her, waved her in the general direction of the skis, and looked back down at the screen. She named the model she wanted and he snarled again without raising his eyes. She named the size she needed and he all but hissed.

Ultimately she found the skis herself and brought them back to the counter and explained somehow that she wanted to give him money in exchange for them. He sighed and growled and shook his head, generally acting as though this was the worst thing that had happened to him all day. Like having to sell a pair of skis was the one thing that he was afraid might occur when he opened the doors that morning, and now here it was. The worst possible outcome of his day at work.

He ran her credit card and said she could pick them up on Wednesday once they got the bindings adjusted. She asked Wednesday morning, and he said if she wanted to take her chances that was fine with him, but if she had any sense she'd wait until Thursday morning. He'd told her Wednesday, which meant Wednesday, not Wednesday morning, in which case he would have said Tuesday night. He wasn't some kind of goddamned miracle worker who could afford to have technicians at her service day and night, was he?

So here she was on Thursday morning, pulling into the parking lot alongside a big white Hummer with out-of-state tags. Maryland. It was rare enough to see any car around here, but if there was going to be one it made sense that it should be a flatlander—from the farther away the better. One who definitely didn't know the score. Good luck to him. Stacey got out of the Subaru, opened up the hatch, and pushed some stuff around to make room for her new skis. The old ones were still back there along with her boots and the rest of her gear, just in case her new best friend Buddy hadn't felt like keeping his promise, but she sure did hope she wouldn't have to use them. She closed the hatch again to keep the boots as warm as she could, and went on in.

Buddy was nowhere to be seen, and neither was the environmentalist from Maryland.

She walked back toward where they kept the skis. Nothing. She came back out front, and looked over among the jackets and ski pants. Nobody. She called "Hello?" and nobody answered. She thought about ringing the bell on the front counter but thought better of it at the last minute. She kept looking. No one was in the snowboard section either, but there was a stairway over in the corner under a sign that read SERVICE DEPARTMENT and she could hear voices from down there. Men. Two of them. Buddy and the guy from Maryland, no doubt about it.

"Hello?"

Nothing.

"I'm here to pick up some skis?"

Still no answer.

She went down. Not fast, just one step at a time, holding on to the railing, waiting for Buddy to yell out and stop her and tell her to go back up where she belonged and he'd get her the damn skis when he felt like it. She was thinking of how the lifts would start turning in forty-five minutes and she didn't want to be late, blaming him already.

She reached the next to last step, ducked her head, and looked to see that there was nobody at the counter. The voices kept on, though, coming from somewhere in the back. She called again, "Hello?" and took a couple of tentative steps across the concrete floor. The place smelled of grease and hot wax and cigarette smoke. The first two she expected and the last was no surprise. If the guy was such a pain, he might as well be a health nut, too. She never understood it when she'd see people out on the slopes—or on the lifts, more likely—sucking away on cigarettes. Poisoning themselves in the great outdoors.

It wasn't Buddy who was smoking, however. She found that out when she followed the voices and made her way back among stacked cartons and heaps of junk and piles of ruined equipment to find the two of them—Buddy and the guy from the Hummer—together at a wooden workbench, transacting some kind of business. Buddy had his back to her. She saw the other guy nearly in profile. Buddy was heavyset, and the other guy was taller than he was by two or three inches and weighed a little less. Solid but kind of rangy, with silver hair immaculately cut to skim the top of his shirt collar. His jacket was flung on a chair and his sleeves were rolled up. He had his weight on his forearms, one of which had the pale ghost of what looked like an old tattoo—not some hip Asian-inspired design, but something he might have picked up a long time ago in a seaport someplace. A heart and an anchor, with chains binding them together.

"Hello?"

They both turned, Buddy with a hard snap of his neck and the silver-haired guy slow as molasses, looking up reluctantly from whatever it was they were studying on the workbench.

"Get lost," said Buddy, looking like he meant it.

She said she was just here to pick up her new pair of Heads. The fat ones. He remembered, right? He'd promised them for yesterday? She didn't mean to interrupt anything.

"I'm kind of occupied," he said. "In case you haven't noticed."

"They're all paid for," she said, as if that made any difference, and she looked from Buddy to the silver-haired guy, thinking maybe he would take her side. He didn't have to, because the sight of him distracted Stacey enough to change the subject entirely.

"Oh, my, God," she said. "It's you."

He didn't deny it. He didn't actually say anything. He just smiled a smile that was a good bit more crooked than Stacey expected it to be, tilted his head a little, and reached up to touch his fingers to his brow in a little pantomime of graciousness. Stacey thought he looked pretty good for his age, but then again it was probably the result of a small fortune spent on plastic surgery. Before she could decide, he swiveled his gaze away from her and gave Buddy Frommer a hard look that got him moving.

"All right." Buddy stepped away from the worktable and kind of bulled Stacey ahead of him, toward the stairs. "Let's get you out of here."

He pushed her on up the stairs, and that was the end of her brush with stardom. Or her near-miss. Or whatever you'd call it.

SIX

Thanks to the delay at the Slippery Slope she didn't make the first chair, but she still came pretty close.

It was a day almost as good as yesterday—a high curved blue dome of sky with just a few puffy clouds, and no wind to speak of. From the top of the main lift the valley spread out below like a diorama in a natural history museum, so pristine and clear and sharp that the distance of it might have been a trick. At the edge of her vision, about as far away as sight would allow, she could see the high white peak of Mount Washington all the way over in New Hampshire. The winds up there were probably a hundred miles an hour or more, but it looked completely lovely from where she stood, putting her gloved hands through the straps on her poles.

"Hey." A shout came from over her shoulder. She turned to see Chip Walsh barreling in her direction from a little distance uphill, out from the spillway of a run from the Northside, which the paying customers hadn't had time to reach yet. She was thrilled to see him but a little jealous, as usual, of the early start that patrollers got. Maybe she ought to give up tending bar and see about a job with the Ski Patrol. She thought she might be almost good enough. Then again she didn't care for the idea of contaminating her ski day with actual work. Where was the fun in that?

Chip pulled up short, his skis sending up a controlled spray of snow. "Don't even think about skiing the Northside," he said. "That movie crew is still over there."

"It's just a commercial."

"Whatever. They've still got the lift all to themselves."

"Dang."

"And a more unhappy-looking crowd you've never seen. On a day like this." He shook his head and pointed to the sky with a pole. "They must be the only twenty people in the state who don't have big stupid grins on their faces."

"Oh," said Stacey as she took off, "I can think of one more." She made him wait until they were on the lift again before he found out she was talking about Buddy Frommer at the Slippery Slope.

That guy," said Chip, shaking his head. "What the heck were you doing in there anyway? Nobody goes in there."

She lifted one of her new skis to an angle at which he could admire it properly.

"Oooh. nice. I didn't know you could get Heads in town."

"You need to go into the Slippery Slope more often."

"No, thanks."

"They're the only place that sells them."

"They're going to have to sell them to somebody else. That Buddy Frommer's too big a pain in the ass for me. I don't care *what* he sells."

She tilted her head, still admiring the new skis. "How does he stay in business, do you suppose?"

Chip raised his eyebrows behind his goggles. "You know what people say."

"No, actually. I don't."

"I don't want to spread rumors."

"Sure you do. Everybody likes to spread rumors."

"I don't know." He shrugged. "You wonder, is all. A big operation like that with no visible customers? Makes you think he might be selling something other than skis."

Stacey's jaw dropped open.

"Come on," he said. "It's possible."

Stacey turned her head his way.

"*It is*. It's possible."

She clapped her jaw shut. "I'm not saying it's not possible. Just the opposite. I'm saying I think I might have just seen it happen." She couldn't believe she'd seen Buddy Frommer and Harper Stone huddled over a drug deal and not even known what she was looking at. Some sophisticated big-city transplant she was.

"You're kidding."

She shook her head and told him everything. The out-of-state Hummer, the empty store, the voices from down in the service department. Frommer and Stone himself at the workbench, up to God knows what. Wow.

"So it's true what people say," he said when she was done.

"Apparently."

"It explains a lot."

"I guess."

"Now I'll know where to go."

"*Chip*."

"Just kidding." They both sat shaking their heads. A rumor was one thing, but this was something else. Leave it to those Hollywood types to find a source for dope even in an isolated little one-horse Green Mountain town like this one. As the top of the lift approached and they raised their skis to slide off, Chip got around to asking, "So how'd he look, anyway?"

"Who?"

"Harper Stone. You know: the mayor of *Murder Town*."

"Not too bad. Well preserved, I guess. Which I guess is what you'd expect, all things considered."

Chip pointed with his pole toward the woods that separated them from the top of North Peak, where the shoot was in progress. "How about we go over there and take another look after all."

Stacey didn't know whether she followed him in order to see Stone or to let Brian see her having fun with Chip, but in the end it didn't make much difference.

They were just standing around like a bunch of statues, all long faces and frustrated looks and contagious gloom. Waiting for snow under that bright blue sky. As she rounded the last couple of long curves and came zooming down the hill, Stacey felt sorry for them—but only a little.

They didn't even have the cherry picker from the electric company fired up today. The whole crew was gathered around a couple of picnic tables set up in back of a catering truck parked near the lift station, drinking coffee and eating donuts and staring at the sky like they didn't trust it. The lifties assigned to run the Northside chair—a couple of bearded old-timers in greasy Spruce Peak jackets and snowmobile pants—were lounging at the tables, too, glad for the easy day, chatting up a couple of cute young production assistants who wouldn't have had a moment to spare for them under ordinary circumstances. Stacey and Chip skied up, stopping where they'd still have momentum for getting to the trail that led back down to the main face, and clicked out of their bindings. The crew brightened up to see them come stamping across the snow toward the picnic tables. A few waved their arms and welcomed them like royalty or visitors from another planet. They were a pleasant break from the routine, if nothing else. Brian didn't seem to be anywhere around, but after a minute or two he stuck his head from the door of the big green fiberglass Porta-Potty.

Perfect, Stacey figured. *Just perfect.*

The crew remembered Stacey from last night at the Binding, and she introduced Chip as her friend. She half expected a few catcalls in Brian's direction—"*I can see why you lost out, buddy boy,*" that kind of thing—but everybody was so depressed and frustrated by the lack of snow that nobody even rose to the bait. It wasn't any great loss. She didn't want Chip getting ideas anyhow. Maybe someday, but not just yet.

There were a few new faces that hadn't been in the Binding last night: the blond actress, an angry-looking guy in a leather coat who sat smoking a cigarette and looking at the sky, and last but not least, the star of the operation, Harper Stone himself, who had just finished doctoring his coffee at the window of the catering truck and was sidling over toward Stacey as if he'd been invited.

"Hey," she said, taking off her helmet. "Remember me?"

Behind dark glasses, Stone knitted his famous brow. "I meet so many lovely women," he purred, "I'm afraid that you have me at a disadvantage."

Stacey looked from him to Chip and back again, and let it drop. "Never mind."

Nevertheless, Stone kept coming, and he took her hand and led her from Chip toward the nearest picnic table and asked the unfortunate guy sitting across from him—Evan, the assistant art director—if he would be so kind as to go get her a cup of coffee. Or would she prefer hot chocolate?

"No, thanks," said Stacey, not in any hurry to sit. "Neither."

"Tea?"

"No, thanks. Really. I'm fine." She extricated her hand and gave Evan a look that told him to stay on the bench. *Please.* That was all right with him.

As long as there was free coffee, though, Chip was all over it. The mountain cafeterias sold you a small cup of thin and burnt-tasting stuff for two bucks and a large one for three, which meant that even with his patrol discount it wasn't anywhere near worth it. Over the last couple of months he'd gotten into Stacey's habit of bringing tea bags from home—hot water was free—but he didn't really like tea all that much and this opportunity was too good to pass up. In a minute he had two cups balanced on a little cardboard tray, one of them doctored to his specs and the other to Stacey's, and he was coming toward her with a huge grin on his face.

"Hey!" he called out. "Isn't that the famous Harper Stone?"

Stone gave him a slow and patented smile.

"It is!" Chip handed the cardboard tray to Stacey and she sat down with it, taking a peek under one of the lids to see which cup—the one without cream—was hers. Chip edged around her with his hand stuck out, heading for the old Hollywood star. "I've seen all your movies, man! All of them!"

"Then you're a glutton for punishment," said Stone, clearly expecting to be contradicted.

Chip didn't let him down. "No! No! They're the best!"

Stone's smile grew a little wider but no less crooked.

"I'm telling you," Chip said, sitting down alongside him and reaching for his coffee, "my dad never missed a single one."

"Your dad."

"Oh, yeah. He took me to all your pictures. We didn't go bowling or play ball or anything like that. He wasn't a real active kind of dad. We bonded at the movies."

"How nice." Stone shifted on the bench.

"He's always been your biggest fan."

"Then give him my regards."

"I will, I will." He blew over his coffee and sipped a little of it.

"He and my mom got Netflix a year or so back, and it's great. You know about Netflix?"

"Who doesn't?" Stone's interest was fading fast.

"They've got everything. I mean *everything*."

"I suppose they do."

"All the classics. Foreign language stuff. You name it."

"I'll bet."

"They've got *Masterpiece Theatres* from when I was about three."

"I'm sure."

"You remember *Afraid of the Dark?*"

Stone's attention returned. "How could I forget? Some of my best work."

"That's the funny thing," Chip said. "According to my dad, Netflix doesn't have it."

Stone looked for an instant like a man having a heart attack.

"You think it went out of print or something?"

"I'm afraid I wouldn't know that."

Chip drank a little coffee and reflected. "How about eBay?" he said after a minute. "Do you think somebody might be selling it on eBay?"

Stone began to rise. "If you'll excuse me."

"Don't tell me you never checked."

"I'm afraid I have no idea."

"Maybe I could try that Half.com or someplace—"

"Excuse me."

"Anyhow," Chip said, "I sure would like to get it if I could find it. He's got a birthday coming up. Wouldn't that be something?"

"Yes. It would be very thoughtful." He was on his feet now, heading for the Porta-Potty. "You're a very thoughtful son."

"One of these days," Chip said, "it might even be a collector's item!"

Stone didn't answer, vanishing instead behind the fiberglass door.

"Nicely done," said Stacey, as the privacy lever clicked over and the indicator showed up red. You could practically see steam rising from the roof of the big green outhouse. With Stone inside it, it reminded Stacey of that famous elevator cab in *Lights Out*, but dirtier.

Chip put down his coffee cup and looked at the people gathered around the table, each face turned his way looking at him as if he were some kind of hero. "What'd I say?"

SEVEN

Snow arrived in the afternoon. It blew in from the northwest unexpected and unannounced, riding in on a mass of Canadian air that the weathermen had said would stay well to the north for another few days. One bad call, and Spruce Peak found itself under a foot of new snow by the time the lifts closed at three thirty. The TV crew made all the progress they could make while the going was good—the skies went gray around noon and the snow that blew in wasn't all that impenetrable until one thirty or two, so they had a couple of hours to grab the shots they'd been waiting for—and they were about half done when the weather closed in tight and they had to fold up for the day.

The gray-haired and black-clad director—a hired gun from New York named Manny Seville, whom Karen Pruitt had worked with before on a chewing gum commercial that never aired—invited everybody over to his Trail's End condo later on to look at what they'd gotten. The technical guys from Rutland said no, they were heading home and they weren't going to come back or stick around just so he could show movies in his condo. Besides, they said, the video gear stayed in the truck; it wasn't going into any hotel room.

He said hadn't they ever heard of burning a DVD and they acted like he was pushing his luck, but after some back and forth they relented.

As for Harper Stone, he just squinted at the sky and said, "I never look at dailies. Bad luck." But everybody figured that he was just chicken to drive himself all the way over to Trail's End from the fancy house that the ad agency had rented for him. Some action hero he was turning out to be.

Dinner was delivery from Cinco de Taco. Brian sent young Evan to the grocery store for beer—"Dos Equis if they've got it, but Corona'll do in a pinch"—and lamented that since there wasn't a proper liquor store in town they'd have to do without mojitos. Karen said mojitos were a sissy drink anyway and Brian said he knew that but he was only thinking of the ladies. Karen said fine, be that way, but she knew the truth. He was definitely the mojito type.

The food was actually pretty good. Better than the raw footage on the DVD, as it turned out, although the more they watched it and the more beer they drank the better it looked. The snow had built up pretty quickly on Stone's eyelashes and it made him look like Andy Rooney or some kind of nutty professor, but there were a couple of takes where that wasn't too big a problem. He'd muffed his lines enough to wear everybody out, including the blond actress, who looked frustrated and annoyed in at least half of the takes. Plus she was clearly young enough to be his granddaughter, which everybody thought was creepy and nobody bothered downplaying since Stone wasn't around anyway. Manny Seville pronounced that there was probably a total of fifteen good seconds in there that they could patch together into something usable, but he wouldn't mind picking up a few more shots in the morning if the weather cleared.

Evan, over by the picture window, pulled back the curtains, cocked his head, and looked out into the night to assess their chances. The snow was still pelting down, great windblown gusts of it that washed across the parking lot and obscured the overhead lamps and had already drifted the cars in pretty well. "I don't know," he said. "It doesn't look promising."

Manny poured himself another beer, shaking his head and giving the television an incredulous look. Stone's face was frozen on it, his snowy eyebrows jutting out every which way. "Damn that guy to hell," he said. "We get half a day's worth of shooting, and this is all he gives us. It never fails."

Brian got another beer, too. "It never fails?"

"Never," Manny said. "We go back, Stone and me. I knew him when."

"When what?"

"Just when," Manny said.

Evan let go of the curtains. "If we can't shoot," he said, "maybe we'll ski."

Brian didn't think that sounded like such a swell idea, but he raised his glass to it anyway.

EIGHT

*T*hank God for the mighty Subaru. It had gotten Stacey home when her shift was over last night, and it would get her to the mountain this morning, and you couldn't ask for more. Well, maybe you could ask for a little help shoveling away the snow that had drifted around it overnight. But Guy was already gone, called out to oversee a fender bender out on Route 100, the schoolkids had a rare snow day to look forward to, and she was on her own. She didn't mind too much. She got an early start and let the work warm her up for what was going to be a sensational day on the mountain. Probably the best of the season.

Between the shoveling and the slow drive through the snow that was still coming down, she got to the mountain half an hour later than usual, and the Northside chair was running when she drew near. She could see sections of it from the access road, emerging from the tree line in places, and though she couldn't tell if there were any people on it, it was definitely in motion. *Nah,* she decided. *That doesn't mean anything.* It sure didn't mean they were running it for skiing. They were probably just getting it ready for the TV crew.

But it didn't turn out that way. When she got into the lodge, the signs warning skiers away from the Northside were down. She asked the guy behind the Mountain Services desk what was up with that and he said the TV crew had called in and canceled today on account of the snow, so she could get in all the Northside action she wanted.

She fairly bounced in her boots.

The snow kept up all day, and the bad roads between Connecticut and the Green Mountain State kept the dilettante flatlanders at home. That's the way it always went, early season or late. Until there were snowdrifts in the backyards of southern New England, nobody got it into his head to drive up here and bother the Vermonters. And once the snow got too deep down there—particularly on a day like this, when the highway patrol was almost as busy as the plowing crews—people just didn't have the nerve to make the trip. All of which was fine with Stacey, who took advantage of the opportunity to ski herself into a stupor.

She saw most of Brian's crew at lunch, but not Brian himself. She didn't ask. Somebody volunteered that he'd stayed back in his condo. Somebody else said something about how he'd forgotten a decent pair of winter gloves and was too cheap to buy new—a story that Stacey believed exactly half of. The first half. Either way, it was good to see that even an opportunity for team-building with the folks from the office wasn't enough to get him on the slopes. Never mind the presence of that blond actress, who was looking kind of forlorn and lonely without Harper Stone around to keep up his constant round of lecherous flattery. Stacey looked around and expected to see him emerging from the men's room or the cafeteria line at any second, but no dice.

"Where's the movie star?" she asked anybody listening as she fished in her jacket for a tea bag and a couple of energy bars.

"Taking advantage of his luxury accommodations, no doubt," said Evan. "Did you get a load of that place?"

"What place?"

"It's the size of a hotel, to begin with."

"What place?"

"The place where they're putting him up. It's this private house on the north side of the ski mountain." Evan folded a slice of pizza in half and began to work on it. "Unbelievable."

"You go in?"

"Nobody went that I know of."

Nods all around the table.

"Why would he invite peons like us over?" Evan said. The pizza looked terrible to Stacey, but he didn't seem to mind. Young guys were like that. They'd Hoover up anything. "Karen and I drove over and checked it out, though. Wow. Incredible."

"You remember where it is?"

Evan didn't know the road but Karen named it. Vista View, one of those narrow winding lanes that vanished quickly into the woods around there, climbing uphill fast and twisting into the trees, promising a kind of housing that ordinary folks weren't even supposed to *see*, much less witness close up.

Stacey thought she remembered the place but figured she'd check it out later. See how the other half lived—the half that didn't even include Brian "Moneybags" Russell. But first she had some more skiing to do.

She finished her lunch and called Pete at the Broken Binding from the pay phone to see if she could start her shift a little late, there being extenuating circumstances and all. Like three feet of snow that desperately needed her attention.

A late start was fine with Pete, since the roads were pretty treacherous. The snow was still coming down, and the driving was probably going to keep the crowds away anyhow. So she kept skiing until the light began to die, then she dug out the car from where the plows had buried it halfway up the hatch and drove back to her rented room for a shower.

The roads definitely weren't good. Pete had been right about that. By keeping the Subaru in the tracks of the cars that had gone before, though, she managed to get back to the house in one piece. She was concentrating hard on her driving when she went by the cutoff for Vista View, squinting through the windshield and wishing she had a better set of wiper blades, but from the quick look she got of it she thought there weren't any tracks on the road or signs of plows coming and going up into the woods there at all. Today would be a bad day to go sightseeing anyhow. She meant to take a closer look on her way back to the Broken Binding, but by then the light was completely gone and she couldn't see a thing. *Next time,* she thought. *Tomorrow.*

NINE

The next morning Karen Pruitt felt like a Girl Scout leader or something, and she didn't like it. Traipsing up and down the halls of the Trail's End condo complex, master list in hand, hammering on doors to make sure that the crew was up and moving around. She'd have called them all if her cell phone was any use—but not only couldn't it hold a decent connection, it kept running out of juice from being on an old-fashioned analog network out here in the woods and hunting for a signal most of the time.

She had to use the landline in her condo to roust Stone out of his mountain aerie. The damned thing had local service only—*how did anybody make long distance calls around here?*—but that was enough to reach the big house on Vista View. All the phone over there did, though, was ring and ring. She leaned up against the wall and looked out the window onto a day of utter perfection marred only by the passage of snowmobiles among the high pines, listening to the phone ring and wondering if that jerk would ever pick up. The house on Vista View was huge, so maybe it was a bit of a walk to the phone. Nah. Not possible. Palaces like that had phones in every bathroom—probably two, one by the john and the other by the Jacuzzi—never mind the bedrooms. So why wouldn't he pick up? Damn him. She'd give him five minutes and try again. If he still played hard to get, she'd have to send Evan over. Or maybe Brian. Yeah. That was it. Brian. It'd serve him right. The two big egos could go head-to-head. Wrangling the alleged talent was a job for management anyhow.

Half an hour later, Brian couldn't even begin to make it up the hill to Stone's place. He didn't even try—not in that shiny new BMW, even though he'd sprung for the four-wheel drive. The main roads were clear enough and they were even almost dry in places, but Vista View was private and nobody had touched it. The plows had piled snow three or four feet deep where it met Route 100, and the drifts beyond that went up into the woods as if into some kind of untracked wilderness. He found a place to turn around—it took a couple of miles until there was a spot wide enough, at an intersection where a front-end loader was working the drifts—and then he drove back into town as fast as he dared.

The crew was stoking up on coffee and lousy bagels at Judge Roy Beans, and they all looked quizzical and frustrated when Brian came in shaking his head.

Karen sighed. "No luck?"

"No luck."

"I don't get it. You mean he wasn't there, or you mean he wouldn't come?"

"Oh, he's there, all right." Brian tossed his hat and his leather gloves onto a chair but kept on walking, headed toward the counter. She pushed her chair back and followed him. "He's there."

"So he wouldn't come. What'd he say?"

"I didn't see him. But nobody's come down that road of his for a while, I can tell you that. Not even in that big new Hummer he's driving." He ordered coffee and a corn muffin, sweet-talking the girl behind the counter while Karen stood alongside him, frustrated. Then he turned back to her. "It's drifted full and plowed shut."

She tilted her head toward the table full of talented and fairly well-paid individuals lingering over their coffee. "This is costing your client money, my friend."

"I know it is."

"A lot of money."

"So?"

"So when something costs the client money, it's been known to cost us the client. That's how it works."

"I know how it works." He shrugged. "I understand. But it's not my fault."

"Of course it's not. But that doesn't make any difference."

He picked up his coffee and muffin and flashed a smile at the counter girl. "So what do you expect me to do about it?"

"I expect you to get that tough guy out of bed and down the hill and on the job. How you do it makes no difference to me. I don't care if you have to buy a shovel and a pair of mukluks and dig him out yourself. *Capiche?*"

Brian stood sipping his coffee, letting reality sink in for a change. He wrapped up his muffin in a paper napkin and pushed the door open and stepped out into the parking lot without his hat or gloves, craning his neck to see if there was a plow handy. God knows half of the locals in Judge Roy Beans looked as if they had ridden there in pickup trucks, but he came up short. No pickups, no plows. There were, however, a couple of snowmobiles parked alongside the building, and they gave him an idea.

"I get that Polaris up to speed with you dressed that way, you'll be froze solid inside of five minutes. Ten at the most." The man who barked these words in Brian's direction was grizzled. There was no other word for it. He was grizzled and he smelled sour and he had a voice that sounded like it hurt, but he sure was getting a kick out of the thought of taking this city kid out for a spin on his snowmobile. He winked at Brian, picked some kind of seed out of his back teeth, and cackled, shaking his gray head.

"You're right," said Brian. "And you know what? I don't think I even *need* to go out there with you. You can go by yourself. Heck, if I go, you won't be able to bring him back."

"Bring who back?"

"The guy who's stuck out there. He's a movie actor. Play your cards right and he might give you an autograph."

"The only actor I got any time for is that Paul Newman."

"It's not Paul Newman."

The grizzled man looked crestfallen.

"It's Harper Stone. Remember him?"

The grizzled man ran his tongue around his teeth and swallowed.

"Remember *Last Stand at Appomattox?*"

The grizzled man smiled as the light dawned. "I know that one," he said. "Shit. A tough guy like that, getting stuck in a little bit of snow. Imagine that."

"Yeah," said Brian. "Can you believe it?"

"Not hardly," said the grizzled man. He drained his coffee and looked at the guy across the table from him, likewise grizzled and grimy and very much his match from head to toe. "How about we all take a run out there?" he said. "Stop at the firehouse and borrow us a snowsuit for the city boy, here. Take both machines. I get dibs on bringing the movie star back, though."

The other guy just nodded. He looked like he did a lot of that.

"Imagine me, little Dickie Burnes, rescuing a big-shot Hollywood hero. Imagine that."

The other guy nodded again.

"I guess that would make me the leading man."

The other guy nodded again, and the three of them left.

The Hummer was there in the driveway, standing like a rampart against the wind, snow drifted nearly to its roof on one side and blown just about clear on the other. So he hadn't gone anywhere.

They pulled the snowmobiles under the portcullis and stopped them over by the stairs, or where the stairs must have been. Even under here the snow was deep and drifted, completely untracked. Nobody had been out the front door, that was for sure.

Dickie and the other guy stayed on their snowmobiles like a couple of cowpokes sitting their horses. One of them tried firing up a cigarette but the wind blew his lighter out on the first five or six attempts. Brian slogged up toward the front door, his borrowed boots filling up with snow. He reached the top step—a more or less snow-free semicircle of some kind of handsome fieldstone fitted together at no small expense—and gave his feet a couple of futile stamps. He reached for one of the door knockers and lifted it. It made a hard bright clanking sound out there in the silent day. He felt like an idiot. How on earth was a house this big supposed to be served by a useless thing like that, even if it *was* roughly the size of a third-grader, forged to resemble a cone-laden pine branch, and worth more than most people in this valley would make in a year? What this place needed was a doorbell, with buzzers in every room.

He waited a few seconds and banged the knocker again. Nothing.

He pounded on the door with both fists. Nothing.

Nothing, that is, except some laughter from either Dickie or the other guy. The one who'd finally gotten a cigarette going. They were both so crusted over with snow that any means he might have had for differentiating them was long gone—and he didn't much care.

The guy with the cigarette hollered, "Try up there!" Brian looked to see him pointing toward a set of drifted-over stairs that led up to an enclosed porch. He slogged up them while the guy sat on his snowmobile, puffing away. The storm door to the porch was unlocked and he kicked away snow from the sill and muscled it open. He went in, stamping his feet on a metal grate that let snow fall to the ground below. This whole side of the house was glass—big floor-to-ceiling sliders—giving out onto the enclosed porch. Must have been nice in the summertime. What a panorama, all those mountains and valleys stretched out practically forever. No wonder the developers came up with a name like Vista View, as stupid as it sounded.

The curtains were drawn but there was a gap or two, and from what he could see the place was a mess. A bachelor pad extraordinaire—and he ought to know—lived in for what looked like six or eight months without benefit of a vacuum cleaner or a dust rag. There were clothes strewn from wall to wall, the throw rugs and cushions were cockeyed, and the pictures were slanted on the walls. It looked like somebody'd been sleeping on the couch.

He knocked on the glass, figuring that he'd get no answer, and he wasn't disappointed. The place was like a tomb. He tried the sliding door. He tried all of them. Each was locked up tight. So even though it was pleasant in here out of the wind with the gorgeous view and all, he gave up and went out and half-slid, half-climbed back down the stairs.

"No luck?" said the guy without the cigarette. Come to think of it, neither of them had a cigarette now.

"No luck."

"We could try around back."

"Let's not."

"Don't be a sissy. We come all this way."

"I'm not walking."

"Climb on."

They repeated the procedure two more times—first at a set of sliders on an elevated deck around back, which Brian reached only by wading through chest-high snow; again at the door by the buttoned-up three-car garage—and they came up short again. Short and freezing and disappointed. Brian turned on his cell and tried to call Karen, but he couldn't get a signal, so he climbed back on the snowmobile and gave the order to go on back to town. Now he owed these guys fifty bucks and he had nothing to show for it. He'd bury it somewhere in his expense report and nobody would be the wiser, but that wasn't the point.

There was one more door, though, and one of the snowmobile guys noticed it as they rounded the house and turned back toward the road. It was underneath the enclosed porch that Brian had checked before, tucked into a little bricked alcove, probably leading to a utility closet or something like that. A dead end even if it was open, but they stopped just in case, for one last try.

TEN

*J*ackpot.

Not only did Brian get in, but the space behind the door was anything but a dead-end utility closet. It was a ski room fit for a sheik, if sheiks indulged in downhill skiing—which they probably did, since they indulged in everything else. It was gorgeous. There must have been twenty lockers along the walls, each one custom built of what looked like solid cherry. Hand-built shelving units up to the ceiling, where soft indirect lighting bathed the whole place in a warm golden glow. Hardwood floors he was ashamed to be tracking snow all over. And in the far corner, a door that without question opened into the main house.

He cracked the door and called Stone's name but didn't get an answer. So he pushed it open and went down the dark hallway until he found the stairs to what he guessed was the main floor. No sign of recent human habitation down here whatsoever. He called up the stairs, waited for a minute and called again, then went up.

What he'd seen through the window was only half of it. This wasn't a bachelor pad: It was a fraternity house at the close of a particularly brutal rush season. All the pillows and cushions off the couches. Plates and glasses and bottles everywhere, with crumbs of food tracked into the carpets and various beverages spilled all over. A decimated pizza box jammed into the fireplace. Picture frames knocked over. Chairs from the dining room upended in front of the dead TV. And at the center of everything, right smack in the middle of the glass coffee table, a smear of white powder that spoke volumes.

He didn't think he ought to look any further, but he tentatively called Stone's name a few times and went looking anyway. There were three bedrooms on this level, and every one of them had been slept in. He went upstairs and found two more—one of them the master suite, roughly as big as New Hampshire—and both of them had been used, too. Either Stone had company, which wasn't likely, or he was fussy about clean sheets. Or maybe he was in the habit of getting himself so messed up on coke that he couldn't remember where he'd slept the night before.

The main thing about all those rumpled beds was that Harper Stone wasn't in any one of them. He wasn't in the kitchen or the library or the formal dining room or the den or the game room or the home theater or any of the half-dozen marble bathrooms either, not as far as Brian could tell. He headed back toward the ski room and stopped at the last minute to pick up a phone and try calling Karen—just like at his condo back on the mountain, long-distance service was disabled. Didn't anybody trust anybody? With his head boiling over with frustration he slammed the phone down and left. It wasn't until he and Dickie and the other guy were halfway back to Judge Roy Beans that he realized he should have called 911 while he'd had the chance.

Sirens in the valley were never a good sign—not in a ski town.

Stacey ran things through her mind and guessed that she had it all figured out. The snow was deep but the roads were pretty well cleared, and the parking lot—when she could get a glimpse of it from the mountain—was filling up with cars. That meant that the traffic was still moving on the one main road into town, delivering a crowd of dilettantes and amateurs and reckless hooky-players sprung loose from desk jobs all over Connecticut and New York. It was only ten o'clock and the late-morning arrivals hadn't pushed their way onto the lifts yet, but she could picture the cause of that siren pretty clearly. Some money manager with a torn ACL, taking a ride down the mountain on a Ski Patrol toboggan. She hoped that was all it was. However you cut it, the sight of the Patrol at work over a fallen skier could cast a real shadow over the day. She loved skiing and she loved the mountain, too, but along with that love went a certain respect. And a skier gone down was a sad reminder of the need for it—even if he *was* an overreaching yuppie flatlander.

Halfway down the Thunder Bowl, she ran into Chip. His skis were planted upright into a drift, and he was picking up a pine branch that the snowfall had brought down onto the margin of the trail. She slid over toward him and stopped, figuring to get the scoop on the sirens in the valley.

"I thought you'd be occupied," she said.

"Hey," he said, "I am."

"No, I mean the sirens and all. They didn't need you? I guess they've got a lot of guys on today."

Chip shook his head. "No—no more than usual." He tapped his walkie-talkie. "I didn't get any calls, though. Whatever happened must have happened in town, not up here."

"That's good news."

"If a siren's ever good news."

"Right."

ELEVEN

That evening, conversation was a little subdued in the Broken Binding. Even Tina Montero, who was a look-on-the-bright-side kind of individual capable of facing almost anything with a lipsticked smile and a glass of chardonnay, wasn't her usual upbeat self.

Word on the street was that Harper Stone had gone missing.

Jack, the highly professional bartender who'd been here since the Germans and was more a fixture than the walnut bar itself, leaned up against the cash register, folded his arms across his chest, and chewed his lip. "I don't know," he said. "It just doesn't make any sense."

"People don't just disappear that way," said Tina.

"Especially not a capable guy like him." He shook his head. "I mean, *come on*. It's *Harper Stone*."

"You don't know," said Tina.

Jack raised an eyebrow. "I guess you're right. The guy could be a pansy. Or maybe he just went soft." He patted his little belly. "We all do, sooner or later."

"Going soft doesn't have anything to do with disappearing into thin air."

"I'm just saying you'd think a guy like that would know how to take care of himself, whatever happened."

"*Whatever happened.* That's the question."

"You're right. There's no telling."

"He was there one minute and gone the next."

"Maybe somebody kidnapped him."

Tina laughed and drained her glass. "Sure. That happens all the time around here."

"I'm just saying."

"You're right. Anything's possible." She was quiet for a minute, thinking. "Then there's the drugs."

Jack wobbled his head from side to side, watching the light in the foyer change as the front door swung open and people came in stamping their feet. "I don't know about that drug stuff. That's just a rumor."

"It's all just rumors."

"I'm saying don't believe everything you hear, is all."

"I'll believe anything."

He rubbed his jaw, rueful. "Not me. You don't succeed in this world the way Harper Stone did without being a pretty square guy."

"You'd be surprised."

He refilled her glass. "You sound like you'd know."

"Six degrees of separation and all that."

"What do you mean by that?" Jack asked, watching Stacey head out among the tables to take orders. It was the TV crew, and if the mood in the Binding was subdued they looked ready to bring it down a little more. "What do you mean 'six degrees of separation'?"

"You know. The Kevin Bacon thing."

"I know that. I've heard about six degrees of separation." He put the bottle back in the fridge under the bar. "How do you suppose Kevin Bacon got mixed up in that, anyhow? He's another one."

"Another one what?"

"Another Hollywood guy. That's all. How'd he get mixed up in it?"

"In what?"

"In that six-degrees business."

"I think because it rhymes, is all."

"Really?" He tilted his head, trying it out to himself. "As simple as that?"

"As simple as that."

"You think he knows Harper Stone?"

"Within six degrees," she said, "there's no question about it. That's the whole point of the game, isn't it? Nobody's that much of a stranger to anybody else."

The crew would be headed home in the morning, there was no way around that. With Stone gone wherever he'd gone, their work was finished. They all looked pretty glum. Not that anybody missed *him* in particular, but you didn't expect things to end this way. It was all very dissatisfying.

Manny Seville was at one end of the long table, waving his hands around and telling Karen and Brian that he'd had another look at the footage during the snowstorm and complaining that he wasn't sure he had enough decent stuff to make the commercial work. Brian was giving him a disgusted look that said he'd damned well better, or else there'd be hell to pay. Karen was putting in her opinion that it didn't really matter, since you'd have to be kind of ghoulish to go ahead and sell mouthwash with poor old Harper Stone's last scenes, if it turned out that that was what they'd gotten on tape. Imagine it. The poor guy's last moments on camera. The famous Harper Stone, looking irritable and old in a mouthwash commercial.

"Don't worry about him," said Manny. "He'll turn up. They always do."

"Do we have insurance for this?" Brian asked.

Karen frowned. "I guess. Maybe." Then she thought a little more and shrugged. "How do I know?"

Manny shrugged, too. "I don't know if you can *get* insurance for this. I mean, the guy disappearing and all. That's an act of God, isn't it?"

Brian gave him a hard look, as if he'd caught him at something. "I thought you said they always turn up. Like you've had experience with this kind of thing."

"Not directly. I mean, I read the newspapers, I watch *Entertainment Tonight*. Just like anybody." He leaned back and swiveled his head, trying to get Stacey's attention. She was at another table, and he'd have to wait. "Anyhow," he said, "when he turns up, we'll come back and get the shots we need."

"Don't bet on it," said Brian. Then, to somebody else at the table, a youngish woman with a pinched look: "That commercial airs . . . when?"

"End of the month."

"The commercial airs at the end of the month, Manny."

"He'll be back."

"We won't."

"But the commercial—"

"The commercial will be perfect." Brian narrowed his eyes and pressed his lips into something that was not a smile. "You'll see to it."

Manny set his jaw as if he had some kind of artistic integrity to defend, but before he figured out where he was going next, he realized that Stacey had come up behind him and was ready to take their orders.

Brian looked past him to her. "In case you hadn't figured it out already," he said, "now you can see why they brought me into this job."

Manny shot a look over his shoulder and then slumped in his

chair, visibly wondering if all of that had been about impressing the girl.

Stacey took their orders and was working on them at the bar with Jack when the front door slipped open on a little gust of wind. Chip Walsh came in. He stamped off his boots in the foyer, hung his coat on a peg, and came over to perch on the stool alongside Tina. He had his black knit cap tugged down to his eyebrows and it made him look stupid, so Stacey took a step away from the taps, yanked it off, and dropped it onto the bar, revealing a case of helmet-head that was pretty remarkable even for Chip. He reached up and pushed his blond hair around, but it didn't do any good. She reached over and gave it a little more pushing, but that didn't help either. He was sitting there with a grin on his face, running the band of his wool cap through his fingers and watching Stacey work, when he picked up the vibe that somebody at the tables was staring at him. It turned out to be Brian—who glanced away the second he made eye contact.

"Hey," he said to Stacey. "That guy." Motioning with his thumb.

She glanced up quickly, still working on the drinks.

"What's his deal?" he said. "You know him?"

"How come?"

"The look he was giving me." He shook his head. "Sheesh."

"What do you mean?"

"I don't know. Like he didn't approve of you touching me or something. Kind of weird."

"Don't give it another thought. It's just Brian."

"Brian?"

"Brian."

"*Brian*, Brian?"

"Brian, Brian."

"*Your* Brian?"

"I don't have a Brian anymore."

"But—"

"I know."

"It's *that* Brian, though."

"That Brian. Yes."

"And you didn't tell me? You didn't mention he was here?"

"I didn't get a chance." She finished arranging the drinks on a couple of round trays. "Besides, what difference does it make? What's the big deal?"

If she didn't know, Chip didn't think he ought to go telling her now. Because he'd probably be wrong, and what then?

The bar filled up and Stacey stayed busy. It figured. Everybody in town had been snowed in the night before, and now that the roads were clear they'd all been set free to enjoy a couple of brews and a bowl of Chex Mix and maybe some hot wings. They obviously intended to make the most of it.

Chip ordered a Long Trail and he took his time drinking it. Every now and then he'd slide a look over toward Brian, and every time it turned out that Brian was looking back. There wasn't anything special about the guy, at least as far as Chip could see. He was all right. He was a type that he'd seen a million times before, back in the offices of his father's lobbying firm in Washington. Smooth, he'd say. Oily but not greasy. In control of things, at least within certain parameters. A guy like that could go his whole life and never know his own limitations, since he'd never attempt anything beyond them. A guy like that could actually believe that he had no limitations—that he was capable of anything he put his hand to. Chip figured a guy like that could stand to fail every now and then. It would improve him, and for that reason, among others, he was pleased that Brian had failed with Stacey.

Maybe it had taught him a lesson. Probably not.

Chip hadn't wanted to go through life that way, believing that he was invulnerable and in charge. He could have done just that, easily, if he'd gone into the family business. He could have ended up like his father the oil lobbyist, thinking that he was in control of the whole world, or at least the big parts of it that mattered. The problem was, if you were an oil lobbyist and you really were in charge of the world, then things were starting to look as if you'd screwed the whole deal up pretty badly. Which is just one reason Chip had left behind the family business and a perfectly good trust fund, and come north to Vermont last year for a stint on the Ski Patrol. After one day in first-aid training, a person with any brains knew that he wasn't in control of things. The world could throw almost anything at you.

With that in mind he got another beer and left the stool alongside Tina's and headed over to the table where the TV crew was sitting, to see what happened when the world threw something unexpected in Brian's direction.

The answer was *not much*, at least not right off.

A few people remembered him from the mountain, from that morning when they'd all sat around the picnic tables drinking coffee. The blond actress in particular. She leaned forward—away from a conversation she'd been having with Brian, as if she were coming up for air—and asked Chip how things were on the mountain. As if everybody at the table hadn't been there all day long. As if he had some kind of inside information. As if his opinion was superior to anybody else's in the room.

He just shrugged.

Evan got up to use the men's room, and she took advantage of his absence to slide over into the chair next to Chip, which also happened to be a notch farther away from Brian. Brian just sat there and watched her go, shaking his head, looking dazed. *Hey*, he asked the room without speaking a word, *what am I, chopped liver?*

People laughed, almost sympathetically but not quite, and the girl smiled back from over her shoulder. Then she turned her full attention to Chip, who'd raised his palms and was giving Brian a bewildered look. Bewildered but definitely happy.

Stacey came back with another pitcher of beer and Brian watched her come. He pointed toward Chip and the blonde. "Looks like the outdoorsy types get all the girls around here," he said. Although she looked over at Chip, Brian didn't. Not for a few seconds, anyhow. He kept his eyes locked on Stacey instead, evaluating her expression. She had a thing for that guy Chip, all right. That was for sure. Although she didn't seem to know what to do about it. Or whether she should be doing anything at all. She just looked at that blond-headed ski patroller and that blond-haired actress, put down the pitcher at the other end of the table, and stood there. Brian had never known her to be at a loss for words—except for that one night in Boston when she'd found him in bed with that friend of hers who hadn't been able to keep her hands off him. Right then she hadn't said a single word, she'd just gone all stony and thrown her stuff in the car and had never come back. It sure looked like she was at a loss for words now, too.

Hmm.

Chip, on the other hand, didn't seem to notice a thing. Whatever subtleties were warring in Stacey's brain were utterly lost on the guy. Mister Oblivious, that was Chip. Then again, Brian thought, who could blame him? It looked like he could have it pretty much any way he wanted it. Maybe what they said about those outdoorsy types was true, incredible as it seemed.

TWELVE

S o where are you staying these days?" Brian. Leaning on the bar with his head tilted to one side in that look of phony sincerity that Stacey had learned, in retrospect, to hate.

"I've got a room."

"Oh. A room. Sounds nice."

"It is."

"*A room of one's own*," he said, as if he knew the first thing about Virginia Woolf. As if he ever might.

"It's nice enough."

"Are you subletting from some old spinster?" He might have meant it as a means of suggesting that she was on her way toward becoming an old spinster herself, now that she'd blown him off; or he might have meant it as a way of discovering if she was shacking up with nature boy over there. Or he might have meant nothing by it at all.

Either way, she didn't bite. All she said was, "When are you going home, anyway?" She was leaning against the back bar with her elbows behind her.

Brian was quick, however, she had to give him that. He turned the question right back on her, making it into an invitation. "When are *you* coming home?" he asked, with that soulful look he could pull out of his back pocket on a moment's notice. She hated *that* look, too.

"I moved out of my folks' place a long time ago," she said. "This is home right now."

"Just you and the spinster."

"More like just me and the sheriff."

"The sheriff?" That kind of changed everything. What about Chip? What about *him?*

"Yeah, the sheriff. The sheriff and his wife and kids. That's where I rent. They've got this spare room."

"Sheriff Ramsey?"

"That's right." She took note of a couple of snowmobile guys in those big yellow snowsuits, trying to get her attention from a table in the back. She gave them a sign to suggest that she'd be right there, and one of them upended his empty glass to show that she didn't need to come all the way over to find out what it was they wanted. Just another round of that Long Trail whenever she got around to it. "You met Guy? What was it, another speeding ticket?"

"No. He came by the condo when we couldn't find Harper Stone."

"I guess he still hasn't turned up, huh?"

"No. Not yet."

"Think he will?" Stepping forward to the tap and pulling a couple of Long Trails.

"I don't know why not," he said.

"So, what did Guy think it's all about? He give you any indication?"

"I don't know. He was more interested in finding out what *I* thought it was all about."

"And?"

"Who knows?" He shrugged, wanting another beer but not wanting to ask her for it. If he'd been in their old apartment back in Boston, sitting with his feet up watching football or surfing the Web, he'd have had no trouble asking her to bring him something. He wouldn't have given it a second thought, but now that there was a commercial relationship involved, it just felt weird. Or it felt as if she might think it felt weird. Which was kind of the same thing, wasn't it? He could do without that beer, no problem. He'd have to.

She made a note on her pad and brought the two glasses over to the snowmobile guys. Then she took a stroll around the room to make sure that her tables were happy before returning to her spot behind the bar.

"When do you get off?"

That Brian. He never gave up.

"Past your bedtime."

"You'd know."

"I guess I would," she said. "Lucky me."

"You off this weekend?"

"I ski during the day, and I'm here nights. The weekends are the busiest."

"Right." He stood for a minute thinking, looking down at the bar, and then he looked up. "I thought I might stick around for a few more days," he said. "Since you and I have a few things we never exactly finished talking about."

"I finished," she said. "But suit yourself."

Guy was still awake when she got home. That was unusual. It was probably the first time ever, come to think of it.

The house was off the main road on its own private lane, past a green street sign that read RAMSEY ROAD, PVT. That was the way things were around here. Half the roads were private, which didn't mean that there was anything special about them. All it meant was that it was up to you to keep them plowed in the winter, to cope with the ruts and gullies that would turn them into treacherous swamps come spring, as well as to fill those ruts and gullies with gravel and fresh dirt come summer. Stacey located the turnoff by means of a pair of red reflectors that Guy had put out there a long time ago, nailed five or six feet up on the trunks of birch trees on either side. In the summer they'd be ridiculously high in the air, but in the winter—on account of the snow that the plows threw in all directions—they were just right.

The woods were thick here, dark and deep, and Ramsey Road had a couple of bends in it that hid the house from the road even though it wasn't actually set too far back—no more than fifty yards, as the crow files. However, this was the first time Stacey could remember seeing a light between the trees as she turned in. Sure enough, the floor lamp in the living room was switched on, and she could see it through the blinds as she rounded the last turn and pulled up alongside the house and parked. The blinds were down and tilted shut, even though there was nobody for miles around, and the light leaked out in thin stripes. She went in through the back porch to the kitchen, left her boots in the boot tray, dropped her things in her bedroom back there—it was in a little square extension, a mother-in-law suite almost, wrapped in raw Tyvek that fluttered in the wind and kept her awake at night—and padded out to the living room to see what was up.

Guy sat in his recliner, wearing striped flannel pajamas underneath his white terry cloth bathrobe, an empty milk glass in one hand and the remote in the other. He wasn't using either one of them, though. He was looking hard at the television, sighting across the room between his stocking feet as if along the barrel of a gun. The television was showing some educational travelogue of what looked like Italy or Greece, but Stacey could see right off that he wasn't watching it. He had the sound turned all the way down and was chewing on his lower lip. The muscles in his jaw were working in the reflected multicolored light of some Mediterranean holiday scene.

He'd hardly heard her come in, but when she said his name he shook off his concentration and turned toward her. "Hey, Stacey."

"You're up late."

"I guess I am." He lifted his left hand to look at his watch and discovered that he wasn't wearing it. He'd probably left it on the nightstand up in the bedroom, where Megan had gone to sleep a long while past. "What time is it, anyhow?"

"Two thirty."

"Wow. I had no idea." He squeezed his eyelids shut and gave his head a little shake as if to clear it.

"Something on your mind?"

"That guy who disappeared. I assume it was the talk of the Broken Binding."

"Yes and no."

"Him being a movie star and all."

Stacey sat down on the couch opposite him. "A movie star?" she said. "Maybe you'd better define your terms."

He poked at the remote without looking at it, and instead of going dark the television switched over to a movie. He'd have known it anywhere, inside of two seconds. *Shane*, with that Alan Ladd. Stacey probably didn't consider Alan Ladd a movie star either. Then again he'd been dead since what, sometime in the sixties. That would be before she was born. At least Harper Stone's career was a little more recent than that, however little there might be left of it these days. "I mean," he said, "the guy *did* make some movies. A couple of pretty good ones, to tell the truth."

"I'd hope so. Given his attitude."

"You met him?"

"I guess you could put it that way."

"What do you mean?"

"He was kind of detached, is all."

"Detached." He studied the film of milk in his glass.

"It was probably just the whole movie-star thing. Ego."

"Maybe." He tilted his glass and watched a single drop of milk slide around the bottom of it, circling and thinning itself out. "Still," he said, "tell me more."

"Starstruck, are we?"

"Professionally curious." He clicked the remote again, killing the television this time.

"Right." So she told him the whole thing. Pretty much, anyhow. She told him how she'd run into Stone in the service department at the Slippery Slope, and how when she'd seen him again later on—not more than an hour or so later, really—he'd acted like they'd never set eyes on each other. How he'd smoothed it over as a result of his meeting so many good-looking women in his life, which was both unctuous and egotistical. Real Stacey bait, ha ha ha. It hadn't worked, as Guy could tell.

But Guy wasn't terribly interested in that part of the story. When she finished telling him everything, he went right back to the part about the basement of the Slippery Slope, to the workbench where she'd seen Stone huddled in conversation with Buddy Frommer. "You sure he saw you there in the first place?"

"Absolutely. I looked him right in the eye."

"That's weird."

"I know."

"What'd he say?"

"Nothing. Not that I remember."

"Buddy did all the talking?"

"He didn't exactly say a whole lot. He kind of hustled me out of there."

"That's Buddy. That's Buddy Frommer."

"Does he always act like that?"

"Like what?" He put his milk glass down on the end table and brought the recliner forward.

"Like he does."

"How's that?"

"Come on. You know how he is."

Guy clearly didn't want to put words in her mouth, but this was getting ridiculous. "Irritable, you mean? Or do you mean secretive? Because—"

She tilted her head. "I hadn't thought about *secretive*, but yeah. That's it. Secretive. *And* irritable. Secretive and irritable both. That would pretty much cover the Buddy Frommer Experience."

"No kidding," said Guy, sitting and shaking his head. "My older brother went all the way through school with Buddy, and he hasn't changed since the first grade."

"How does he stay in business?" Thinking that maybe Guy would mention the rumor Chip had suggested, how Buddy might have been selling drugs out of the Slippery Slope. She didn't want to leap to any conclusions, but it sure did make sense, what with that transaction over the workbench and all.

But Guy kept his own counsel on that issue. "He comes from money," is what he said. "His parents bought him a brand-new Camaro when he and my brother were juniors in high school. Regular kids were driving around in third-hand VW Beetles and rusty Ford Falcons and God knows what else. Anything with wheels. Anything that moved. And Buddy got a Camaro for his birthday. I was maybe eight or ten years old, but I still remember it. You can bet my brother never forgave him."

Stacey could see that it still stung.

Guy sat staring off into space, remembering. "It was red. Cherry red."

"Wow," said Stacey.

"Anyway," said Guy, shaking loose that sour old memory and getting back to business, "the bottom line is Stone didn't talk to you."

"No."

"So maybe he didn't see you at all."

"Oh, he did. He saw me. He kind of acknowledged me a little as I was leaving." She touched her brow and moved her hand away slowly. "You know, like that."

"Right. But later on it was as if he hadn't seen you before in his life."

"It's probably nothing. Just his way of making himself feel like a big shot."

"Sure." Guy ran the back of his fingers over the stubble on his chin. "That's probably what it was."

"I wouldn't make anything of it, Guy. Really."

He shifted forward in his chair, either ready to call it a night or just getting started, she couldn't decide. "Tell me," he said. "Did you get a real good look at him? I mean later on, not in the shop. When you were on the mountain."

"It depends on what you mean by 'a real good look.'"

"I mean was there anything . . ." He shrugged his shoulders.

"Do you mean was he . . ."

No clarification from the sheriff. No clarification at all.

"Do you mean was he high or something?"

"You tell me." Folding his hands.

"He didn't act it."

"And you'd know."

Stacey stood up. "Come on, Guy," she said, at a volume that was tilting toward sufficient to wake Megan and the kids upstairs.

He smiled. "No. Sorry. Didn't mean to sound like I was interrogating you."

"Hmph."

"Really. I mean, we're trained to notice things. Behavioral stuff. Physical stuff. I was just thinking out loud. I'm really sorry."

"That's all right."

"No offense. I didn't mean to suggest that you had some kind of experience in that area."

"I know."

Guy got out of the chair and scuffed in his slippers toward the kitchen, and she followed behind him. He turned on the tap and stood rinsing out his glass and she went on past, toward her room.

"Anyhow," she said, "I don't see how a person would be high at nine o'clock in the morning."

"Then you haven't seen as much of the world as I have," Guy said.

THIRTEEN

Guy shared a secretary with the town clerk, a little Scotsman named Archie MacGregor. The plain truth was that MacGregor, who was long retired from his maple sugar business but spent most of his time working at it anyhow, got the better end of the deal. His secretary was supposed to devote two hours a day to the sheriff's paperwork, but she usually fell short because Archie wasn't around to look after his own business more than a couple of mornings a week and she ended up doing it for him. The secretary was his sister-in-law, Mildred Furlong. This morning she was in early, stoked on black coffee and ready to go when Guy showed up.

"I've looked everywhere," she said before he could even get his coat off, "but I can't find the forms you'll need."

"The forms I'll need for what?"

"To file a report on a missing person."

He hung his coat on the hall tree in the lobby and walked through, past her desk and into the records room, toward the hall-way that led to the kitchen and his little office. "What happened?" he said over his shoulder. "You lose somebody?"

Mildred clutched her sweater around her neck. It was a cardigan and she had it pinned with one of those little chains that nobody but deeply unfashionable women of a certain age even remembered wearing, much less still wore. "Why," she said, "I'm referring to *Mister Stone*."

In the kitchen, Guy rinsed out his mug, poured coffee into it, and shook in some sugar. He stirred it with the common spoon and called back to Mildred, "We've got a little ways to go before anybody declares Harper Stone missing."

"I went ahead and called his rental house again this morning," she said. "There wasn't any answer."

"Who authorized that?"

"Now, Guy—"

"Did I authorize that?"

"It was just a telephone call."

He stood in the hallway, sipping at his mug, raising his eyebrows.

"There wasn't any harm in it."

"Did I say there was?"

"You implied it."

"But you were just trying to help."

"I was just trying to help."

Guy opened the door to his office, and didn't even switch on the light. He stepped back to the records room doorway and said, "What you could do to help, if you've got the time, would be to get around to typing up that report I left in the bin yesterday."

Mildred picked up her glasses—they were on another chain around her neck—placed them on her nose, and looked at Guy through them. "Do you mean the one that's right there on your desk?" she asked. "That report?"

He switched on the light and smiled. "Yeah," he said. "I guess that's the one."

"Happy to help," said Mildred.

"I appreciate it," said Guy.

"You're entirely welcome," said Mildred.

The report wasn't long.

It detailed how the sheriff and another individual—Luther Per-kins, who owned Mountaintop Rentals and managed the place on Vista View, and had keys to all of the nicest places in town—had ridden out to the property on Luther's snowmobile, knocked at all the doors and tried all the windows, then finally unlocked the front door and gone inside. The scene was exactly as the caller, one Brian Russell, up from Boston on business, had described it. The Hummer out front. No lights on. Tracks all over the place—footprints and snowmobile treads both—from Russell himself and from the guys who'd taken him out there, Dickie Burns he'd said and somebody else whose name was missing. There'd been two snow-mobiles. Guy and Luther had had to circle around a good distance from the house in order to see that there were no prints or tracks either coming or going, other than their own and those that Brian and Dickie and the other guy had left.

It was kind of a mess, if you cared about it being a mess. If it mattered. Guy didn't happen to think it did, but that wasn't in the report. Unless he missed his guess, Stone hadn't disappeared from the house the night before. Not at all. He hadn't even been in the house the night before. He'd been somewhere else. He hadn't come home, so he hadn't wandered off. So none of this mattered, but Guy went through the motions anyhow. It was what you did. It was part of the job.

The report covered how Guy and Luther went inside to find the house a disaster area. Again, everything was just the way Brian Russell had described it—with the extra advantage of Russell's having walked around contaminating it all, too. The beds were un-made, the kitchen was a wreck, the furniture and throw rugs and

pillows in the various family rooms and public spaces were all
tumbled as if somebody had tossed the place looking for something.
Nobody had. He was pretty sure of that. So it was more as though
the fanciest property in town, a house that rented by the week for
more money than Guy took home in two or three months, had
been lived in by a bunch of cannibals unaccustomed to the norms
of human habitation. Go figure. The way people lived, you just never
knew. It was all Guy could do not to square up the dining room
chairs, fluff the pillows on the couches, and close the cabinet doors
in the kitchen. He'd been raised that way and Megan had kept him
on the straight and narrow at home. By now it was second nature,
but he'd been careful to leave everything just the way he'd found it,
including the picture frames gone cockeyed on the walls. Including
the fireplace with that half-crushed pizza box jammed into it, and
the glass-topped coffee table—with the dusting of white powder
smeared around in the middle.

To tell the truth, though—and that's what the report did; it told
the whole truth and nothing but—he did mess with that last a little.
He scraped a little bit of powder from the glass and swept it into a
ziplock bag, sealed the bag shut, and stuck it into his pocket. Harper
Stone would be back soon enough, he figured, and when the movie
star showed up he'd want to ask him a few questions about that
stuff. Guy was lots more interested in the cocaine on the coffee
table than he was in Stone's whereabouts, actually. One of them was
a law enforcement problem; the other, so far anyhow, was merely an
annoyance.

They had checked the bedrooms upstairs and the game room
down by the garage—Guy had never had much interest in pool,
but the table down there was enough to provoke envy even in the
disinterested—then they moved on to the ski room before heading
out. The report said this was where Brian Russell had entered the
building, and sure enough there were deep tracks in the snow out-

side and the flagstone floor was wet in spots. The ski room was all heavy wood and indirect lighting and gleaming surfaces, like a locker room in some golf club nicer than any that Guy had ever had the opportunity to visit. Like a museum. Like a mausoleum, come to that. The lockers were all shut. Hung on the wall opposite the outside door was a collection of snowshoes that Guy couldn't decide represented a supply or a display. Probably a little of both. All different sizes, all different types. Old wooden jobs with leather straps maintained just like new. New ones made of aluminum and plastic that looked like fat little aircraft carriers. One pair was missing. One of the new ones, to judge by the placement of it. A big pair, too, the size a grown man would need. Its absence from the orderly array on the wall looked like the gap left by a missing tooth. Guy didn't think anything much of it, but he made a note of it anyhow and it ended up in the report. He was just built that way.

"So what are we going to do about Mr. Stone?" Mildred asked. She was a broad woman, nearly as wide as the doorway she blocked. Guy had the impression that she'd been waiting somewhere for him to turn the last page of the report before materializing there with her question.

"What are *we* going to do?" He put a lot of emphasis on that *we*. "Not much. Not today."

"But—"

"No buts, Mildred. Just because it involves Harper Stone, it's not like we're playing in some Hollywood movie here."

Mildred, just slightly overwhelmed at the mention of Stone's proximity, rolled her eyes and fanned herself the way she used to do when she was having hot flashes. Guy didn't remember how long ago that had been, but it was a while. The two of them sure had a history. *"Harper Stone,"* she said.

"That's how all the sweet young things like you say it." He

tapped the sheets of the report on edge to line them up, and slid them into a file folder. "He'll turn up when he's ready."

"But Guy," she said, "what if it's like in *Night Train,* and he's gone off to rescue somebody who's in trouble with the mob and ended up getting in worse trouble himself? What then? He could be in over his head."

"I don't think there's a whole lot of mob activity around here, Mildred."

"You know what I mean. It doesn't have to be the mob, just because it was the mob in *Night Train.*"

"And there isn't any passenger rail service up here anyhow. Just freight. Two trains a day. Unless you go all the way to Rutland."

"It doesn't have to involve a train."

"Or you could go to Albany, I guess."

"Guy."

"People do."

"Guy, really."

"Really, Mildred. I'm not going to get all worked up over a fellow going missing from his condo. He's a grown-up. He's a big boy. He can take care of himself." He slid his top drawer open and rummaged around in it as he talked. "My read on things is that he's just dropped out of sight for a little while." He found what he was after in the drawer—a pair of black sunglasses—and he put them on. "Maybe to evade the paparazzi," he said, looking at Mildred through their dark lenses. "Your hero's just gone incommunicado for a couple of days."

"There aren't any paparazzi around here."

"You've got a camera, don't you?"

"No. Walter used to have a Polaroid but they stopped making film."

"You've got a cell phone."

"I don't know how to use it. I mostly leave it at home."

"It's got a camera in it."

"If you say so."

"See?" said Guy. "The paparazzi are everywhere." He reached for his coffee mug and pretty much drained it in one gulp. "I'm telling you, Mildred: You're the reason he's gone underground."

FOURTEEN

Guy tried Stone's phone number a couple of times as the next hour went by, but no dice. It wasn't like he didn't have anything else to do. A farmer out on the west side of town had reported his new snowmobile missing, and Guy had a pretty strong feeling that the fellow's brother-in-law, a known troublemaker from way back, might have been involved. He ought to get on that. Then Bud Wellman from over at Bud's Suds—the Laundromat in town, right next to the pizza joint—called to complain about a couple of Jamaican guest workers from the mountain who he thought had been jimmying his change machine. This was a complaint that Bud filed about once a month, and Guy knew that it had less to do with the change machine than with a problem Bud had with seeing faces around the Laundromat that weren't quite as pale as his own. He needed to swing by the Laundromat and go through the motions and explain to Bud one more time how all men are created equal. If anybody was jimmying the change machine it was that Danny Bowman, the more or less homeless Vietnam vet who spent more hours a day in Bud's place than Bud did himself. Besides, they'd grown up together, Bud and Danny, right here in the valley where they both still made their way through whatever nonsense life threw at them, which made things different. Bud wouldn't go calling the sheriff on Danny Bowman.

He also needed to drop in on a couple of the TV guys up from Boston, see if they'd heard anything about Stone. Checkout time in the condos was 10:30, so he figured he ought to get on that. The snowmobile and the change machine would have to wait.

When he pulled into the little lot at Trail's End—most of the parking was underground, but there were still a few spaces outside for visitors—the automatic door was just beginning to rise and a car was waiting behind it. New York plates. Could have been anybody. Guy put on his flat-brimmed hat, got out of the car, and approached the door, his feet crunching over hard snow. The door kept rising and the car behind it was revealed inch by inch to be a late-model Jeep Grand Cherokee, filthy as anything, with automatic headlights that clicked off when the door got high enough. Guy couldn't see into it; the sun was bouncing off the windshield and the angle was wrong. So he stepped out of the way and pressed the brim of his hat between his thumb and forefinger and waited, squinting through the driver's-side window as the big SUV pulled forward.

It was Manny Seville, the director. When he'd come by the day before to chat with everybody on the job, Guy hadn't realized that Manny was a New Yorker. He'd figured he was up from Boston like the rest of them, but it made sense now that he thought about it. Why not? Everybody figured that the best of everything in the whole world came from New York . . . unless, on the other hand, the car was a rental, which it probably was—like that Maryland-tagged Hummer parked on Vista View. Manny Seville didn't look like a Grand Cherokee kind of individual, not even this newish one with the leather everything and that big colorful GPS screen glowing away on the dashboard. Guy could see it through the dried mud on the windows. It looked like a movie screen.

Guy lifted the brim of his hat just the slightest and Manny stopped the SUV. He stuck an unlit cigarette between his lips and fumbled with his left hand for the switch to lower the window, then fumbled further with his right to put the car in park. It was definitely a rental, no doubt about it.

As the window began to crawl down Guy said, "Why don't you pull on ahead a little bit, just get her out of the way of the door?" But Manny was busy horsing around with the lighter now, and before he got his cigarette lit and returned his focus to the shifter the door had started to groan back down its track. Guy put up both arms to see if he could stop it but the thing didn't slow down in the least. It just kept coming, like a guillotine in slow motion. That was a safety violation right there, no doubt about it. He'd have to tell the fire marshal, have him look into it. It was always something.

Since he couldn't stop the door he stepped aside, out of its path and into the lot, and watched while Manny threw the Jeep into drive and hit the gas. It was all too little, too late. The Jeep almost cleared the lowering door but not quite, and the point of impact was the sloped rear window. The frame bent and the glass exploded, showering a million pieces everywhere.

"Aww, shit," said Manny.

Guy didn't say anything. He just wondered why people insisted on driving big monsters like this one. If it'd been a regular car, closer to the ground by a foot maybe, Manny would have had time to slip it out of the garage without a scratch.

"For Christ's sake," said Manny, "if you hadn't stopped me, this never would have happened."

"I believe I actually told you to pull forward," said Guy.

"Still." He'd moved the Jeep out into the parking lot and stood behind it, puffing furiously on his cigarette, scowling at the damage. "Of all the shitty luck."

With a heavy groaning of cables the door began to rise again, and Guy walked over toward it. "Let me see if I can find a broom," he said.

"Fat lot of good that'll do me."

"To clean up the concrete. We don't want any flat tires. Even with that safety glass, you never know."

"Oh," said Manny. As if the idea that there were other people in the world who might be worth caring about was a news bulletin.

Once the door was up high enough Guy raised a hand and got the car behind it to stop. Behind the wheel was a fat, middle-aged guy from Connecticut, ski racks loaded up and a mad-bomber hat screwed down on his head, heading out of town for a day over at Killington or someplace. These people paid extra for ski-in/ski-out, and then they went looking for greener pastures. Go figure. The fat guy looked alarmed at the sight of the sheriff in his flat-brimmed hat. Guy smiled and the fat guy cocked his head. Guy pointed to the glass all around and the fat guy settled back in his seat. There was a broom against the wall that Guy used to push the glass and various bits of metal and hard red plastic out of the way. There was always so much more of it than you'd expect after a crash. Things fell apart and in the process they somehow got more complicated. The good news was that the garage door looked as if it had made it through pretty much unscathed—or at least no more damaged than it had been to start with. That was a plus. He'd mention it to the fellow who managed Trail's End—it was Luther Perkins's brother-in-law, and they shared office space in town—when he got the chance.

When he was finished with the broom he signaled for the fat guy from Connecticut to come on through, which he did. At no point had the fat guy even rolled down his window to make a little small talk. Guy shook his head thinking about it. What got into people? Did they think everybody in the world was there only to wait on them? Probably. He leaned the broom against the wall and watched the fat guy leave the parking lot and turn hard onto the access road without even slowing down, tires squealing, gunning the engine to cut in front of a minivan full of kids from the mountain school. Just making up for the time he'd lost waiting for Guy to sweep up. The nerve. If Guy had been in his car instead of standing here flat-footed, he'd have given him a ticket fast enough to make his head spin—and the fat guy knew it, no question.

Manny was still looking sore when Guy came back. He was leaning against the Jeep, getting his long leather coat dirty, hollering into his cell phone as if volume would improve the lousy connection. "I'm telling you I can't drive this thing all the way back to New York the way it is," he was saying, "and I can't wait until the day after tomorrow for you to get me a replacement." He pulled the phone away from his ear and glared at it. "Hey," he began hollering at it again, "can you even hear me?"

Guy took him by the elbow. Manny looked irritated and shook his hand off. Guy took him by the elbow again and walked him up toward the building and around the side, onto the little railed stoop that served as an entranceway. Nobody used it on account of the underground parking, and it was just barely shoveled, but cell reception was better up there. Guy had a detailed map of the whole county in his head, showing spots like this one. That was half of what law enforcement was about in Vermont—keeping track of where you could make a call.

Manny begrudged him a sharp little smile, but he still didn't stop hollering into the phone. "Where do you think I am, that you can't get me a goddamn car? On the fucking moon?"

A gust of wind blew up from out of the north, and Guy fastened the top button on his coat against it. He figured that for all the good that Manny's shouting was going to do, they might as well be on the moon as here.

"I don't care that somebody has to drive one up from Albany. They can drive one up from Miami for all I care. As long as they get here by two o'clock this afternoon." He stabbed the connection off and jammed the phone into his pocket, then stood looking out at the mountains. He wasn't really looking at them, but he definitely wasn't looking at Guy either.

"Connection's better over here, no?"

He had to admit it. "Yeah. Thanks."

"So when's your car coming?"

"Your guess is as good as mine."

"My guess is tomorrow, maybe the next day."

"Damn," said Manny. He waited a minute, then he said it three more times for good measure.

"When're you due home?"

"I was due the day before yesterday, but the weather wasn't co-operating and the shoot was going overtime so I moved some things around. Worked it so I didn't have to be back until tomorrow."

"Tomorrow early?"

"Tomorrow first thing."

"Maybe you'd better move some more things around."

"I wish I could. I wish it was that easy."

Guy watched another car leave the underground garage. It was an old junker with Maine tags. "Maybe somebody else can give you a lift."

"They're all gone. All but that Brian guy."

"So ride with him."

"He's not going."

"Then I guess you're going to have to enjoy our hospitality for a little while longer."

"Great," said Manny. "That'll be just great."

FIFTEEN

Winds were always high on the backside of a storm, but that was yesterday. This morning conditions on the mountain were just about perfect—if you didn't count the crowds up from the flatlands, or the extensive work that the groomers had done on their behalf the night before. Ninety percent of the mountain was groomed down into picture-perfect corduroy, smooth and skiable as anything in this world or the next. Which was fine with Stacey, as far as it went, but what made her happiest was finding a cache of untouched powder—either in the gladed runs like Blowdown and Hold Tight, or off-piste on the far side of the North Peak. She always felt a little guilty ducking under the fence and setting off beyond the official boundary of the ski area, and she knew that if she got in trouble over there she'd be by definition on her own, but a couple of runs couldn't hurt. Especially once the crowds began to build up at 10:30, when even the bumps on Watch This! and Devil May Care began to get scoured clean.

There would sure as heck be plenty of snow over there, though, and there wasn't much chance she'd get lost. People said you could see town from most every angle as long as you got clear of the trees, and that there were lots of places from where you could see the lifts running up the face of the main mountain, so it wasn't going to be that big a deal. Besides, she happened to be a pretty darned good skier.

So she went.

And holy cow, was there ever snow over there.

Buckets of it. Mounds of it. Drifts and piles and waves and clouds and shoals and fields and mountains stacked upon mountains of it. Talk about *first tracks*. As often as Stacey had made sure to be among the first paying skiers down Spruce Peak in the morning, she'd never experienced anything quite like this. It was complex and clean and easy and difficult all at once. It set her legs on fire and it turned some animal part of her brain loose.

This, she decided after no more than forty-five seconds of bliss, *was skiing.*

The trees were far enough apart to be fun, not treacherous, and the underbrush was buried beneath so many feet of snow that she didn't even have to consider it. She swooped through the long curves and whooped through the short ones. She skied where the mountain wanted her to, not where some team of engineers and lumberjacks had decided that she should. It was, in short, heaven. It couldn't last forever, but she sure did wish it would.

The line at the bottom of the North Peak lift, when she dropped out of the trees above it and found herself legal again, was longer than she'd have liked. There was even a wait for the Porta-Potty, which was never a good sign. And the singles line, which generally went faster than the main line even though it looked longer, didn't seem to be moving at all. So she skated around to what seemed like the lighter of the two sides and settled in for the duration. The sun was bright and she had worked up a sweat in the deep snow off the trails. Standing still cooled her off. The break was nice, but she could have used a little less of it.

Between the two main lines was a gap, marked by orange plastic cones, where patrollers and people taking lessons could get to the lift without waiting in line. She saw Chip zoom into it. He pulled up short behind an instructor doing his best to manage what looked like a pair of twin girls, probably four or five years old, all bundled up in pink and purple. Stacey saw him offer to help wrangle them onto the lift and watched them climb on together, the lift operator slowing down the chair to make it easier. Chip got the girls settled and then looked back over his shoulder, and Stacey was pretty sure he'd caught sight of her. It turned out she was right, because when she finally got to the top of the mountain—it seemed like half an hour later, but it was probably fifteen minutes—he was waiting for her.

"Here comes trouble," he said when she skied over.

"What do you mean, *trouble?*"

"I mean as in skiing out-of-bounds can cost you your ticket." He raised his goggles and squinted at her, trying his best to look serious.

"Come on. It was just a *little bit* out of bounds. And hey, you wouldn't pull my ticket."

"You never know."

"I do know." She grinned, settled her goggles on her face, and adjusted the straps of her poles. "Anyway," she said, "what makes you so sure I was out of bounds to begin with?"

"It doesn't take a rocket scientist. You see a person coming back *in bounds*, you figure that person's been *out of bounds*."

"Well, I had to get to the lift."

"I could see that."

"I sure wasn't going to hike up."

"I guess not." He pulled his goggles back down, too.

"So there you go."

"There you go." One after another, he clapped his skis on the hardpack to knock the snow loose. "So tell me," he said just as he was looking about ready to take off. "How was it over there?"

"It was gorgeous," she said. "And there was nobody. That was the main thing."

"You sure about that?"

"About what?"

"About there being no people?"

"Sure I'm sure."

"Because ticket-pulling isn't the worst that could happen."

"I know."

"A person goes over there, he could ski into a tree and knock himself out and nobody'd ever find him."

Stacey grinned at Chip. "Maybe you'd better go check, huh?"

Chip permitted himself a tiny smile.

"Maybe you'd better go see if somebody's in trouble over there," she said.

"You know," said Chip, "I think maybe I'd better."

"Just to be on the safe side."

"Right."

"I mean, *what if?*"

"*What if* indeed."

"You need some help?"

"I'd hate to involve a nonprofessional," he said, "but the buddy system is always the safe way to go. Come to think of it, you'd be doing the Patrol a great service."

"Am I invited?"

"Would you mind?"

"It'd be my pleasure."

"When we get near the bottom," he said as they pushed off, "I can show you a much less conspicuous way out of the trees and back to the lift."

Manny and Guy were in a booth at Judge Roy Beans. The place was empty except for the two of them. Even the counterman was gone, having slipped outside to grab a smoke while the crowd was light.

"So anyway," said Guy, "since you're still here and all, I was wondering."

"What?"

"You heard anything from that guy Stone?"

"Nah."

"Nothing?"

"Nothing."

"No call?"

"I'm the last person he'd call." Manny took a sip of his coffee and winced. He put it down in front of him and looked at it as if it were poison.

"I guess," said Guy. "Why call the director, huh?" He was giving Manny a look that Manny wasn't going to like much.

"You don't understand. The director isn't in charge of anything, except on the set. He doesn't run the project. Not by a million miles."

"Is that so?" Guy looked surprised and a little bit impressed. The world was full of arcane knowledge.

"Absolutely. The director's a hired hand, just like everybody else."

"Just like Stone."

"Try telling that to *him*."

"How do you mean?"

Manny sat without saying anything for a minute. His gaze flicked over to the window and back again. He looked like a man who wanted something and couldn't have it.

Finally it occurred to Guy that that's just what he was, and that what he wanted was a cigarette. Manny clearly envied the counterman, outside in the cold wind in just his shirtsleeves, enjoying a smoke. Guy could have invited him to go on out and satisfy the urge—he could have gone out with him—but he didn't. He just kept thinking about Stone and Manny and the relationship between them, and he waited a beat or two. "You don't seem to like the fellow very much," he said at last, when Manny didn't seem to feel like telling him anything more. Like that might jog him a little.

"Who does? He's a schmuck."

"Really."

"First class. Top shelf."

"Is that so?"

"Absolutely," said Manny. "He always has been."

Guy pulled at his lip and didn't make any other response.

If Manny thought he'd said too much with that last, he didn't show it. Then again the sheriff didn't look like he'd noticed it either. After a minute Guy even seemed to let him off the hook. *"Always,"* he said. "So that's, like, a well-known thing, huh? Stone being a pain in the neck?"

"It sure is."

"I'll be. The stuff you people in the business know."

"Right."

"A guy like myself, I'd never get wind of that. It's like how they said Rock Hudson was gay. I'd never have known that unless I read about it in the papers. And if a guy is just a pain in the neck or something—I mean just a regular pain in the neck, not a child abuser or a drunk driver or a dope fiend or something on that order—if a guy is just kind of irritating, I guess that wouldn't make the newspapers."

" 'Kind of irritating.' That's putting it mildly."

"You said a 'schmuck.' That was the word you used."

"From the word 'go,' Sheriff. A Grade-A schmuck." He drank a little bit more and twisted his mouth as if the taste of it actually hurt. "How about I go out and have a cigarette while you finish up your coffee?"

"I'll come with you."

"You smoke?"

"No," said Guy. "I used to, but I gave it up a long time ago. I just like the fresh air."

SIXTEEN

"You're off tonight, right?"

Chip and Stacey were riding the lift alone. It was lunchtime on the slopes—lunchtime lasted from eleven thirty until maybe quarter to two—and the crowds had all gone indoors to fill up on lousy clam chowder and cold chili dogs and rubbery hamburgers, all of it overpriced by a factor of three or four. If there was one thing any serious skier knew, it was that on a busy day you had your lunch either before everybody else or after. If you had lunch at all. The best skiing was first thing in the morning, before the flatlanders showed up. The second-best was over lunch, when they stormed the cafeterias and got out of your way.

"Yeah," Stacey said. "Tonight's my night off."

"Got anything in mind?"

"A proper dinner," she said. "A girl can't live on free hot wings alone. Not for long, anyhow."

"There's always Chex Mix."

"Right. Chex Mix."

They rode in silence for a little while. Stacey thought he might be fixing to invite her to go out and get something for dinner, but then she changed her mind and decided he was waiting for her to invite him. Either way, neither of them spoke up. They rode on side by side, looking down at a few kids who were trying to kill themselves on the terrain park underneath the lift. Chip kept a professional eye on them, but Stacey just shook her head.

Chip began. "How about later on we—"

At last, Stacey thought, *here it comes.*

But he cut himself off in mid-sentence, wincing at the sight of a kid dropping off the edge of a rail and cracking the back of his head on the hard edge of it. Thank God for helmets. Still, Chip kept watching—turning around almost 180 degrees in the chair—and he didn't resume what he'd been saying until the kid had stood up and shaken himself off. And even then Stacey had to jog his memory.

"You were saying? About later on?"

"Oh. Yeah. Right." He straightened himself in the chair. "How about we get together after supper and do some *real* off-piste skiing?"

Hmm. So there was no dinner invitation after all. But that was fine, because the off-piste skiing invitation was plenty more interesting than mere food. She gave him a quizzical look. "Everything's closed after supper, though. Everything closes at quarter of four."

"Not everything. There's a whole world out there, Stace."

"Stacey." Brian was the only one she'd ever let call her Stace, and she wished she hadn't.

"There's a whole world out there, Stacey. And there's going to be a full moon to light it all up."

"What're you talking about?"

"Not a cloud in the sky, either. Look at that. Not right now."

"Enough with the meteorology. What are you talking about *doing?*"

The lift station was getting closer. They lifted the bar, tightened their grip on their poles, and raised the tips of their skis. "You've got to plan ahead for night skiing, is all. You've got to watch the weather. Especially if you're going for those huge stashes of powder underneath the power lines." He pointed with his poles as they slid down the ramp. Stacey followed their angle, past the abandoned fire tower, up over the trees, to the spot where a line of transmission towers stalked over the mountains like giant robots from another planet. She'd seen them from town a million times but had never noticed them from here. It had never occurred to her that you might reach them, much less get over there and use the bare swath of land under them as your own personal, untouched, pristine, virginal ski slope.

"You're on, pal," she said. "Oh, you are *so* on." She stood gazing up in wonder, and before she knew what she was saying she had asked him to have a quick bite to eat beforehand. Or maybe afterward. Whatever.

How was he supposed to refuse? So now dinner was on, too.

"Hey, Sheriff." The counterman, in shirtsleeves and a white apron, was working on his second or third cigarette. He turned to see Guy and Manny come out, both of them just as underdressed for the temperature as he was.

"Hey, Earl."

"You need something? Can I—?"

"Nope. Mr. Seville, here, just thought he might like to grab a smoke."

"Right. Gotcha."

Manny fired up.

"You need anything, though—"

"Thanks. We're covered."

The sky was bright and blue and cloudless, and they stood in a line against the plate-glass window looking at it. They couldn't see the runs from here, but every now and then a car passed and turned up the access road to the mountain.

Manny sucked on his cigarette and blew smoke from the corner of his mouth. "You got someplace else to be?" he asked Guy.

"It doesn't look to me like a heavy crime day."

"You never know."

"How about you, Earl?" Guy turned to the counterman. "You seen any criminal activity this morning? Anybody suspicious lurking around the place?"

The counterman just laughed, blowing smoke.

Guy turned back to Manny. "I'll have you know that Earl, here, is one of my top informants. So I guess I've got a little time on my hands after all."

Earl laughed, then shouldered the door open and went back inside, saying he had to use the john.

When they were alone again, Guy cleared his throat against the cold and without turning his head to Manny said right out, "So he's a schmuck, huh?"

"Earl?" said Manny. "That guy runs the place?"

"Not Earl, no. And Earl doesn't run the place. He just runs the counter, five days a week. Kind of like you and the commercial."

"Ah."

"I'm talking about Harper Stone. You said he was a schmuck."

"I did."

"How would you mean that?"

"Hey," Manny said, "is this an interrogation? It's no crime not liking a person."

"I know that," said Guy. "I know that full well."

"So is this an interrogation?"

"I don't think so," said Guy. "Does it seem like an interrogation to you? I'm just trying to learn everything I can about Harper Stone, and right now you're the best source of information I've got." He watched Manny grind out his cigarette on the concrete, and kept watching him until Manny got self-conscious and picked up the butt, making sure it was cold before putting it into the trash can. Some people needed law enforcement coverage all the time. "That's kind of a shame, don't you think?"

"What?"

"That you're the best source I've got. A guy comes to a strange town where he has no friends or family or anything, and he disappears off the face of the earth. Leaving a guy like you—a business associate who knew him for what, maybe a long weekend?—the only one I can talk to about him."

"There's Brian."

"There's Brian. Right. Right you are."

"Besides, everybody knows Harper Stone."

"Not everybody," said Guy, thinking of Stacey. "To tell you the truth, I'm afraid that the days when Harper Stone was on everybody's radar are long gone."

"You sound like his manager."

"Do you mean that? You know his manager?"

"Sure."

"So you two go back a ways. Or is that something else I don't understand about your business? You all know each other."

Manny said no, that was right. He'd known Stone for a lot longer than the weekend.

"No wonder you're so confident about what kind of person he is."

A spotless black Audi pulled up and two men in business suits got out. They came across the lot toward the coffee shop and greeted Guy, who swung the door open and pointed out that Earl might still be in the men's room. They'd have to wait for a second. That seemed fine with them.

"Look," Manny said, "I'm beginning to be sorry I ever said anything negative about the guy. I didn't mean anything by it."

"Don't be. Other people—people who maybe just ran into him in town, is all—other people said he was kind of a queer guy, too."

"Not like that. He wasn't—"

"I don't mean *queer* queer."

"Right."

"I mean the kind of guy who might look you in the eye and not even notice you."

"Aha," said Manny. "That's him, all right." He lit another cigarette. "That's Harper Stone all over."

"You think maybe it's just ego?"

"Sure. If by 'ego' you mean *cocaine*."

Guy looked shocked. "No," he said. And then, "Really?"

"Really."

"I'll be. I thought that stuff appealed to a younger crowd."

"There's younger and there's younger. You can be younger than Stone and still be in the nursing home."

"I guess you're right."

"Which is his whole problem."

"Really?"

"Sure. The guy's a has-been. Washed up. That's got to be hard to take, after you've been on top."

Guy bit the inside of his lip and nodded, watching a couple of cars turn up the access road to the mountain. When he'd processed everything, he said, "If you don't mind my asking, tell me how far back you two guys go."

SEVENTEEN

Manny Seville and the former movie star went almost all the way back to when Harper Stone's name was neither Harper nor Stone. In fact, on the day they'd first sat down on the concrete steps in front of his seedy Hollywood apartment to watch the girls go by and share a couple of beers and a pack of cigarettes, the mailman had handed Stone a stack of junk and bills and said, "Nothing here from Otto Preminger, Mr. Schwartzmann. Better luck tomorrow."

The incipient movie star flashed his teeth at the mailman and said, "Very funny, very funny."

The mailman seemed to think it was, since he kept laughing all the way up the steps. He was still laughing as he opened the door and went in to distribute the mail, and was at it still when he came back out and walked down the street.

Once he was out of earshot, Manny tipped his bottle back and swallowed. "Mister Schwartzmann?"

"So I haven't had a chance to get legal. Sue me."

Manny grabbed an envelope. "Howard?"

"You never heard of a stage name?"

"Howard Schwartzmann?"

"You know what John Wayne's real name is? Marion. Marion Morrison. And that Cary Grant? He used to be Archibald Leach, until he got wise." He drained his beer. "*Marion. Archibald.* So don't start making fun of your friend Howard." He set the bottle down on the step beside him. "And never, *ever*, let on that you know."

"Of course not."

"Or you're a dead man."

"Of course not, *Howie*." Manny made his eyebrows jump.

"My mother calls me Howie. Don't you."

"Fine. The whole thing'll be our little secret."

The two of them had known each other for six months or so. They worked together on the back lot at Warner's, two chumps from nowhere trying to break into the movie business. In Manny's case, "nowhere" was the Bronx. In Schwartzmann's, it was some county in Nebraska where the grass grew high and the sun hung higher still, and there was nothing within a thousand miles to interest a big dreamer like him. How his parents had landed there he would never know. They would stay there forever, his mother calling once a week to beg him to come home, his father slipping a few bucks into an envelope every month and mailing it off to this apartment building either to keep him going or to keep him gone. It didn't matter which. Even when he finally got legal with his new identity, Stone didn't tell his father and the envelopes kept coming—addressed to his former self. How could you cut that off? So what if it meant the end of the noble Schwartzmann line? There was no reason for his old man to be the wiser.

The two of them were runners on the back lot, errand boys in the grand tradition. Manny wanted technical work and he was getting closer to corralling some of it. He sucked up to every assistant director and lighting guy and cameraman he ran across, and a couple of them were starting to recognize him. It was a start. Stone had bigger ideas, of course. He wanted to be a movie star, and at the moment he figured the best way to do that was to stage a performance every day as the very best errand boy in the whole wide world. The smartest, the sharpest, the handsomest, the best-natured, and the most efficient. As a result he was getting a reputation as a real first-class errand boy, while Manny was on the verge of stepping up in the business.

"So what was it?" Guy asked. "You loan him money or what?"

"Worse than that," Manny said. He pursed his lips around his cigarette and stood there looking as if he wanted to suck the whole thing right down into his lungs. Like that would put an end to something.

"Worse than money?"

Manny dragged on the cigarette, took it from between his lips, and scrubbed it out against the heel of his boot. He took a step forward and tossed the butt into the trash can, then stood there in the entryway breathing out smoke, letting it out so slowly and over such a long period that it seemed as if something inside of him might have caught fire. "Worse," he said finally, not looking at Guy. "It wasn't money. It was a girl."

"A girl."

"Only you don't loan a girl. And a person like Harper Stone, he isn't much on giving them back when he's done."

"I gather that his star was finally beginning to rise," Guy said.

"Not with me it wasn't," said Manny, still rueful after all these years.

Stacey and Chip had ended up taking a late lunch—if you could call a cup of lukewarm tea and a squashed granola bar "lunch," which she certainly did—after the crowds had returned to the slopes and the cafeteria had emptied out. That meant they could put off supper until after they'd skied the power lines. In the mountains the sun

went down around quarter to four, and it would be fully dark by five.
All they'd have would be the moon, plus a couple of headlamps that
Chip kept in his backpack. But that would be all they'd need.

"Let's see," he said as he took off his boots in the Patrol shack at
the bottom of the mountain. "We've got two choices. If you want to
do it the hard way, we can skin all the way up and ski back down.
Or else we can spot a car at the top and the bottom."

"If we drive," Stacey said, thinking, "do you think we could ski it
more than once?"

"I don't see why not."

"Then never mind the hard way."

"I second that."

"But how do we drive up there?"

"There's an access road around the back side of the mountain.
Goes to this cabin? All set up with a windmill and solar and everything? Real off-the-grid stuff, about three-quarters of the way up to
the peak. Pioneers."

"You sure it's plowed?"

"I think the guy who lives there works over in Rutland someplace. I see him around. He comes and goes all the time. We'll leave
your car down where the power lines come into town, there by the
park, and we'll take mine up past the cabin as far as we can get.
Climb up the rest of the way, and we're in business."

"Have you done this before?"

"I've thought about it plenty."

"That's good enough for me."

They met in the park around seven, their cars loaded up with
heavier and warmer gear than they'd have worn in the sunshine.
Nothing on earth was much colder than night skiing, moonlit or
otherwise. People around here didn't do it much. None of the Vermont mountains offered it on a commercial basis. There was no

market for it, at least not among the sane. You had to go south into New York if you wanted that kind of thing, down to the Catskills where the slopes were so crowded you felt like a sardine. Or all the way to the sorrowful Poconos of Pennsylvania.

Stacey pulled up behind Chip's Wrangler, checking the clock on her dashboard and hoping she hadn't made him wait too long. The Wrangler was an old army-green wreck with a sagging canvas top that was no use against the wind and the cold. He wasn't in the car, though. He was on a bench in the park, sitting there in the darkness and admiring the mountain through the moonlit trees. She went over and sat beside him, shivering a little bit already. On the mountain the groomers swarmed from trail to trail, little points of light moving against pale snow and black woods.

"It's cold," Stacey said.

"Yeah."

She thought he might take advantage of the opportunity to put an arm around her—boy and girl, park bench, freezing cold, darkness—but he didn't. She wasn't sure how she felt about that.

He pointed toward the groomers on the mountain. "Those guys aren't cold, I can tell you that. They're riding in the lap of luxury."

"I'll bet."

"I'm not kidding. Leather seats, cup holders, big honking stereos—the works. I've never been in one, but Andy Paxton's told me all about it."

"I forgot. You two are like this." She held up a mittened hand. Chip had to take it on faith that she had two fingers crossed inside of it.

"We are. Andy and me."

"I know."

Andy Paxton was the patriarch of the family that owned Spruce Peak. It had been in his family for generations. He'd raised two sons on the mountain, both of them as different from their father as people could be and still be walking around upright. One of them, in fact—David, the younger of the two—wasn't actually walking around upright anymore. He'd died earlier in the winter, a month or so back. And the other—Richie, the older one, the philanderer and egomaniac—had had more to do with the reasons for it than anyone could ever be entirely comfortable with. No wonder that as Chip's path had crossed with Andy's they'd recognized each other as kindred spirits. The father and the son that life had denied each of them, delivered better late than never.

"Andy's my *other* night-skiing buddy."

She knew all about how Andy and Chip liked to skin up the mountain after the groomers were through and sail back down on the freshest of corduroy. So now she was Chip's buddy, just like old man Paxton. She wasn't sure how she felt about that, either. "Right," was all she said.

"How about we get going?" Chip said. So they stood up and walked to the curb and swapped her stuff into his car.

EIGHTEEN

A light in the woods. It was the cabin Chip had mentioned, yellow windows glowing through the leafless trees. Stacey saw it as they rounded a switchback on the road that led up the back of the mountain. She was amazed at how empty and dark it was back there. Compared to the front side, which had been civilized with trails and lift towers and lodge buildings and condos galore, the back side was pretty much a wilderness, except for this narrow and barely plowed road, and that light in the trees up above.

"What is it, a couple of miles up here?"

"Seems like it," Chip said. "The odometer's busted, so it's hard to say."

"There are some hiking trails back here someplace, aren't there?"

Chip said there were, although he'd never given any of them a try. He was more the biking and kayaking type.

"We'll have to check them out in the summer," she said. Kind of trying that out.

"We will," he said. "We'll bring a picnic."

A picnic. That put her a step ahead of Andy Paxton. All right, then.

Stacey's instinct was to expect a road like this to get narrower as they went up, but that was pretty much impossible. The road was basically a tunnel through three feet of packed snow, precisely the width of two passes of a pickup-mounted snowplow—one going up and one coming down. It didn't get any wider than that and it didn't get any narrower, either. They rounded a few more bends, the lights of the cabin flickering into view and out of it again, and then the road straightened out and made directly for the cabin. Just a hundred yards or so, and they'd be stopping.

The Wrangler's headlights, dim as they were with age and a crusting of ice, must have cast some illumination on the inside of the cabin, because before they'd gone so much as fifty feet past the curve a black silhouette appeared in the front picture window.

"Uh-oh," said Stacey. She crouched down instinctively in her seat.

"What?"

"I don't know. It's just—is this private property, or what?"

"Who knows?" He didn't slow the car. "Everything's fine, though. Trust me. We're not causing any trouble."

The cabin was on Brian's side of the car, the uphill side. In the window where the first shadow had appeared there was now another, this second one materializing slowly from the dimness on the other side of the room. Perhaps from down a dark hallway, or from out of an ill-lit kitchen or someplace. There was a sheer curtain across the window that shifted and swayed a little with the movement of the two figures, growing dense in places and airy in other places. It gave the whole prospect a ghostly look.

"I guess he's got somebody there with him," Chip said.

"Probably he's married."

"Could be. Probably. I don't know."

The second figure was at least a head shorter than the first, and broader in every dimension. Stacey studied the two of them, man and woman, and imagined the painting *American Gothic*. She saw her as a farm wife living a hard existence here on the mountain. It was better than picturing her as second in command to an ax murderer, or some kind of Mother Bates, ready to work mischief.

While she was persuading herself, the first figure ducked out of sight. The farm wife stayed put as the Jeep drew nearer, standing stoically behind the curtain, not moving a muscle that Stacey could see. Chip flashed his lights, trusting that it would be taken for a friendly greeting. A little tip of the hat, a neighborly wave. Hoping further that the figure in the window might raise a kindly hand in return.

Nothing.

"Why would you live all the way up here, anyhow?" said Stacey.

"I guess because you wanted your privacy."

"Great," she said, leaning forward to peer through the windshield and wondering if the figure in the window could make her out past the headlights. "That's great."

The road was plowed for a little distance past the cabin, up to a shack that wasn't quite big enough to be a garage and probably held tools, a snowmobile, maybe a little powerboat for trolling on the lakes come summer. Either that or chain saws and meathooks and bloody carcasses, swaying ever so slightly in the cold night air. Stacey shivered at the thought and a porch light snapped on, throwing light across the cabin's front yard and pitching the shack behind it into deeper darkness. The paintless old pickup truck that had cleared the road was pulled up in front. The only real color in the whole stark tableau was the blade of the plow mounted on the pickup, a swath of wrenchingly brilliant yellow against the darkness. It looked like acid, ready to eat through something.

They looked back toward the window to see the woman standing there still, planted like a fireplug. She may have actually moved back a step or two now that the porch light was on. Her silhouette had taken on a little bit of color in the light of the room, but her presence had become vaguer yet, blurred and shadowy. Then the front door cracked open and the man swarmed out onto the snowy porch. He was even taller than they'd guessed, long as a scarecrow and just as thin, and he hollered something at them that they didn't hear over the noise of the Jeep. He jutted his chin up and snapped his head back and shouted it again, and this time Chip cut the engine.

"Not a good idea," Stacey said. "We want to stay mobile, right?"

Rather than take her advice, Chip had started rolling down the window. "Don't sweat it," he said. "I don't think turning around right now is much of an option anyway. And I'm sure as heck not *backing* the whole way down." He got the window open—the night air was frigid even compared to the inside of the Wrangler, thanks to the constant blast of the heater—and he stuck his arm out. "Howdy!"

"You're either lost or crazy," said the tall man. "Which one is it?" He stood on the porch in a T-shirt and an orange down vest, grinning like a sphinx at Chip, both hands jammed deep into his pockets.

That's a step in the right direction, Stacey thought. *At least he doesn't have a gun.*

"I don't believe I'm crazy," Chip said, "but I'm hoping like anything to get a little bit lost."

"There's only one way down. You turn right around and go back where you come from." He circled his finger around, making the universal symbol for U-turn. Stacey decided that he seemed reassuringly ordinary, now that she was getting a good look at him. Well, maybe not *reassuringly* ordinary, but at least ordinary. Which covered a lot of ground.

"I think I'll do it the hard way," Chip said. He pointed with his thumb back over his shoulder. "We've got skis."

"Oh, for the love of Mike." The tall man sighed. "Another one."

"Another one?"

"This ain't no rescue mission," the tall man said. He came down off the porch and walked toward the car and leaned forward, almost but not quite sticking his head in the window. He tilted it and bobbed it this way and that, sizing up Chip and squinting at Stacey in the dark, trying to get a look at the gear they carried. His breath emerged sour and strong, even from the other side of the car, and Stacey realized he'd been drinking. "If I'd known how many morons'd be wandering around these woods, knocking on the door at all hours, I don't think I'd ever built this place. There's times I've got half a mind to shut off the lights and let 'em freeze." He drew one hand from his pocket and put it on the door to steady himself.

"Lost skiers. You're talking about lost skiers."

"Damn straight, I'm talking about lost skiers. They go out of bounds and get a little bit mixed up, and the next thing you know they're banging on my door. It's like I'm running a ranger station up here."

Chip offered the tall man a big smile, grinning right into the gusts of his whiskey breath. "See," he said, "we mean to do just the opposite. We're going to hike *up* to the peak, and ski *down* under the power lines. We left a car down there. In town."

The man took his hand off the car door and ran his palm over his buzz cut. "There's a new kind of idiot born every day of the week."

"Really. It's OK. I'm on the Ski Patrol."

The man raised his eyebrows. "Oh," he said. "A *professional*. That makes all the difference, now, don't it?" He rapped his knuckles on the doorsill and moved away, backing off toward the porch. "Suit yourselves," he said. "I guess it's a free country. Ten thirty is lights-out, though, so don't come knocking after that or I might have to run you the hell off."

"Understood," said Chip. He rolled up the window, started the

Jeep, and pulled it past the cabin and next to the shack, just as far up the hill as it would go until the plowing ran out and the snow-drifts set in.

The groomers were just finishing as Stacey and Chip crested the peak, a dozen pairs of taillights in a long line far below, snaking across the lower slopes toward the maintenance shed. They winked on and off through the trees, one last intrusion of civilization against the wilderness, going black two by two.

There was a lot of snow up here, but it wasn't consistent. Whole swaths of the mountainside were blown bare over broad expanses of naked rock, and the base of the fire tower with its jumble of boulders was almost entirely clear. In other places, it was God knew how deep. And everywhere the wind was a killer—brutal and bit-ing and without mercy, even at this hour.

They slogged over to the fire tower and perched on the rocks to sip a little water, eat a couple of energy bars, and get set for the trip down. They unholstered their skis from their packs and clicked in. They swapped their knit caps for helmets, and stashed the caps in their packs. There was no need for headlamps up here, not with the moon as bright as it was. They'd needed them under the tree cover on the way up from the cabin, no question. And soon enough they would need them again, as they struck out beneath the trees toward the power lines.

It was a straight shot across the ridgeline, and on skis it didn't take long. The trees and underbrush didn't exactly thin out as they neared the edge of the clearing; it all just stopped dead, leaving Stacey and Chip to break out into a bright and moonlit right-of-way marked by dark woods on either side and a long march of elec-trical towers down the middle. They could see what looked like the whole world—make that *worlds*, since you had to include the in-finite space that spun over their heads, blue space full of more stars than Stacey had ever seen in all her years in Boston. Not to mention the mighty Milky Way itself, a phenomenon which, prior to coming to the Green Mountain State, she had considered nothing more then a lovely rumor.

The town and the valley were spread out below them. There were great dark patches that were forests and small darker spots that were houses, and there were great swaths of gleaming white that were pastures and fields and open spaces, fresh and untracked still. Scattered all around were tiny yellow lights like gemstones, some of them moving and some of them fixed, and all of them heartbreakingly beautiful and faraway.

"Wow," said Chip.

"Yeah," said Stacey. "If I weren't freezing my butt off, I could stay here forever."

"You're right," he said. "You want first tracks?"

By way of answer, she clicked off her headlamp and pointed her skis downhill.

The snow was magnificent—light as air, deep as a well, smooth as butter. It practically skied itself, choosing Stacey's line and modulating her speed, making her turns with no intervention at all on her part. All she had to do was keep her weight centered over the skis and lean a little bit to the right or the left. She wasn't even sure she had to do that much. It was as if the mountain wanted her there. As if it understood what she was after. As if the line between the woman and the run, between the athlete and the trail, between the skier and the skied, no longer existed. Or at the very least as if it was of no consequence.

Everything, in other words, came together.

Stacey had taken great runs before. *Fantastic* runs. A handful of them here in Vermont, once or twice out in Utah, and maybe a time or two up in Quebec somewhere. She'd had her share, make no mistake about that, but those runs had had a different quality about them, a quality that if you could name it, it would have to be something like an awareness of the limits of their greatness. Midway through each of them, she'd begun not just looking forward to the next run down the same slope, but analyzing what she could do to make that next run even better. *Maybe the drifts will be a little softer over there near the trees. Maybe the fall line on the left side will be just a bit steeper.* The kind of thought process that indicates analysis over engagement.

On the other hand, this time she wasn't thinking. She didn't have to.

At least not until her skis hit something—hard—and stopped dead.

Her bindings released and she pitched forward, going briefly airborne before plummeting into the snow in a burst of white powder, then finally tumbling twenty or thirty feet down the mountain. Her skis were back where she'd left them; her poles came loose and flew free. In short, it was what the smart alecks call a yard sale: gear everywhere, wall to wall. By no means would every piece of it, given the light and the deep snow, be easy to find.

"Rats!" She righted herself, stood up, and shouted into the night, "Rats, rats, rats!" She felt as if she'd been awakened from a dream, and an outstanding dream, at that.

Chip was a few yards above her on a line of his own, but stopped short at the sight of her explosive plunge into the snow. He heard her shouting and figured that she was probably all right. He sidestepped toward the spot where her skis had gone under, and she started slogging up in his direction. "That's OK," he said. "You stay where you are, and I'll bring the skis down."

She stopped, grateful.

"You all right?"

"Yeah, I'm all right. You fall in this stuff it's hard to get hurt."

"What'd you hit, anyhow?"

"I don't know. A log, maybe. A limb. Something."

He was clicked out of his own skis now, and up almost to his waist in powder. He hadn't expected it to be that deep, but he didn't mention it. "I think I see where they went in," he said. Then, a few seconds later said, "I *think*."

"Don't think. Just do."

"Roger that one, Yoda."

"And while you're busy with that, I'll look for my poles."

Which was fine with Chip. He was moving slowly through the snow, jamming his own poles in, then lifting them out again and jamming them back in, probing for any sign of her skis. He'd already obliterated any trace of the path they'd taken into the snow, and in the moonlight he was afraid that he was getting a little bit turned around. He backed up and started again, unsure whether he was going over new ground or old. He started breathing hard.

"You all right up there?" Stacey asked.

"I'm fine. I'm just not getting anywhere. Not yet." He looked up from the snow and was struck by how far she was below him, vertically speaking. From here, she was pretty much straight down. Damn, this right-of-way was steep. Steeper than he'd thought.

"Got the poles," she said. There was a little triumph in her voice, and a little teasing, too.

He shook himself and concentrated on the snow before him, trying to rid himself of a twinge of vertigo. It was just a passing sensation, no question. A short-term freak-out that could have happened to anybody. "Great," he said, "Good for you. I'll just be a minute."

Below him, Stacey turned to look out over the valley. She planted her poles and whistled appreciatively between her teeth, then she called up to him over his shoulder, "I sure wouldn't want to walk down."

"You won't." He said it, but he wasn't feeling it.

"Good. Because I think it'd kill me."

He looked up for himself and felt his stomach turn over and thought the same thing—that it would kill *him*—but at the same moment one of his poles stabbed something hard. He smiled, put the pole down, and started digging.

He threw snow like a madman, and didn't stop . . . until he saw the corpse's face. Then—breathless, vertiginous, sick to his stomach—he passed out.

Stacey saw him go. One second he was up and the next second he was down, vanished into the powder. She couldn't believe her eyes. She called his name, thinking he'd stumbled somehow—maybe over the edge of whatever log or limb she'd hit in the first place—then she started up toward the spot where he'd disappeared.

NINETEEN

T hat's what I like about this job," Guy said to Megan and the kids over the supper table. "I mean, it's not every day you get a guided tour of Hollywood."

"You mean *old* Hollywood," Jim said. He was fifteen years old, and anything that predated *The Dark Knight* was old. *Star Wars* was an antique. *Murder Town* was positively prehistoric.

"Granted," said his father. "Although *old* is a relative term, sonny. My point is, you never know what stories people are going to tell. This guy Seville, he was there when it all happened. When they shot all the great stuff from when I was growing up. He was what they call the technical director on *Lights Out*. Can you believe it? That elevator scene? With the cables?"

"They'd CGI that these days and it'd be better. You'd think it was real."

"It *was* real."

"*Dad*. You know what I mean."

"I do, but I don't understand it."

• • •

Chip didn't think he'd exactly passed out. At least not for long. He was sitting up, wiping snow from his goggles with the thumb of his mitten, when Stacey worked her way up to the spot where he'd fallen. "Sorry," he said, before she could ask. "I'm fine."

"You're fine."

"Really. I'm fine." He pointed toward the spot where he'd been digging. "That guy, on the other hand . . ."

She looked over and saw nothing.

"He's definitely not so good." He drew himself to his feet and leaned on her shoulder, putting more weight on her than he meant to.

She stiffened and pushed back against him. "Huh?"

"That guy. In the snow. He's the thing you hit, I'm pretty sure."

"There's no guy in the snow."

"There sure is. He's a *dead* guy, but he's there, all right."

They pushed together toward the spot, and bent to clear away the snow. Stacey switched on her headlamp and Chip did, too, but soon enough they both wished they hadn't. "It's Stone," she said, aghast and a little out of breath. "It's Harper Stone. Oh. My. God."

His face was blue in the blue LED light, pale as the snow that covered him. She thought it looked as though one of her skis had slid across the skin just above his eyebrows, the sharp metal edge cutting flesh that was too bloodless and too frozen to bleed.

She stopped but Chip kept on digging around Stone's body, pushing snow away from his arms and legs, clearing out a margin around his torso. He was working fast, almost a little frantically, and Stacey reached out a hand to make him stop. "Leave him," she said. "It doesn't matter. You can't do anything for him now, and they're not going to want us to disturb anything." By "they" she meant Guy Ramsey, the state troopers, whoever else might want things left the way they'd found them. At the edge of the cleared area in the snow she saw the tip of one ski, and went after it. The other was right alongside it, and she dragged them both from the loose snow.

Chip stood up straight, panting. "The good news, I guess, is that he's not a missing person anymore."

"We found him," said Stacey, bursting in through the kitchen door, red-faced and blowing steam. "We found Harper Stone."

Guy had a mug of coffee and a piece of yellow cake on a little plate, and he was heading toward the front room to watch the news. He shot a quick look over his shoulder when he heard Stacey's voice, then he vanished through the door into the foyer, saying, "Hey there, Chip," as he disappeared. Raising his voice as he went farther on, "Where'd he turn up? Where's he been?"

They heard the low electronic burp and hum of the television coming on.

"It's not like that," Stacey said.

The television came roaring on at whatever volume Jim had been using to play some video game after school, and Guy cut it back with the remote. He walked back into the foyer and stuck his head around the door frame, chewing cake. "What does *that* mean?"

"We can't just leave him up there till daylight." Guy had pulled on his snowmobile gear and was standing by the kitchen door, scratching the stubble on his chin. He wished he'd had a chance to finish that yellow cake.

His wife, Megan, sat at the table in front of her coffee, shaking her head.

"Some animal'd find him for sure. The bears might be sleeping, but those woods are full of foxes and fisher cats and God knows what else. All of them starving this time of year. Hungry as bears."

"Just be careful," she said.

"I will." He took a step toward the door and looked over at Chip. "You ready?"

"Why him?" said Stacey. "I'm the one who found the body."

Chip didn't dispute that. He started to, but before he got very far Stacey saw something pass across his face that looked like relief. The realization that he might not have to see that dead body again after all, which seemed to suit him fine.

It took a while to get ready. Guy and Chip had to gas up Guy's snowmobile, load it onto a trailer, and back the patrol car up to hitch it on. They agreed that Chip would take Stacey's car home; they'd work out getting his car from the other side of the mountain tomorrow sometime. The state troopers would want to talk with him, but since there were only two seats on the snowmobile, they'd have to wait.

"Did I miss something?" Stacey asked as they got into the patrol car. "Did you call it in?"

Guy had the engine running all this time. It was hot in the car and he turned down the fan. "I'm not going to call it in until I've seen it for myself."

"You don't believe me?"

"Oh, I believe you all right." He waved to Chip and waited for him to pull down the lane, then he followed him out onto the main road.

"So?"

"So, about half an hour after I make that call, this whole thing is going to turn into a circus. It won't be just a handful of staties from Rutland. It'll be the coroner's office, the VBI, you name it."

"The VBI?"

"Vermont Bureau of Criminal Investigation."

"I get it," said Stacey. "Like the FBI."

"Kind of."

"The VBI. That's funny."

"Not to them."

"I guess not."

Ahead of them by a half dozen car lengths, Chip neared an

empty intersection. He switched on his turn signal and came to a careful stop, and Guy blasted his horn at him and kept moving, slowing down only enough to keep Stacey from grabbing the door handle for support. "For crying out loud," he muttered, "this is police business. Come on!" Then he turned and grinned at her to show that he was at least half kidding. "Anyway," he said when they'd gotten up to speed again, "add Harper Stone's celebrity into the mix, and you've got something pretty irresistible to law enforcement."

Stacey thought for a minute, then she finally went ahead and asked it. "That wouldn't be why you want the first shot all to yourself, would it?"

TWENTY

Chip stopped by the park to help them get the snowmobile off the trailer, but Stacey shooed him away and they did just fine without him. She'd never ridden a snowmobile before, and was astonished at how inhospitable the thing was. It was like riding a motorcycle in a meat locker. Why anybody wanted to own one for anything other than emergency purposes was beyond her.

They found the tracks that she and Chip had left and followed them up the hill under the power lines; in no time they were at the place where she'd fallen. The place where the body lay in its snowy grave, bathed in moonlight and the gleam of the snowmobile's single yellowish headlight. Guy switched on a flashlight. They both climbed off and went wading on over through the deep snow.

He passed the flashlight's beam over Stone's body. "I'm glad you guys didn't dig him out any more than you did," he said. He stopped when the beam lit on Stone's forehead, focusing in on the long thin bloodless gash. "*That's* interesting."

"I think I did that. With my ski. When I, you know, when I *hit* him."

He poked around with the light, following the tracks down the mountain and figuring. "Could be," he said. "Could very well be."

"I'm sorry."

"Don't be."

"I mean, I'm not sure what I'm sorry for. But it's just—"

"Your skis are in your car?"

"Yeah."

"The staties are going to want a look at them."

"I guess. But isn't that just my luck? I save up for a new pair of skis, use them for one day, and the next morning they're 'evidence.'"

Guy grimaced. "Don't worry. You'll get 'em back in a year or so. Don't give it another thought." He put the flashlight beam back on the corpse and bent over, looking down hard and making a study of the details. "I guess that's Harper Stone, all right."

"Told you."

"He still looks pretty good, considering."

"Guy!"

"I know, I know. Thing is, how'd he get up here? What was he doing?"

"How'd he end up dead?"

"Right," said Guy. "That's the main thing. How'd he end up dead?"

Stacey just about froze to death herself before the troopers arrived, she and Guy stamping their feet in the snow down past the body, more or less in the spot where she'd landed after striking Harper Stone. No sense contaminating the tracks higher up, however much that was worth. Guy was adamant that anything you could do to keep from pissing off the state troopers was worth the trouble. Not that the original tracks that she and Chip had made were going to mean squat, seeing that they were in three or four feet of snow that had fallen since the time when Stone went down. The condition of the snow wasn't going to tell anybody a whole lot.

For whatever lucky reason—it may have been the electrical towers or it may have been the elevation or it may have been the bad weather that was starting to move in—Guy had gotten a good cell signal right off and reached the barracks in Rutland with no trouble at all. So now the two of them waited as the moon sank and the night got darker. A cloud bank built in from the west. Come morning everything would be dreary and gray and oppressive, low clouds and a high overcast thick as soup; not the greatest day for skiing. Stacey was about to lose that brand-new pair of Heads anyway, and if she didn't watch out the troopers would have her tied up all day tomorrow on top of that. So bring on the clouds, she thought. It couldn't get much worse. Besides, whatever happened, she had a leg up on Harper Stone, the famous movie star. The dead famous movie star.

The troopers surprised them by roaring over the top of the mountain and down, instead of coming up from the park. It sounded like an aerial assault, a half dozen of them on the biggest and angriest machines imaginable. Somebody must have GPS'd the location and decided that the closest road was the one by the cabin where Chip had left his car, and before they knew it they'd obliterated any trace of Chip's and Stacey's tracks. No great loss, but still. Guy quit hugging himself and stuck out his arms to flag them down before they did any more damage.

The troopers tumbled off like Harper Stone and his dauntless SWAT team in *Big City Heat*, like Harper Stone and his brave cavalrymen in *Last Stand at Appomattox*, like Harper Stone and his toughguy platoon in *The Ne'er-Do-Wells*. Chances were that at least half of them, the older guys anyway, had grown up studying the moves and attitudes that Stone had made famous. Too bad they'd come too late. Instinctively and against all ordinary practice they gathered around the white grave, bundled up like spacemen in their snow-mobile suits (*Mission to Antares,* 1969), lifting their clear goggles and bowing their heads. One or two of them may have shed a manly tear—not for Stone, but for some part of the innocent past that was now gone forever.

A trooper identifying himself as Thompson was in charge. He took Guy aside and after they'd talked for a little while Guy directed him to Stacey. There was something surreal about the whole thing as far as she was concerned. The swarm of serious men clambering over the mountain with their flashlights pointing at crazy angles; the clicking and flashing of cameras everywhere, like a swarm of lightning bugs on this black night; the flat and impersonal tone that Thompson adopted as he questioned her about what she'd found and how she'd found it (and yes, they were going to have to confiscate those brand-new Heads of hers for a while, if she didn't mind); the two troopers apparently charged with cordoning off an appropriate chunk of real estate as a crime scene, running yellow tape from tree to tower to tree and back again. As if the place would be crawling with curiosity seekers by morning.

After a quick debriefing and a promise that they would get back with her tomorrow, one of the troopers took her home. As far as she could see there'd been some low-key dispute as to who would get the duty. Thompson seemed to have been voting for Guy, claiming authority over the case and wanting to brush him off as rapidly as possible, but in the end the sheriff stuck around. One of the men who'd been putting up that useless yellow tape, a tubby guy that Stacey had a tough time getting her arms all the way around on the snow-mobile, took the job.

TWENTY-ONE

Come morning, Harper Stone was slowly defrosting on a steel table in the Rutland hospital—and the whole world seemed to know it.

A reporter from the little NBC affiliate in Burlington was right in the middle of his fifteen minutes of fame when Megan Ramsey turned on the tiny old black-and-white TV that hung over the microwave in the kitchen. The sound came on louder than she'd expected and it woke Stacey up. Megan apologized when her boarder opened the door to her bedroom and came out blinking. There was a disorienting moment when Stacey was pretty sure she was still dreaming, because on that little screen it looked for all the world as if the Burlington guy was talking with somebody from the *Today Show*. Then she realized that he was, at least via satellite. He was standing outside the hospital in Rutland, the skies behind him gray and a little bit of sleet whipping at him from on high, acting as though he knew something about the death of Harper Stone, when he probably hadn't even known the old movie actor was even in the state. Or still alive, for that matter. Until just now.

She poured herself a cup of coffee and watched while they switched over from live coverage to a taped overview of Stone's life and work. The segment began and ended with the rousing trumpet theme from *Last Stand at Appomattox*, and it covered everything from the early black and white adventures he'd shot for Warner's to his disastrously failed comeback in the long-forgotten *Cannonball Run IV*. Titles flew past like birds. Stills of Stone through the years, playing golf and riding horses and just monkeying around with the people who had once made up his usual crowd—Joey Bishop, Richard Nixon, Bette Davis, Billy Graham—flickered by in sepia tones, grainy and sad and vanquished. As if the world had been less colorful in those bygone days. At one point a sour-looking Burt Reynolds, his hairdo visibly newer than the rest of him by a decade or two, reminisced about learning his trade at the great man's inspirational knee—which was either a false memory or an exaggeration meant to suggest something about their relative ages. Then it was back to the studio in New York, back for a quick bobble-headed nod from the reporter in Rutland (who was still getting sleeted on), and finally on to the actual news of the day.

Stacey walked back toward her room with her coffee, and found a note from Guy taped to the door.

"He didn't make it home until a couple of hours ago," Megan said. "And even then he just came and went."

"Sorry."

"It's not your fault. He's going to have a long day, is all."

The note said he'd brought her car back from Chip's. It said he wasn't trying to be a good Samaritan or anything, it was just that the state troopers had wanted to get their hands on those skis she'd told them about, and he figured while they were at it he might as well. It also suggested that she might want to keep a lid on what she'd seen until she'd talked with the boys from Rutland again.

• • •

"Wherever I go," said Brian, "that's where the action is." He had a look of bland arrogance on his face that made it seem as if he actually believed it, and he probably did.

He was standing ahead of Stacey in the long line at Judge Roy Beans, and there was nothing in the room to prove him wrong. Just the opposite, in fact. It was only quarter of eight in the morning, on a weekday, and the place was a beehive. Camera crews down from Burlington and up from Boston; print reporters from every little tabloid in every little mountain town; rubbernecking skiers who'd left their condos and their kids and their coffeemakers early just this once. Somebody had come in with a rumor that Meredith Vieira was flying up from New York at this very minute, but nobody believed it and it died down fast. Meredith wouldn't be coming all this way for Harper Stone.

Would she?

Still, there was something festive about the whole thing, with the smell of the hot coffee and the bright morning sky through the windows and the buzzing crowd and all. Something so contagious that even Stacey got caught up in it—forgetting for a moment both the physicality of the dead thing she'd seen the night before and the misery of being this close to her old fiancé. Lifted up by the cheerful atmosphere and empowered by the freedom she'd created for herself by coming to the mountains in the first place—and still a little bit psyched and sleepless from her adventure with Chip and Guy and the state troopers—she shouldered Brian like a football player and said, "So it's all about you, is it?" She was feeling tough, resilient. Like the kind of person who could discover a dead body in a snowbank and not be fazed by it in the least. Like the kind of person who could be cheated on by a loser like Brian and just let it slide right off. She felt good.

"I've gotten used to it," he said. "You, on the other hand, might forget what it's like hanging out with me."

"I'm trying to," she said, taking a step forward and pushing him ahead into an empty space he'd been too self-absorbed to notice.

"Very funny."

"I had it down pretty well, until just now. The forgetting."

"Too bad."

The door blew open and a half dozen more people came in from the parking lot. It was going to be a good day for Judge Roy Beans. The way it looked, Earl wasn't even going to get a smoke break. If business kept up like this for a week or so, they might even make rent.

Brian scanned the chalkboard. "Once folks find out I'm pretty much the only guy in town with a connection to Harper Stone"—he said it a little bit louder than was strictly necessary—"I've got a feeling I'm going to keep right on being the center of attention."

The couple in line behind them lowered their voices to a whisper and cocked their heads forward. One of those old E. F. Hutton commercials from when Stacey was a kid, come to life by the power of morbid curiosity.

"Is that why you came over here? To make yourself available to the waiting world?" She couldn't believe it. She felt her blood pressure climbing, just the way it had when she'd found him in bed with what's-her-name, the Boston blonde.

"You underestimate me, Stace." He ran his fingers through his hair. "I came here in hopes of running into *you*."

She didn't believe it for a second, but she let it go.

"Also because I was out of coffee in the condo."

"Now *that* makes sense."

The couple behind them had given up on Brian, the woman no doubt having decided that he was a jerk and the man having decided that she was right.

They were almost at the counter now, and Stacey lowered her voice to drop the bomb that Brian had coming. "I'll tell you what, Mister Authority on the late Harper Stone: I'll do you one better."

"One better? How's that?"

Earl saw her coming and gave her a wink and got busy with her usual double espresso—boiling hot, overwhelmingly caffeinated, and easy to get down in a couple of fast swallows so that she could get to the mountain and begin her day. "You may have been one of the last people to see him alive," she said, raising a finger to her lips to make sure that he knew this was a secret, "but I was pretty much the first to see him dead." *Take that, Mister Center of Attention.*

"What?"

"You heard me." Looking away from Brian. Smiling across the counter at Earl.

"You were—"

"That's right. Well, it was either me or Chip, depending on how you want to look at it. I guess technically he was the first one to see him, but I was definitely the one who found him."

As usual, Brian went straight for the important stuff—that is, the stuff that was immediately relevant to his personal life. That was perfectly fine with Stacey. She didn't plan on telling him much more about Stone anyway. She just wanted to let it be known, between the two of them, that he wasn't the top dog. "What is it," he said, "with this guy Chip?"

"He's a friend."

"*I* used to be a friend."

"Yeah. Once upon a time. But you lost that privilege."

"It's not the only privilege I lost."

"You're telling me." She put her knuckles on the counter and waited for her double shot.

Earl asked Brian what he'd like, and Brian launched into a specification so detailed and multilingual that it left the counterman blinking like an ox that'd been hit over the head with a two-by-four. Earl pointed to the list on the chalkboard and asked Brian if what he had in mind was anywhere close to something they had up there in plain sight and Brian said no, and Earl said then maybe the line would move along faster if he could adjust his expectations a little bit to match what was available. Rather than endure the disdain of half of the people in town—including another dozen camera-toting individuals in big-city black who'd just blown in through the open door—Brian settled for a cappuccino. Half-caf. Skim milk. One packet of Equal and one of Splenda. With a little fresh cinnamon ground over the top. And maybe some shaved chocolate if they had any. Extra dark. Just a touch of it. If that wasn't too much trouble. And oh, yeah, he'd pay for Stacey's double shot while he was at it. By then he was too late and she'd already put enough money down on the counter to cover both of them—her own and whatever his finally turned out to be. It put a big dent in her budget, but he didn't need to know that.

One of the booths was emptying out—four gray-haired retirees on their way to the mountain, looking silly in Spyder jackets, all angular red panels and creepy black arachnids—and Stacey and Brian took their places. They were almost instantly joined by a father and son from somewhere out of town, the man eager to get to the mountain and the boy—a five or six-year-old bound for a day of glorified babysitting in the Ski School—beginning to pick at a chocolate chip muffin the size of his head. It was going to be a long morning for those two. Anybody could see that.

Stacey and Brian hunched their shoulders against the newcomers and angled their faces toward the wall by a few degrees. "So what's the deal?" he sad, sniffing at his coffee cup. "You said you *found* him?"

"Yep."

"How was *that?*"

"It was . . . sudden."

"I guess." He looked at her the way he'd have looked at a stubborn faucet. "But there's got to be more to it than that."

"I don't think I'm supposed to be talking about it a lot. Not right now. Not until—"

"What're you? A person of interest?"

"Don't be silly."

The dad next to Brian was well into his coffee already, while the kid opposite him was busy inspecting his first chocolate chip as if it were some kind of gemstone. The dad was audibly grinding his teeth.

"So what's the big deal? What can you tell the police that you can't tell me?"

At the sound of the p-word a half dozen heads turned their way—including the dad's, since it looked as if he was going to be stuck here for a good long time anyhow—so Stacey dropped her voice further. "I don't know. It's just—"

"Somebody told you to keep things quiet, right? And if a person can count on anything, he can count on you to be a good girl." Brian said it as if there was something wrong with that. "Who was it, your landlord?"

Stacey wasn't interested in answering. "So what's wrong with being a good girl?" she said.

Brian shrugged. "Nothing. Nothing at all. Except where's the fun?"

"There isn't any fun. There's no fun."

"I thought that's why you came here, babe."

"Don't call me *babe*."

"Stace."

"Don't call me *Stace*."

"Jeez. I thought that's why you came here. To cut loose. Break out of the old routine." He raised his complicated coffee in a toast. "To live a little."

"Boy, did you miss the point. I should have slammed the door a little harder on my way out."

The dad winced, and not entirely on account of the way his son was sucking on that chocolate chip.

"Never mind about that," Brian said. "You can tell me: How'd you find him? What were you two doing up there in the woods, if that's not too personal?" His eyebrows jumped.

"We were skiing. Which is what some people come here to do. It's what *most* people come here to do."

"But I thought Stone was somewhere off the mountain. Off the ski mountain, I mean."

"He was."

"I don't get it. You can't just ski *anywhere*."

"Actually, you can," Stacey said. "If you've got the skills, and if you want it enough, you can go for it. It'd be a mistake not to."

Brian brightened. "Good for you! That's the same way I look at things."

"I know. Believe me."

"If you want it, go for it."

"Brian."

"Go for the gusto."

"Brian."

"I mean it."

"Look. Brian. You're not helping your case."

"Oh. Right. Well. You know what I mean. Good for you." He gave her a little salute.

"Anyway," she said, "how'd you know Stone was off-piste?"

"*Off-piste.* Is that like piste-off?"

"It's French. It means out of bounds. Off the trail map. In the woods."

"How'd I know? Word gets around."

"The news report I saw just said he was on the mountain. Nothing more than that."

"Stace."

She grimaced.

"Stacey. Come on. I followed the blinking lights off the access road, is all. It's kind of hard to miss. All those police cars, the snowmobiles all over the place, the camera crews."

"Oh. Right."

"Right. It's not like it's a big secret where they found him."

"Where *I* found him."

"Exactly. Anyhow, I pulled over and tried to tell a cop that I was up here on a shoot with the guy, but he just waved me past."

"Poor Brian," she said. "Your time will come." Despite or perhaps because of the irony, she had a reflexive urge to reach out and touch the back of his hand—but she caught herself at the last minute, and tossed off the last of her espresso instead.

TWENTY-TWO

'll be a monkey's uncle," said the tall man, folded up into a chair in front of his TV, in that remote cabin on the backside of the mountain. He couldn't have gotten out and gone to work if he'd wanted to, on account of the half dozen state police cars still strewn up and down his winding lane.

"What is it?" came the answer from the kitchen.

"The TV just said those two old Harper Stone pictures, *Murder Town* and *Lights Out*, are number one and two at Amazon."

"Really?"

"Number one and number two. The DVDs, I'm talking about."

"What's number three?"

"They didn't say. Probably some kind of Hannah Montana crap or something. Anyway, they're freaking sold out. Unbelievable."

It was going to be a while before the authorities came up with a cause of death. Manny Seville's people had been in the refrigerated transport business back in the Bronx—some of them were probably in it still—and growing up he'd seen enough frozen meat to last a lifetime. With a day to kill before his rental arrived and no way out of town, he'd pushed up the pillows on the bed into a big pile and finished off the contents of the cereal carton and the milk carton and the orange juice carton, too, flipping from *Today* to *Good Morning America* to *The Early Show* to whatever it was they called that thing on Fox. Harper Stone was turning out to be big news on all of them. Everywhere he turned they were showing little snippets of action from his pictures, promotional photos and backlot stills whose colors had all bled out, and now and then an old head shot that went back to the days when they had been just a pair of innocent kids, scrambling around Warner's, looking for a way to make something of themselves. Amazing. Nothing ever goes away entirely.

It never occurred to him to get dressed and walk into town to check things out for himself. Televised was better. What did the hicks around here know about anything? By later on in the morning, though—when Regis Philbin and that blond girl had come on, taking up the story and adding embellishments of their own (Philbin claimed to have run into an inebriated Harper Stone at Cannes many years back, and who could deny it?) he was starting to get a little stir-crazy. Hungry, too. So he got dressed, pulled on his coat, and made his way down the mountain road. The day was brightening up and getting a little warmer. Car traffic on the blacktop had cleared patches in the newly fallen sleet or snow or freezing rain or whatever it was they called it. The road was gray and sloppy and his feet got wet through his boots, but at least he wasn't watching Regis Philbin anymore. There were limits to what a man needed to endure, even on behalf of an old compadre like Harper Stone.

There were plenty of places to grab a bite in town, but not a single one appealed to him. Through the hazy plate-glass windows at Mahoney's Luncheonette, every surface looked mired in some kind of greasy yellow film. Vinnie's Steak-Out didn't look half bad, but it wasn't open yet and although the early bird special they had posted in the window sounded all right, he sure couldn't wait until four o'clock. He'd already had enough Cinco de Taco to last him a lifetime, and the Whippi Dip was buttoned up tight for the season. He didn't want ice cream anyway and kept walking.

There was one decent-looking restaurant up a side street, a phony French place called Maison Maurice, but that was closed, too. He almost hit the pizza joint out of desperation. He came even closer to stopping at the grocery store for some cold cuts and a loaf of bread, but by the time he figured out that he could make his own lunch he was past the entrance to the parking lot. He thought maybe he ought to give it another ten minutes or so, get all the way to the edge of town in case there was some kind of fast food or something out that way. Something with a name brand on it anyhow. Something you could trust as a known quantity.

He was scuffing along the sidewalk, dreaming pathetic dreams of a lowly Burger King, when a gigantic Japanese SUV cut in front of him and zoomed down a driveway, hitting a pothole and splashing him from head to toe with a muddy mixture of half-melted snow, road grit, and rock salt. He did what any good New Yorker would have done. He didn't hesitate, and he didn't get angry, he just stood his ground and nailed the rear bumper of the SUV with the hard heel of his boot. It left a mark—not just a mark, really, but a boot-sized impression in what turned out to be a plastic panel—and he capped it off with a picturesque profanity and a one-fingered salute. God, he was hungry—and now he was wet and cold, too. What was wrong with people?

The SUV belonged to Buddy Frommer, and the driveway led to the Slippery Slope, and that's what was wrong with people. Frommer skidded the thing to a stop in the best space in the unplowed parking lot, right in front of the entrance (What was the point of owning the place if you had to save the good parking spots for customers? And there weren't usually many customers anyhow.), and he opened the door and climbed down, his face twisted into an ugly knot. He shot a quick look at the rear bumper, and then plunged toward Manny with his index finger jutting out like a knife. "I guess you ain't from around here, are you?"

"I get it," said Manny. "If I *were* from around here, I'd know to watch out for the big Nissan with the asshole behind the wheel."

Buddy's face got even redder than usual. "You'd know to look out, let's leave it at that." He drew near to Manny, following the trajectory of his pointing finger, and came within an inch of reaching out and taking him by the collar but stopped at the last second. He turned, still pointing, and directed Manny's attention to the rear of the SUV. "And you wouldn't pull *that* kind of stunt, that's for sure."

A car with Massachusetts plates pulled into the lot and a woman got out and tried the front door, only to find it locked. She studied the hours posted behind the plate glass, pushed back her sleeve, and checked her watch. She tunneled her hands and held them against the door and peered inside. Then, frustrated, she looked over at the two men arguing on the sidewalk and shrugged by way of asking if they knew what was up.

Buddy, distracted for a minute from his fury over the damage to his car, hollered at her, "This town is full of ski shops, if you're in such a goddamned hurry."

"I'm picking something up," she called, looking helpless. "I can't just—" Then, slowly, she tipped her head to one side, beginning to realize who it was she was talking to.

Frommer had turned his attention back to Manny by then. He put his red face right up to his and began saying he had half a mind to call the cops on account of the damage he'd done to the SUV with his boot, but stopped halfway through because he got distracted by the way Manny was studying his upper lip. He peeled off his glove and rubbed at the spot beneath his nose with his thumb and forefinger, pushing at it and squeezing his nose and sniffing.

"I've got an idea," said Manny, brightening up and forgetting about lunch entirely. "How about *you* don't call the cops, and *I* don't call the cops either."

Frommer, bullish and fuming, lowered his head by a few degrees and looked at the flatlander from underneath his eyebrows. He still didn't get it. Not entirely. Or maybe he thought he could still brazen it out.

Manny reached up a gloved finger and swiped it along Buddy's upper lip. The move couldn't have shocked Buddy more if his hand were a cattle prod. Then he drew back a step to show off the little white smudge across the tip of his finger.

"You missed a spot," he said.

TWENTY-THREE

ina Montero was devastated. She'd watched the news reports
in the morning before heading to work, and then contrary
to every principle of relaxation and mindfulness she had
kept the TV in the Green Mountain Massage waiting room tuned to
CNN all day. As a result she and her customers—sophisticated
ladies from New York and Connecticut in the morning, passing the
time while their husbands went skiing and their kids pined away in
ski school; then belligerent and foul-smelling men from the same
places in the afternoon, all pulled muscles and regret—were wound
up tight as watch springs from the nonstop barrage of bad news.
Not just about Harper Stone but about everything else: the econ-
omy, the Middle East, you name it.

She was wired when she locked up after the last client and she
was wired when she finally got her car to start and she was wired
when she hung her coat on a peg at the Broken Binding and made
for her usual stool. Jack, behind the bar, recognized her distress without looking twice, and he had her chardonnay all set before she
even sat down.

He bent forward with his elbows on the bar and his hands

folded, giving her a look of professional concern. "Aww, sweetie," he said. "What is it?"

"It's everything. It's every damned thing."

He nodded. "I know."

She took a sip and gave him a ravaged look. "Have you had the television on?"

"No. But I heard. I heard." He paused, took a deep breath. "No question: It's the end of an era."

"It's not just Harper Stone," she said, raising her glass in a toast to him anyhow. "It's Afghanistan and Israel and the health care system and—"

"Whoa," said Jack, holding up his hand like a traffic cop. "Somebody's had herself a little too much MSNBC."

"CNN."

"Oh, my God. There isn't enough chardonnay in the world to cure a CNN overdose."

"You're telling me."

Jack smiled big. Tina had never noticed that he had a couple of gold teeth halfway back on one side, but she noticed them now. "We're just going to have to talk you down," he said. "Nice and easy. That's all there is to it."

Before long a tiny bit of the old sparkle returned to Tina's eyes. Stacey saw it happen as she pushed through the swinging door from the kitchen, a bucket of ice in each hand. "What's up with you two?" she asked.

"Tina's feeling the weight of the world."

"Tell me about it," Stacey said. Jack slid the steel door open for her and she emptied the first bucket into the bin.

"You haven't heard?"

"Oh, I've heard all right." She tipped out the second bucket, and raised her voice over the crash of ice cubes. "Haven't you heard?"

Tina looked puzzled. "Heard what?"

"I thought everybody knew by now. I mean, I wasn't in any hurry to let it get out, but I spent the better part of the afternoon telling the state troopers and all—"

"Let what get out? Told the state troopers what? I haven't heard *anything*." Tina had a desperate look on her face that said *one more piece of bad news, and this woman will go straight back to the edge and over it.*

Stacey slid one bucket inside the other and set them down on the perforated rubber mat that covered the floor behind the bar. By the end of the night that mat would be slippery with spilled beer and melted ice, slimy with stray bits of Chex Mix decomposing into a wet goo, but for now it was pretty dry and even relatively clean. "I figured everybody'd know by now."

"Know *what?*" The suspense was about to drive Tina crazy.

"That I found him." She slid the door to the bin shut with a practiced swipe of her rear end.

"Who?"

"Harper Stone. I'm the one who found him. In the snow. Underneath the power lines."

"*No.*" Tina was so aghast that her grip all but cracked her wineglass.

"Well, Chip helped. Hadn't you heard?"

"I've been watching the news all day, and all they said was that a couple of skiers—"

"That would be us."

"But they didn't know who—"

"The state police didn't want me telling anybody. So I spent most of the day on the hill, and then I drove to Rutland to answer some questions, and then I came back here."

Jack stood marveling. "You, my dear, are on your way to becoming one of the great bartenders of the western world."

"Really? I don't know a Kahlua and Cream from a White Russian."

"You know how to keep things to yourself," said Jack. "That's the main thing."

"Don't give me too much credit. I did let it leak to Brian—"

Both Jack and Tina cocked their heads.

"—to my old fiancé, Brian, just to kind of one-up him. He had this whole thing going on about how he was one of the last people to see Harper Stone alive. I figured being one of the first to see him dead would beat that by a mile."

"Damn straight it does," said Jack.

"Then again, you can tell Brian *anything*. As long as it doesn't involve him personally—you know, as long as it isn't about *him*—it just kind of bounces off." She picked up the buckets and headed back into the kitchen. "So telling Brian doesn't count."

When she came back, Tina and Jack were dying for her to spill everything she knew. It turned out to be tougher than talking to the state troopers had been. The troopers already knew everything about the scene where she'd uncovered Stone, while here at the Broken Binding she had to reconstruct the whole deal from scratch. All kinds of details came up that the troopers hadn't needed to ask about.

Was he out in the clear or back in the woods? Out in the clear.

What was he wearing? She wasn't certain. It had been dark up there on the hillside in spite of their headlamps, and he'd been covered all over with snow. Crusted with it. He'd had on a wool hat, she was pretty sure about that much, with clumps of snow stuck to it. He'd been wearing gloves or mittens, probably. She could pretty much swear to that, but the more she thought about it the more she figured that she might have been just imagining it. He *should* have been wearing gloves or mittens, so maybe she pictured them. Her mind filled in what should have been there. Gee: It was a good thing the troopers knew what Stone had been wearing, since she'd have mistrusted her memory and gotten confused and made a mess of things. Probably incriminated herself. She did remember a dark jacket, though. It was dark for sure, maybe black or navy blue, unless it had just gotten wet from the heat of him as he lay dying in the snow and then frozen over. Yecch. *That* was a hideous thought.

Was he carrying anything? She couldn't remember. She didn't recall that he was holding ski poles or anything like that in his hands, although her growing uncertainty about the gloves or mittens kind of threw some doubt into that equation anyhow.

The afternoon grew later and the crowd around the bar picked up. She kept on answering questions, remembering everything she could and criticizing herself for the gaps.

How about a backpack or something? He'd been lying on his back, that much she knew. So if he'd had a backpack, she wouldn't have been able to tell. Unless she'd seen the straps, which she couldn't say one way or another.

Skis? Wow. Skis. That was anybody's guess, now that she thought about it. The way that they'd found him was she'd skied right over his face—

Eeeeewwwwwww.

Right. She knew. Horrible. Anyhow, she'd skied right over his head without even seeing it, assuming when she hit it that it was a log or a boulder or something, and she'd taken a great big yard sale of a fall, and Chip had recognized that it wasn't a log or a boulder but an old movie star instead. She left out the part where Chip passed out in the snow. She'd even left that part out when she'd talked to the troopers. If Chip wanted to tell them about it, then that was his own business.

Anyhow, back to the question of skis. Chip had kind of started digging the body out, at least until it occurred to her that the troopers might want things left just the way they'd found them, so although in the end his torso was exposed pretty well and Chip had worked some on his arms and legs, they'd never gotten far enough to see if he was wearing ski boots. Or if there were skis stuck somewhere in the snow alongside him. So she couldn't say.

Snowshoes? How about snowshoes? She didn't remember anything sticking up. But then again she couldn't be sure about the depth of the snow.

Had it bled, where she cut his face with the skis? No. She didn't think so. She thought he was (A) pretty thoroughly dead by then, and (B) pretty much frozen solid. It was more like whacking a brick of frozen hot dogs with the tip of a knife, and the tip goes in through the plastic but instead of separating two of the dogs it kind of slides into one of them. Just opens it up a little bit. That's all. Or like trying to cut through a frozen pork chop or something like that. He always was a ham actor.

That's not nice. Don't speak ill of the dead.

Manny Seville didn't look like a man who was in any special hurry to leave town. He looked, on the contrary, as though he was enjoying himself all to heck.

Guy was crawling the streets in his patrol car, watching the sun go down over the mountain and waiting for the valley to fill up with darkness. That was when he saw Manny walking between the Slippery Slope and the Broken Binding. Manny and Buddy Frommer, strolling along the sidewalk like a couple of jolly pirates. Guy had never seen Buddy walking there before. As far as he knew, these days Buddy only existed behind the desk at the Slope and behind the wheel of his SUV. Maybe down in that house he and his wife had somewhere in Londonderry or wherever. But not out on the sidewalk. And certainly not out on the sidewalk practically arm in arm with another human being, their heads tipped together as if they were engaged in some kind of conspiracy.

On top of everything else, he was pretty sure that Buddy was actually smiling—although he'd never swear to it on a witness stand. It might have just been a new variation on his usual grimace.

Guy watched them come and he nodded in their direction just in case they had taken note of him through the tinted glass—they hadn't—and then he turned the car into the lot opposite and backed it around and faced it toward the street. He switched the headlights on against the lowering dark. Just keeping an eye on things, as far as anybody could tell. Just keeping an eye on Manny and Buddy, to tell the truth.

It was only a short distance between the ski shop and the restaurant, maybe a quarter of a mile, but the two of them looked as if they might not ever make it. Every eight or ten steps one of them would stop, pulled up short by something he'd spotted on the ground or in the field alongside the road, or else by some idea that had popped into his brain. He'd point or pontificate or both. They looked like a pair of old philosophers or lunatics, one or the other. There was no distinguishing between the two.

So maybe, Guy was thinking, it was true after all—what people said about Buddy Frommer and how he made his money. How he kept the place going in spite of having no customers and not seeming to want any. Guy had always figured maybe he was a day trader or something along those lines, watching his stocks on the computer he had set up behind the counter. But maybe not. Maybe he was selling some kind of dope after all. It made sense, given what Stacey had said about seeing Stone in the basement of the shop with him, huddled over the workbench. And now this. Manny Seville had mentioned cocaine. Leave it to him to sniff out a supply of it—maybe through that Stone, whom neither one of them seemed exactly overwhelmed about missing. That was worth thinking about, wasn't it?

He sat with his hands on the wheel and watched their stumbling silhouettes merge with the long shadows creeping down from the mountains. He kept on watching until they turned together into the parking lot at the Broken Binding.

TWENTY-FOUR

The gray-haired early dinner crowd was paying their checks and drifting toward the door, the après-ski scene in the bar was starting to get fueled up and raucous, and Stacey's former fiancé was nursing a drink at the table by the jukebox, talking up a local girl who looked like she had a lot to learn about guys like Brian Russell. The kind of girl who'd gone to college up in Burlington or maybe over in Manchester, New Hampshire, some town not too far from home in whose bars she'd picked up the famous freshman fifteen and a handful of other unfortunate habits, all of which she figured she could shake through the magic of a couple of years back home living in this little nowhere burg with Mom and Dad—what with the clean living and the fresh air and all that. The kind of girl who hadn't run into Brian's type before and no wonder: Even Brian hadn't been entirely Brian yet when he'd gone off to college. It had taken more than an accident of genetics and a privileged childhood in his parents' fabulous house to make him into the creature who sat before her now. It had taken patience and time and a whole lot of practice. But he was pretty sure it had been worth it.

"That's right," he was saying with a disdainful little smile, raising a finger to signal Jack behind the bar that they were ready for another round. "Harper was in my employ when it happened."

He'd begun the day telling anybody who'd listen that he and Stone had been working together, which he'd thought would give him a kind of Hollywoodish sheen. Around lunchtime he'd upgraded the story to their having been what he called *business associates*, which he figured could mean anything from the movie business to investments to God knew what. But just now he realized that if he was going to get anywhere with little Susie Chap-Stick he was going to have to do better than that, so he'd fallen back on the oldest trick in his book and the most automatic: the power of being in upper management. Nothing in the world beats a corner office, and the idea that he got there by climbing on the back of old-time Hollywood royalty like Harper Stone was just icing on the cake.

"Really? He was working for you?"

"Oh, yeah. I'd hired him for a project we were shooting—over on the mountain."

"What kind of project?"

Jeez. How stupid can you get? Who doesn't know that when a person in the business says "project," that's as specific as he has any intention of getting? A *project* could be anything. If it usually turns out to be something considerably less impressive than it sounds, then so be it. That's why God invented words like *project*. Brian took a sip and gave it some thought. "Well," he said after a second or two, "it wasn't a science project, that's for sure. Unless you consider whatever technology that old guy used to preserve himself as something worth looking into."

"Hey," she said with a grin, completely distracted, "I guess he's even better preserved now. Freeze-dried and all."

"Yeah, right." It sent a chill up his spine. "Freeze-dried."

. . .

At a table way in the back, in a dim corner lit only by a sputtering votive candle, Manny Seville and Buddy Frommer had gone from goofy to morose. Right now they found themselves at a decision point, trying to figure whether they ought to stay in the bar and continue on toward flat-out drunk, or head into the dining room to cut the booze in their stomachs with a little prime rib. Manny was angling for the prime rib, since he hadn't had lunch and a person could go only so far on Chex Mix and complimentary hot wings. Buddy was undecided.

Stacey came by to see if she could freshen their drinks, and they looked up at her like a couple of weary owls. "I think we're going to hit the dining room," said Manny, and Buddy didn't seem to be able to muster any argument. For a change.

What he did was point at Stacey and say, "Don't I know you from somewhere?"

"Yeah." She brightened professionally. "I bought a pair of skis from you."

"That's nothing to brag about," he said. "The world is full of people who've bought skis from me. I don't think I'd remember you on account of *that*." He dropped his hand to the table and cupped his drink.

"It was only a couple of days ago."

Buddy shrugged. "Sue me." Then he lifted his glass and eyed its contents. He started pushing his chair back and turned a bloodshot eye to her and said, "I'm bringing this with me. And don't worry, sweetheart. You'll get your tip."

Yet Stacey wasn't worried about that, not in the least. What she *was* worried about, suddenly and severely, was her own mental health. Because as Buddy raised his glass, she saw on his forearm the tattoo that she was certain she'd seen before on Harper Stone. A heart. An anchor. Chains. Hadn't she taken note of that down in the service department at the Slippery Slope? When Stone and Buddy had been swapping lies or dope or whatever? Hadn't she seen it on Stone's arm, not Buddy's?

Answering everybody's earlier questions about finding Stone had made her doubt her ability to remember anything, and this was the capper. "I trust you," she said. Then, collecting herself as best she could and fearing the worst from this wobbly pair as they set out for the dining room with glasses in their hands, she added, "How about I carry those drinks for you?"

They refused, of course. Now that she had a couple of months at the Binding under her belt, Stacey was beginning to see that drunks *always* refuse help of any sort. Denial is their default mode. Pete Hardwick had a rule that the bar staff was supposed to deliver customers' drinks from one room to another, but there was only so much a person could do. So she let them go, clearing the table behind them and making a mental note to replace that votive candle with a fresh one, then looking up at the television over the bar just in time to catch a closed-captioned announcement by Harper Stone's beleaguered publicist: Apparently the dead man had left no will at all, at least none that anybody had been able to dig up yet. Add to that the fact that he had no known living relations, add the widely-held suspicion that he had a half dozen illegitimate children scattered all around the Western world, add the understanding that he had multimillion-dollar estates in exclusive communities from coast to coast, and top it off with the suspicion that his dwindling movie career and his expensive tastes had left him with about a zillion dollars in unsecured debt, and you had a world-class legal struggle in the making.

She took a step backward and found Manny and Buddy standing there behind her still, transfixed by the television. They jumped and she jumped, too. Manny's face went slack and his mouth dropped open as the story crawled past on the bottom of the screen.

Buddy sneered up at the television and said how great it would have been if Stone had lived to see himself finally getting some decent publicity after all those years.

"The state police wanted me to tell them everything, of course."

The girl leaned toward Brian, rapt. "Did they put you in one of those interrogation rooms, like on TV?"

He laughed it off. Mister Tough Guy. The Voice of Experience. "Hardly," he said. "In fact, quite the opposite. They visited me in my condo."

"What did you tell them?"

"I told them what I know. Background information, mostly. Personality issues. Behavioral stuff. Performance on the job."

"Like if he'd been acting strangely? That kind of thing?"

"You've got it."

"Well, had he?"

"Had he what?"

"Had he been acting strangely?"

"Hard to say." It was hard, on account of Brian had only been on the job with Stone for a couple of days. Even then they hadn't exchanged more than ten words. Prior to that he'd never met the guy. He'd never even seen one of his movies, other than on one dimly-remembered Saturday afternoon in junior high, stuck over at some friend's house in the rain, bored half to death and seeking salvation in a cardboard box of old VHS tapes. As he recalled, it was either watch *Murder Town* or sit through some Clint Eastwood cowboy picture they'd both seen a hundred times already.

The girl poked at the votive candle between them. "Did he have any enemies or anything?"

"Wow," said Brian. "You could be a police detective yourself."

She beamed.

"Really. Have you thought of going into law enforcement?"

"I took a couple of classes," she said.

"No kidding."

"So they asked you that? They asked you did he have any ene-mies?"

"Oh, you bet they did." They hadn't asked him anything of the sort. Once they'd gotten the lowdown on how little he knew about Harper Stone, they'd taken his contact information, given him a business card as a courtesy, and tipped their hats good-bye.

"And?"

"And a person like Harper? With his profile and his status and his wealth?" (All of them, the profile and the status and the wealth, being things that he'd already trumped by claiming himself the guy's employer.) "Why, he's *bound* to have enemies. Don't you think?"

"That's why I asked."

"I told them a few things. Let's put it that way." He sipped his drink. "Let's leave it at that, OK?"

The girl leaned forward. "Aren't *you* the mysterious one?"

"Sometimes," he said, as mysteriously as possible.

Brian had been doing so well. When he went off to use the men's room, though, everything changed: the people, the dynamic, his prospects, the works. He'd washed his hands and combed his hair and fixed his shirt collar just right, but when he came back to the table he found two more chairs pulled up and a couple of laid-back guys draped over them—guys younger than him by as many years as Susie ChapStick was, guys who looked like they might have gone to high school with her, guys who were just bursting with bullshit stories about their heroics on the mountain. There was no way in the world he could compete. He sat down and introduced himself, stayed put for as long as it took to finish his drink and salvage a little bit of his dignity, then excused himself for an empty stool at the bar. He hated like anything to drag himself over there in plain sight of Stacey, but she was pretty occupied anyhow.

Jack was right there when he sat down. "No luck?"

"It's not about luck," Brian said.

"I guess not." He didn't look like he meant it, though. He pointed to Brian's empty glass. "Another one of those for you?"

"Sure," said Brian.

Everything that Stacey might have had to say about finding Harper Stone beneath the snow was pretty much common knowledge by now. Brian sat quietly, letting that third drink work on him, feeling the information ebb and flow around the bar. It was nothing but locals, as far as he could tell. Somebody'd have a question for Stacey and Stacey would be too occupied to answer it entirely—she was either consulting Old Mr. Boston on the fine points of a drink she'd never made before or carrying a tray of Long Trails over to a table of snowmobile dudes who couldn't seem to get enough—and somebody else would take up the thread on her behalf. There was a rhythm to it and a kind of comfort, too. All these people finishing each other's sentences and filling in each other's blank spaces. He had nothing to add, really, and it made him feel kind of low. Kind of jealous. Not on account of Stacey's connection with anybody in particular—none of the men here filled that bill; it was only the bartender and some porky middle-aged guy who looked like a car salesman, and an old farmer whose gray hair stood straight up like it was scared of something—but because of how she seemed to be fitting in here better than she'd ever fit into his life. It made him wonder about things, until he decided that it was probably just the alcohol.

TWENTY-FIVE

Maybe the troopers were just throwing Guy a bone, but maybe not. Maybe they really *were* interested in his personal take on the local angle. Either way, it was going to give him something to do instead of the usual, which mainly consisted of bolstering the township's budget by snagging flatlanders who thought that the road between here and Rutland was their own private speedway. Every time he issued a ticket he included a friendly and even faintly apologetic lecture about traffic safety and narrow roads and the stopping distances required by these treacherous wintertime surfaces, but everybody involved in the process knew the truth. As a general rule, it was 75 percent about the money. The money funded a lot of good things—including his own salary, without which the highways around here would definitely be more dangerous. So there you had it.

Anyhow, the lead-footed flatlanders were going to be getting a holiday today. God bless 'em, there'd been a little bit of fresh snowfall, and they'd be in an even bigger hurry than usual. Guy Ramsey, though, had other fish to fry.

• • •

He started at the Slippery Slope. Buddy's big Japanese SUV was where it usually sat, in the parking spot right in front of the door. For a change there were five or six other cars, too, all of them from out of state. People coming and going with skis and poles over their shoulders and boots dangling from their gloved hands. Guy backed his patrol car into a space across from the door, killed the engine, and sat for a while watching folks come and go. It was actually kind of comical. You'd see somebody getting out of his car, a spring in his step and a smile on his face as he looked forward to a day on the mountain, and fifteen minutes later—when he came out of the shop with a pair of freshly-tuned skis over his shoulder or a sack of gear in his hand—that same guy's face would be twisted into a mask of impotent rage. He'd be shaking his head *never again, so help me God, never again*. That, in a nutshell, was the special magic of Buddy Frommer. He'd made the Slippery Slope into a homey place, provided that home was an institution for the criminally insane.

Guy waited until the crowd thinned out, turning on his engine every few minutes to warm up the cabin and defog the windows, and when the rush was over he got out and approached the store.

Buddy was behind the counter with his head down, scowling at numbers on a computer screen, and he wasn't in any hurry to look up as Guy came through the door. When he did raise his eyes, though, it was clear that either he'd sneaked a peek and known that Guy was coming all along, or that the old off-the-cuff nastiness that Guy and his brother had always hated him for had not abandoned him in middle age. He tilted his head toward Guy's muddy patrol car and smiled his poisonous smile. "I see you're still driving a Ford," he said.

"Company car," said Guy.

"So's mine." He was talking about that big white Japanese SUV.

"I guess," said Guy.

"Only I own the company."

"Right," said Guy.

He stood in front of the elevated counter with his boots draining onto what looked like a pretty high-end hardwood floor, and reminded himself not to care. He had other things to think about. The immediate problem was that all the trappings of authority that he carried with him everywhere he went—the razor-sharp uniform, the flat-brimmed hat, the scrollwork badge, the holstered gun—all of the things that ordinarily established an air of authority around him and produced a kind of settled and automatic confidence in his heart, all of these elements suddenly felt not just meaningless but downright silly. Like he was a kid wearing a costume for Halloween. Like he was Michael Jackson dressed up in one of his flamboyant Sergeant Pepper outfits. All because of Buddy Frommer and his attitude, Buddy Frommer and his dad's bank account, Buddy Frommer and his damned Camaro, thirty years in the junk yard. Some things never changed.

Buddy sighed, craned his neck, and twisted his shoulders like they hurt. He had a big head, that Buddy Frommer. It was a head like a bull's head, one of those big belligerent oversized heads like John Travolta had. His hair had gone thin on top a long time ago and he'd covered it up with a comb-over for years, but lately he'd begun shaving it instead. Now it just looked kind of naked. Big and naked and raw. It wasn't a good look. Guy took off his flat-brimmed hat and ran his fingers through his own dense flattop, feeling a little better about that if about nothing else. You took pleasure where you could find it.

"You're not here shopping," Buddy said. He said it as if it was an accusation, as if Guy was just one more irritating flatlander, arrived to waste his time looking at skis for an hour and then to splurge a couple of bucks on a ChapStick.

"No," said Guy. "I'm not." Running his hand through his hair again for good measure, and putting his hat on the counter.

"Hmm." Buddy gave his computer screen another quick look and then switched it off, a move that Guy observèd without looking directly at it. "Then what *do* you want?" he asked.

"A couple of questions, if you don't mind."

"I do mind. I mind very much. How's that?" Turning back instinctively toward the dead screen and reaching around the back of it.

"I'm going to ask them anyway. How's that?" Guy forced out a smile.

Buddy just grunted.

"I understand you've been making some friends in the media lately."

"Is this one of the questions?"

"Yes."

"Then ask it straight out."

"Nothing specific. I was just wondering if you've been making some friends in the media lately. Movie people. Like that."

"I have no idea what you're talking about."

"Come on."

"Really. No idea. You're going to have to get a whole lot more specific."

Guy started small. "A director from New York. A fellow by the name of Manny Seville."

"Never heard of him."

"Come on."

"No. Really. Never heard of him."

"He came into your shop yesterday."

"A lot of people do."

"You left with him."

"People buy enough of this crap, I help them out to their cars. Give 'em a hand."

"No, you don't. Not the Buddy Frommer I know. You've never given anybody a hand in your life."

"Sure I have. A guy with a couple thousand bucks' worth of skis. A little old lady." He shrugged. "I'm a Good Samaritan. Sue me."

"This guy didn't buy skis."

Nothing from Buddy. Not even the passage of some hidden recognition behind his eyes. His big dull face on his big head was a blank.

"This guy Manny left and walked to the Binding, and you had dinner with him there."

"Jeez. Am I under surveillance now or what?"

"No. People just notice things. Me included."

"Goddamn small town busybodies."

"So you *did* spend a little time with Seville."

"I never knew the guy's name. Or else I forgot it. Sorry."

"I see."

"We had a few drinks. Had a few laughs. I'm a friendly guy."

"Sure," said Guy. "But never mind that." He was thinking that there was obviously more to be learned about what Buddy was up to around here, but now was not the time to do it. "I'm not really interested in Seville anyhow. Who I *am* interested in, in case you haven't guessed, is an old friend of his. Harper Stone? The movie actor? You do know *his* name, don't you?"

"I haven't spent my whole life under a rock."

"I guess not."

"Remember in high school?" Buddy's eyes, sunken into that big head, actually got a little dreamy at the recollection. "A bunch of us took Bernie Johnson's mom's car—that big Eldorado—up to the drive-in for a double feature? *Murder Town,* it was. And that army one."

"*The Ne'er-Do-Wells.*"

"Yeah. That's it. That's the one. *The Ne'er-Do-Wells.*"

"That was my brother," Guy said. "My brother Bill. You were in *his* class, remember?"

Guy didn't say anything. He was too busy marveling at how movies had the power to change history. To rewrite not just their own subjects but the content of life that went on around them. There was no question in his mind that Bill Ramsey hadn't been in that Cadillac with Buddy and Bernie and their pals. He'd been doing his homework, probably, or running his paper route. Working, anyhow. Like his little brother Guy did. It was how they were raised.

"Must have been a dozen kids jammed into that car. Four or five of us in the trunk."

"Bill never mentioned it," said Guy.

"What a night," said Buddy, shaking his big head back and forth in a fog of misremembering.

"I guess."

"Those were the days."

"Right," said Guy. "Anyhow, what I'm wondering now is if you had a chance to see Stone when he was in town."

"I wish."

"You wish."

"You bet."

"So you didn't see him."

"Nope."

"You didn't sell him anything."

"Nope." The notion of making a sale seemed to pull Buddy out of his reverie of that long-ago night at the drive-in. He raised his big head and looked around the shop: at the stacked skis, the racked helmets, the hanging jackets and pants. "To be perfectly frank," he said, "and not to bite the hand that feeds me, I think a big shot like Harper Stone would go for equipment a little higher-end than this crap."

Guy waited a half a second. He knew there was some risk in the path he was about to take, but he took it anyhow. "So you didn't sell him the same stuff you sold Manny Seville?"

"Who?"

"The director. From New York."

"I didn't sell him anything."

"No?"

"No," Buddy said, with a harder edge. Anyone could see that bringing Manny into the picture—Manny and whatever it was that he and Buddy had partaken of prior to their drunken-sailor walk to the Binding—had snapped him out of his Hollywood reverie and restored him to his usual pugnacious self. Too bad, for the sake of the questioning—and the sake of the next customer. Whoever came in the door next was due for an extra dose of that old Buddy Frommer magic.

"All right," Guy said, "I'll take your word for it. And you never met Stone, either."

"Nope." A little trace of that starstruck gleam passed over his face, but it didn't last. "I'd sure as hell remember *that*."

TWENTY-SIX

One side of the mountain:

Here comes Stacey, racing down the steeps at the top of Oh, Brother! with Chip right behind her. When they stop at a catwalk to catch their breath and look up at them, their separate paths through the overnight snowfall will cross and recross like a double helix. *A thing of beauty,* Chip will say, although the real beauty is always in the making of it.

The other side of the mountain:

Here goes Guy, cranking his patrol car up the narrow and winding trail to the cabin where Stacey and Chip brought the car on that fateful night. The state troopers said that they'd gotten nothing out of the guy who lived there, except a report about how two kids had shown up after dark and gone hiking over the peak on skis. A couple of crazy kids. The new snowfall makes things treacherous but Guy perseveres, taking the untracked white stuff as a sign that when he gets to the top there'll probably be somebody home.

There was a pickup in front of the cabin with a big yellow plow mounted on the front of it, the whole deal covered over with snow.

Just as Guy had imagined. Past the pickup was a woodpile of epic scale, three or four cords at least, stacked neatly and covered over with blue tarpaulins against the weather. He pulled the patrol car up in the shadow of it and got out, the snow at this elevation well up over the cuffs of his pantlegs. The cabin sat in a clearing with a view of the sky that must have been just right for getting satellite television, to judge by the dish mounted under the eaves and pointing skyward. Guy remembered when a satellite dish was a satellite dish, when people with money around here—people in the woods, where cable didn't go—had big black bowls in their yards that looked like something out of a science-fiction movie. All steel latticework and sharp antennas and heavy-duty cables snaking through high grass. Something fit to capture signals from the deep-space crew of *Mission to Antares*. Not anymore, though. These days everybody had their own little vest-pocket dish, just as nice and compact as you please. Mount it under the eaves to keep the snow off, and you were in business. Things changed.

The front porch of the cabin was loaded with junk. It wasn't trash, at least not most of it, but it was definitely junk. Guy always made a distinction between the two. Trash was garbage. Junk was old beat-up stuff with some use left in it, at least in somebody's mind. The junk in this particular collection included a couple of aluminum folding chairs, a gas grill without a tank, a pony saddle, a busted recliner, and a snow shovel that he wished somebody'd used before he got here. There was some newer stuff mixed in, too. A Garden Weasel. A pair of aluminum snowshoes. A Crock-Pot still in its packaging.

He stepped onto the porch, stamped his boots off, went to the door and knocked. There was a television on inside, loud, and he could hear it through the glass. Nobody answered the door so he knocked again, louder. This time there were footsteps inside and the creaking of a chair and the slamming of a door. The volume on the television went down and footsteps approached. Guy adjusted his hat, squared his feet on a novelty doormat that read COME BACK WITH A WARRANT, and put on a businesslike smile.

"Yeah," said the tall man as he opened the door wide. Just that. "Yeah."

"Sheriff Ramsey." Tilting his hat. "Guy Ramsey."

"How you doing."

"All right. You?"

"All right." The tall man looked as if he could keep this up all day.

"Mind if I come on in?" He cocked his head to see behind the tall man a little. A cold wind swept around him and around the tall man and into the living room, flipping the pages of a copy of *Guns & Ammo* that lay on a big wooden industrial spool that Guy figured must be a coffee table.

"How come?"

"I've got a couple questions for you."

"Troopers've already been here."

"I know that."

The wind blew again and the pages of *Guns & Ammo* kept turning until most of them had flipped over; then the magazine fell off onto the floor. The tall man didn't budge and he didn't say anything.

Guy went on. "The troopers and a local guy like me," he said, "we kind of look at things from different directions."

The tall man narrowed his eyes. "If it's their case, then you got no authority."

"You've been watching too many cop shows."

"Sue me."

So help him, if Guy heard that expression again today he was going to have to kill somebody. He squared his shoulders against the cold wind, put a hand on the open door, and said, "How about we just go inside and quit heating up the outdoors."

Rather than stand in his way, the tall man stepped back.

Stacey and Chip were on a chair with one of the ski instructors and a little kid who looked to be no more than four or five years old. Stacey hated riding with little kids, and if left to her own devices she wouldn't have done it. She was always afraid that they were going to slide forward under the bar and plummet to their deaths— either that, or slip rearward below the seat back and dangle by their skis until they finally wriggled loose, and *then* plummet to their deaths. What a nightmare. Often enough some instructor who'd gotten overburdened with kids would be standing in the lift line trying to pawn them off on unwitting skiers one or two at a time, but Stacey always said no. Actually, it was more like, "No, really, I just can't, see, I'm, uh, I understand, but, uh, I mean, you know . . ." until the chair came and she could get on and make her escape. The thought of losing some helpless little five-year-old from the seat of a chairlift was simply too much to bear, and it was one of the things that kept her from ever becoming an instructor. That and an unwillingness to let the sport that she loved so much get tainted by the stigma of *work*. That would ruin everything.

Stacey was on one end of the chair and the instructor was on the other, with the little kid and Chip in between them. That was all right. If the kid went, there was no way she could be held responsible. Plus Chip was on the Ski Patrol, so he'd know what to do—if you could do anything other than wave good-bye. Argghh. She closed her eyes and waited for the ride to be over.

Chip nudged her with his shoulder. "What happened to those new Heads?"

"Gone," she said.

"Somebody steal 'em?"

"Hah. I almost wish. Then I could claim them on my insurance or something." She picked up the tips of her old skis and studied them, clacking them together to knock off the snow. "Actually, it's kind of the opposite of theft—but it comes to the same thing in the end. I'll probably never get them back. They're evidence."

"What?"

"You heard right."

"No."

"If you're talking about the new Heads that I skated across Harper Stone's forehead with, yes."

"Unbelievable."

"Well, they did do some damage."

"I know, but—"

The ski instructor leaned forward, one hand on the little kid's chest to keep him from going anywhere. He was an old man with a gray mustache all icicled over, and when he spoke his Long Island accent gave his whole life story away. He'd retired from someplace in New York, moved up here to get away from it all, and taken up instructing to fill the empty hours. It happened all the time. He held the kid and looked past Chip to zero in on Stacey. "Are you the one that found him?"

"Hey," Chip said, a little hurt. "What am I, chopped liver?"

"Never mind you," the old man from Long Island said. "I heard it was a girl. That's what everybody's saying. *Some girl found him*, that's what they say." Then, lifting his hand and pointing at Stacey, "So it was you, huh?"

"It was both of us. Kind of."

"I'll be." Without the pressure of the instructor's hand on his chest the kid leaned forward a couple of inches, pushing out his tongue toward the metal safety bar. "Hey, kid," the old man barked, pushing him back. "Quit acting like an idiot." The kid settled back with a dazed and disappointed look.

"That kind of thing could hurt your tip," Chip said. "Calling a little kid an idiot."

"What the hell do I care about a tip? Besides, I bring him back with half his tongue ripped off, you think I'll get a tip for that? Huh? You think these yuppies are handing out tens and twenties to guys who bring their kids back at the end of the day all disfigured and everything? Not on your life." The old man sat chuckling into his icy mustache for a minute, and then he remembered about Harper Stone. "So you're the ones found that old bastard, huh? Tell me all about it."

The whole morning was going to go pretty much like this.

The tall man's name was Frank Schmidt. Guy took out a pad and pencil to get the spelling right, then he put them away rather than give Frank the idea that this little conversation was anything more than the neighborly visit it seemed like. You never got anywhere with that.

Apparently, Frank was a lineman for the electric company. That would explain the giant spool that he used for a coffee table, the even bigger one that looked to be serving as a kitchen table in the next room, and the little one that stood against the wall with a toolbox on it. It would also explain the hard hat hanging on a peg by the door where Guy had left his boots, and the filthy orange storm gear hanging alongside it. You didn't exactly have to be Sherlock Holmes. Today was Frank Schmidt's day off, he said in a much softer voice than Guy had expected once they got inside and sat down. Almost whispering. Guy was lucky to have found him home, he said.

"I was pretty sure there'd be somebody—" Guy started, intending to explain that the absence of tracks on the lane suggested that no one had gone out this morning, but Frank lifted a finger to his lips and shushed him gently.

"The little woman's still sawing wood," he said.

"Sorry," said Guy, thinking of how the television had been blaring just two minutes ago.

"It's my day off, and she's the one sacked out. Ain't that the way?"

"I guess it is," said Guy.

Schmidt shook his head, long-suffering, and ran the flat of his hand over his buzz cut. "Anyhow," he whispered, "like I said, the troopers been here already."

There was coffee on in the kitchen and Guy sure could have used some of it, but Frank wasn't going to offer and Guy wasn't going to ask.

"Right," said Guy. "And you—"

"—didn't see nothing but them two kids. It ain't like this place is Grand Central Station or nothing." He laughed between his teeth, hissing.

"Sure. I can see that." Guy looked down at his stocking feet, cold on the hardwood planks. "The little woman didn't see anything either?"

"Not a thing."

"You sure about that?"

"Not before and not after. She was up here all day and I got off early around lunchtime. I come home and we watched a video."

"What'd you see?"

"I told you we didn't see nothing but them two kids."

Guy cocked his head. "The video. What'd you see?"

"I don't remember."

"Just curious. Maybe you saw something good."

Frank lifted his hands.

Guy laughed, softly, and scratched his head for effect. "Let me get this straight," he said. "You remember not seeing something you didn't see, but you don't remember seeing something you did see."

"I can't explain it," said Frank. "It must have been some chick flick."

"Fine," said Guy. "Just kidding. It's funny how your mind works, though, isn't it?"

"Right. It sure is."

"What about the day before, then?"

From behind the door came a creaking of bedsprings, and Frank lowered his voice another notch. "The day before? I think we watched something on HBO."

"No. Sorry. I didn't mean on the television. I meant did you see anything suspicious the day before."

Frank smacked himself in the head. "Sorry. No."

"Any tracks in all that snow?"

"Nothing."

"Anybody up here that shouldn't have been?"

"Wait a minute. Was that the day it come down so hard?"

"No. The day after."

"Right. I was stuck here all day the day it come down. Couldn't get out."

"Not even with that plow?"

"I'd have gotten out if they'd called me. If there'd been an outage or whatever."

"Lucky you," said Guy.

The bedsprings sounded again, accompanied by a mild cough mostly muffled by a pillow.

"You mind if I stay around and ask your wife a question or two? Just confirm she didn't see all the same things you didn't see?"

Frank laughed out loud. "She ain't never coming out as long as you're here." He pointed to a little hallway that ran past the bedroom door and led into the back of the house. "Bathroom's back there. Until that woman gets the curlers out of her hair, she don't think she's fit for company."

"I'm not exactly *company*," said Guy, and he realized from the impatient look that was coming back to Frank's face that it was true. "How about I leave you my card," he said, knowing a dead end when he saw one, "and you folks give me a call if something comes up. If you remember anything. Anything at all."

"Sure," said Frank, taking the card and sliding it into his pocket. "Will do."

TWENTY-SEVEN

Stacey ran into the Long Islander again, not long after lunch. The one thirty lineup, where the instructors picked up a new batch of students, had come and gone—and now the old man with the icy mustache was back on the lift. This time he wasn't riding with a little kid. This time he was saddled instead with something even worse: Brian Russell. Complete with his barf-yellow Columbia jacket and dinosaur hat.

"Hey, Stace," Brian said, fumbling with the safety bar. "Fancy meeting you here."

"Everybody knows this little gal except me," said the instructor. "Where've I gone wrong all my life?"

Brian turned to him. "Stacey and I have something remarkable in common," he said.

Stacey swallowed hard, thinking that he was going to give away their history. She didn't even know the old man from Long Island, but she sure as anything didn't want him finding out she'd ever been engaged to this guy. A person could never live a thing like that down.

But Brian didn't betray her after all. He wasn't in the process of

claiming her as his one-time fiancée. He was in the process of an-
nouncing that he, like Stacey, had a connection to the late Harper
Stone. "She was the first person to see him dead," he said, "and I
was about the last person to see him alive."

"Guess again, buddy boy," said the instructor. "How I figure it,
the last person who saw him alive is the same one who helped him
end up dead. You interested in making that claim? Hmm?"

"You know what I mean."

"I'm just saying."

Stacey leaned toward Brian and cupped her mitten around his
ear. "Tell him his attitude problem is going to cost him his tip."

Brian bailed out on his lesson after half an hour or so—without
giving the old man an extra nickel—in order to chase Stacey into
the main lodge. He and the old-timer were just skidding into the
lessons-only line when he saw her out of the corner of his eye, and he
figured it was now or never.

By the time he'd dumped his skis and caught up with her she had
her boots off, her bag packed up, and was ready to go. "Short day?"
he said, clomping up in his rental boots like Herman Munster.

"That would depend on what time you got started," she said.
She barely looked at him. She was busy checking around for any
sock or gaiter or glove liner that might have gone missing under the
table—everything was black, which made things trickier—and
squaring a ball cap on her head. "I'm always on the first chair," she
said, "if I can help it."

"And you're off to work now, I'll bet."

"Yep."

"Too bad. I could use some pointers."

She convinced herself that nothing was hiding under the table,
and she looked up at him from beneath the brim of her cap. On the
front of it was a logo he didn't recognize. Something to do with ski-

ing, no doubt. "Pointers?" she asked. "From me? What happened to your lesson?"

Brian shrugged. "He said he'd taught me everything he could."

"Right." What he meant, if it had any connection to reality whatsoever, was not that he'd exhausted the instructor's knowledge of ski technique, but that he'd exhausted his patience. Stacey knew it, naturally. You couldn't teach Brian anything, on account of he knew everything already. She'd blame it on that Harvard degree of his, but he'd been that way for as long as she'd known him. It just took her a while to see it.

"To tell the truth," he said, "I only took a lesson on account of you."

"Me?" She took off her ball cap and set it on the table.

"I thought it'd be nice if I tried to keep up with you. You know, you enjoy this stuff so much. I thought maybe if I—"

"I get it."

"Honest! Being here in town made me want to spend all the time I can with you. And if this is what you enjoy the most, then so be it."

She pushed her hat around on the table and looked him square in the eye, looking for something she used to think was there. Just in case. Just to understand it, the way a medical examiner might look for something during an autopsy. After a minute she picked up the hat and put it on again. "This is the whole reason you came here, isn't it?"

"Yeah. To take a lesson. So I could keep up with you, maybe."

"No. I mean the reason you came to Vermont in the first place." It was about time she called him on it. "I'm talking about why you came on the shoot."

"Oh, that," he said, with an airy look. "It's my job."

"Don't give me that. You've never done a thing in your life that you didn't want to do. You've never done anything that wasn't your own idea."

"All right." He sat down, finally. "Guilty as charged."

"No big surprise. But at least you've come clean. That's more than—"

"Guilty as charged," he repeated, interrupting her. "But it's only because I missed you."

"Brian."

"I did, Stacey. I missed you. I *miss* you. Present tense."

She could tell he was really giving it his best, because he'd had the presence of mind to call her "Stacey" instead of "Stace." It didn't mean he was sincere, though. Not by a million miles. What it meant was that he was *selling*. The realization hit Stacey hard. Six months ago—actually, at any time in their relationship prior to the big breakup, when she'd found him in their shared Back Bay bed with that stealth slut she'd thought of as a friend—she would have registered his navigating the Stacey/Stace distinction as a sign that he cared about her. Now, she saw it for what it was: a sign that he cared about himself. There was a small part of her that wished, as Bob Seger used to sing, that she didn't know now what she didn't know then.

"If you *do* miss me," she said, "you'd better get used to it. Because that's the way it's going to be."

"I've changed, Stacey. Really."

"No. You haven't. It's not possible."

"I think you might be mistaken."

"People don't change. Not that much, anyhow. Not enough. Not you."

"They do. I did." He pushed away from the table a little. "Look at me, out here taking skiing lessons just so—"

"It's not a change, Brian. Following me out here, renting the gear, taking the lesson—it's not a change. It's just a strategy."

"Ow." He clutched at his heart. "That's cold."

"I'm not being cold. I'm being realistic. I have to be."

Brian brightened. "Because there's still something there, isn't there?"

"No." She turned her head away from Brian and his awful yellow coat to watch a little kid at the next table, six or eight years old and beginning to work on a huge chocolate chip cookie.

"Come on. You can feel it, can't you? That little something."

She just kept watching the kid.

"It's still there, isn't it?"

Stacey made no response at all. She just looked at the kid. How could a guy with a dinosaur hat be saying these things to her now? How could she have ever listened to him?

"I sure can feel it," Brian said. He slid his hand toward hers, there on the table. "I never stopped feeling it."

Blame it on peripheral vision or whatever, she drew her hand back as his came nearer, and dropped it into her lap as she turned away from the cookie-eating kid and fixed Brian with a hard stare. "Don't," she said. "Just don't."

Taking that as a good sign, he changed the subject and asked if she'd mind keeping him company for a minute while he had a snack. That cookie looked pretty good.

As long as Brian was buying, she went for one, too. White chocolate macadamia, although she could never quite tell which bit was a chunk of white chocolate and which bit was a macadamia nut. Who cared? It was all good, and she never splurged on this kind of thing for herself. She couldn't afford it. Three bucks for a cookie. It was robbery.

Brian snarfed down two of them and a large hot chocolate. "So," he said between bites, "has your friend the sheriff got any suspects lined up yet?"

"He doesn't tell me," she said, "and I don't think he knows too much about it anyhow. The state troopers are on the case. It's kind of out of his hands."

"Too bad. It'd be nice to have an inside track, don't you think?"

"I guess."

"Me, there's one guy I've got a funny feeling about. That guy Manny? The director? Up from New York?"

"I don't know him."

"He came up with the rest of us, but when the crew went home he stuck around."

"Maybe he likes it here."

"Maybe it's one of those scene-of-the-crime things."

"Brian."

"Really," he said.

"A lot of people like the mountains."

"Not Manny. He doesn't like anything. I can tell. He's that kind of guy."

"It takes one to know one," she said, watching him finish the first cookie.

"Hey, I like plenty of things." He looked for a minute as if he were about to throw caution to the winds and mention that one of those things was Stacey Curtis, but in the end he didn't. He just repeated himself, meaningfully: *Plenty of things.*"

"Right. And those things all cost a fortune."

He didn't take the bait. He just lifted his eyebrows as if the two of them shared a secret, and then he started in on his second cookie. Through a crumbly mouthful, he returned to the subject of Manny Seville and Harper Stone. "Thing is," he said, "they went back."

She leaned forward. This was interesting. "They went back where?"

"Not to a place. No. Sorry." He mopped cookie crumbs from his lower lip. "They went back in *time*. They had a history."

"What kind of a history?"

"I don't know exactly. They worked together a long time ago."

"A lot of people work together. That doesn't mean anything."

"There was friction."

"Friction? Oh, boy. Wait until I tell Guy. *There was friction.*"

"It's something. Otherwise all we've got is this old has-been movie actor in a town where nobody knows him—"

"Everybody knows him."

"Nobody knows him *personally*, I mean. And he ends up dead a mile or two out in the woods in the middle of a blizzard with no reason to be there in the first place, so who did it?"

"Maybe nobody. Maybe he was just out there and he died."

"Not that guy. Not Stone."

"How come?"

"He wasn't the type."

"So now you know all about what type he was."

"I know what I know. He wasn't exactly outdoorsy."

She laughed. "Right. There was friction, and he wasn't the outdoorsy type. I hope you shared these insights with the state troopers."

"I did."

"Then they must have the case pretty well solved by now."

Brian dunked the last of his cookie into his hot chocolate and popped it into his mouth. Then he drank off the rest and put the paper cup down on the table. It made a little hollow sound. "I wouldn't know," he said.

TWENTY-EIGHT

That night at the Binding, Stacey was simply going through the motions. She made a sweep of her tables and saw that nobody needed another drink, then she went back toward the bar, thinking of Harper Stone and Manny Seville and Buddy Frommer—three men that the world would have been better off without. And Brian Russell, too, while she was eliminating people. Just for good measure. Tina was leaning back in her stool to get a better look at the silent television that hung over the bar, shaking her head and clucking away. "My God," she said as Stacey came past. "I guess I missed my chance."

"What chance would that be?" She lifted the gate and let herself back behind the bar and leaned against the cash register.

"The chance to have married a movie star and come out of it a millionaire. Better than that, a *millionaire widow.*"

Stacey stood on her tiptoes, leaned over the bar, and craned her neck, but she couldn't see what Tina was talking about.

"All I had to do was follow my dream, go out to Hollywood, hunt up Harper Stone, and be the last one to marry him. I'd be worth a fortune right now. I wouldn't be breaking my back in the spa, that's for sure."

Stacey let herself back down. "That seems like kind of a long shot, Tina."

"A gal can dream, can't she?"

Jack looked up from washing out some glasses. "Wasn't he still married to what's-her-name? That Estelle Whatever? The one from *Afraid of the Dark*? With the low-cut dresses?"

"I thought so, but it turns out I was wrong. Seems they had a quiet divorce a long time ago."

"What was her name, anyhow?"

"Estelle."

"I know that. I know Estelle." He stood staring straight ahead, dumbfounded, scratching his little potbelly with one finger. "Estelle *What*, though?"

"Estelle Gardner."

"That's it. Estelle Gardner. Good for you." He resumed washing out glasses, bending over and looking up at Tina from over his glasses. "They have any kids?"

"Apparently not," Tina said. She pointed to the screen. "They're saying he left no next of kin whatsoever. Now, isn't that sad?"

"Very," said Jack. "And it's a shame, too—when he could have had you."

Tina finished her chardonnay, set the glass down, and sighed. "He never knew what he was missing," she said. "And it's too late now."

"Poor guy."

"Poor him," said Tina. Then, looking at some numbers flashing past on the silent screen, she added, "Poor me, too. I'd have made quite the merry widow."

Because according to the numbers, Harper Stone's movies were the top five bestsellers at Amazon. *Lights Out, Murder Town, The*

Ne'er-Do-Wells, *Night Train*, and *Last Stand at Appomattox*, in that order. The latest DVD from Pixar was in position six, followed by *Mission to Antares* and *Big City Heat*. She read them off as they scrolled past, marveling at poor old Harper Stone's reversal of fortune.

"Yeah," said Stacey. "According to Chip, you couldn't even get them on Netflix a week or so ago. Now he's everywhere."

Jack began drawing a beer for somebody, saying, "Turns out it's a good career move, I guess. Dying, I mean. Who would have thought?"

Stacey hoped that Guy would still be up when she got home, but it wasn't likely. Their two businesses—bartending and law enforcement—tended to run on vastly different schedules, at least out here in the woods. Back in Boston, the police were on duty twenty-four/seven and an awful lot of the trouble occurred around places where people were drinking into the wee hours. Here, though, it was different. Unless some drunk ran his car off the road in the middle of the night, there wasn't any reason for Guy to be up and about. Even if somebody did run his car off the road, it would be a long wait until somebody else found him and reported it. There was just so little traffic.

So the Ramsey place was shut up and dark when Stacey pulled into her parking spot beneath the kitchen windows. Just a little green gleam from the microwave, that was all. She let herself into the back porch and took off her boots before going on through to the kitchen. Nothing was locked. Nothing ever was. Not out here. What would be the purpose of a lock? To keep out bears? To discourage a hungry moose?

Still, there was somebody at large out there who had something to do with the unfortunate death of Harper Stone, so after she had washed up and brushed her teeth in the tiny hall bathroom, she went straight into her own room and shut and latched the door with the tiny hook and eye. It wasn't anything close to secure, but it was all she had. Only then, with the window shades pulled down tight against the enormous blackness outdoors, did she slip into her pajamas and jump into bed. After a few minutes she stuck one arm out from under the covers and into the cold to set the alarm. She usually didn't have any problem waking up in time to make it to the mountain for one of the first chairs, but she didn't want to risk missing Guy in the morning again.

"I think there's a drug connection," she said over a cup of Megan's coffee.

"You're talking about Stone."

"Yeah." She sat at the table and watched him stir his oatmeal over a low flame. "Stone."

"What makes you think drugs?" He said it without looking up, and he said it as if he hadn't been thinking the same thing for a while now. Just as casually as you please.

"Remember what I said about the Slippery Slope? That guy Buddy, and how I saw them downstairs?"

"I remember."

"The two of them? Looking at something? Like something on the table was changing hands?"

"The Slippery Slope's a retail store. Things change hands." He put the lid back on the pot and put the sticky spoon down on a little ceramic holder.

"It looked suspicious."

"Buddy always looks suspicious. It's part of his charm."

"You don't mean that."

He stuck his hands in the pockets of his bathrobe and said, "No. No, I really don't. Buddy has zero charm. He's the least charming man on the face of the earth, but that doesn't mean he's dealing drugs—or killing people."

"You haven't given any thought to what I said, then? To what I saw?" She looked disgusted.

Guy lifted the lid, peeked inside, and put it down again. He was thinking about something, and he wasn't in any hurry to give Stacey an answer. Satisfied with the oatmeal's progress, he put his hands back in his pockets and leaned against the stove, like Jack against the back bar. "I've thought about it hard, Stacey," he said. "I've taken it very seriously."

"You have?" She was still heated up, thinking that maybe this was worse. That he hadn't rejected her idea out of hand, but had thought about it for a little while and *then* rejected it. That was worse, wasn't it? Maybe. Maybe not. She didn't exactly know, but she stayed heated up over it anyhow.

"I did," he said. "In fact I took it so seriously that even though it's none of your business, I went and checked out the guy. He tells me he's never met Harper Stone."

"He's lying."

"I don't think so. I don't think he was lying. He was pretty persuasive."

"*He's lying to you, Guy*. I saw them. Together."

"I don't know." Guy remembered the starstruck look that had slid across Buddy's ordinarily impassive face at the mention of Harper Stone's name. He remembered how Buddy had said he would have remembered making Stone's acquaintance, sure as hell. "I just don't know."

"*But I do know*." Stacey said. "I know what I saw."

Guy shrugged just the slightest, noncommittal, and shifted his balance as if he were about to head toward the front hall. He was usually up in the bathroom right now, brushing his teeth. He was a creature of very regular habits, and veering away from his usual routine made him uncomfortable. Plus all four members of the Ramsey family had to get ready for the day in that one little bathroom, each in turn, before the school bus arrived.

Frustrated, Stacey tried another angle. "Did they find any drugs? In his body, I mean? Because that would mean—"

"I don't know what they've found. I don't guess they've even gotten that far yet. I don't have any idea how long it takes to thaw out a body, but I'm thinking a pound of hamburger meat takes the better part of a day."

"Ewwww."

"Yeah. Ewwww." He pushed himself away from the stove entirely.

"But if there were drugs in his system, then he might have gotten them from Buddy. Which would give Buddy a reason for lying about having met him. Right?"

"Are you fingering Buddy for a dope dealer, or a murderer?"

"I don't know. Couldn't he be both?"

Guy grinned. "You just don't like him."

Now it was Stacey's turn to shrug.

"Join the club," Guy said. "Unfortunately, being unlikable isn't a crime. Not that I know of."

"But what if Stone died from an overdose?"

"We'll see. You've got to wonder, though: Would that be Buddy's fault, even if he was the one who sold to him?"

"You're the lawman," she said. "Not me."

"True."

"But there's been a crime committed either way," she said. "Whichever."

"You've got a point." The pot of oatmeal behind Guy burped and its lid chattered a little bit, jumping. He reached over to turn the heat way down. Upstairs, somebody else got into the bathroom and started the shower running. Guy checked his watch and frowned and opened the cupboard over the sink to take out a cereal bowl. Everything was entirely out of whack now, and all he could do was go with it. He got some maple syrup from the fridge and a spoon from the drawer, and stood watching the oatmeal pot.

Stacey drained her coffee. "So now you think he might be a dealer, after all?"

Guy set the syrup and the spoon on the table. "Stacey," he said, tightening the belt of his bathrobe and sitting down opposite her, "the truth—just between you and me—is that I've been considering that as a real possibility. That's why I went over and talked with him."

She straightened up. "All right," she said. "All right, then. Good."

"Yeah. What you said helped."

"I appreciate it."

"I've been living right alongside that guy ever since I was a kid, and seeing only the same thing over and over: a rich kid living high on his dad's money. It never occurred to me that he might have had other sources of income all along. There've been rumors for years, but I've always believed in looking for the most obvious and reasonable answer."

Stacey finished her coffee and sat opposite him, looking awfully pleased with herself.

Guy clacked his spoon on the table, chewing his lip and thinking. After a moment he confessed. "There's one more thing," he said. "It wasn't just what you said about him and Stone in the basement."

"No?"

"No. That helped jog my mind loose. But it wasn't all of it."

"What else was there?" She leaned forward.

"There was another guy. You might have seen him in the Binding with your friend Buddy."

"Who?"

"You tell me. Did you see Buddy in there a couple of nights back? With a guy from out of town? A flatlander?"

Stacey remembered. She remembered what Brian had said about the guy on the crew who didn't go home. The director. "Wait a minute," she said. "It was Manny Something. That's it. Manny."

"Exactly. Manny Seville. Another big shot with a Hollywood story."

"He and Stone knew each other." The way she said it, it could have been either a question or not.

"They did know each other. And they might have some shared habits that aren't exactly wholesome."

"The two of them had a history, I know that."

"A history," said Guy. "How did you know?"

"My old fiancé told me. Brian."

"*Brian.*" Guy got up, turned off the heat under the oatmeal, and scraped it into his bowl. "Did he tell you I talked to him?"

"Yes."

"He's a good argument for a long engagement."

"I know what you mean."

"I think you did the right thing. You know—" He sat down with the bowl, poured some maple syrup over the oatmeal, and stirred it in.

"I know." She didn't need him to tell her that.

"Is he still in town?"

"He sure is. He won't go away."

Guy ate a couple of spoonfuls, tipped in a little more maple syrup, and stirred. "I wonder why that is."

"You know why."

"I guess I do."

"He can't let things go."

"I guess I understand that." The oatmeal seemed more to his liking now. "Anyway," he said, "next time you see him, have him tell you what he saw on the coffee table at Harper Stone's rental house. You might find it interesting."

Stacey thought for a half second. "It was cocaine, wasn't it?"

"He already tell you that?"

"He didn't have to."

TWENTY-NINE

Stacey sat in the lodge, putting on her boots, checking out a copy of the Rutland *Herald* that somebody had left behind. It had a story about what the troopers found in Stone's rental house. She figured the article was far from complete, and she was right. There was no mention of what Brian might have noted on the coffee table, for example, unless Guy was referring to empty Harpoon I.P.A. bottles and some magazines and some greasy napkins, which didn't seem likely. What the troopers did tell the *Herald*'s reporter was that the house was in terrible disarray, as if it had been occupied by a bunch of irresponsible and high-spirited fraternity brothers on winter break.

Frank Schmidt didn't get the paper delivered to his cabin in the woods, but he was getting basically the same information from CNN. They didn't have a reporter on the scene anymore—there wasn't exactly a scene for the reporter to be on, not up here in the Green Mountain State and not out west in Hollywood, where the absence of next of kin was combining with the absence of a body to yield pretty slim pickings in the way of newsworthiness—so CNN picked

up network feeds of affiliate feeds of coverage of absolutely no consequence. Some reporter standing in the snow in front of the Rutland hospital, her breath blowing steam. Frank sighed, picked up
the remote, and flipped around.

Manny Seville couldn't believe it. The *Today Show* was back to re-
porting on elementary schoolkids stealing their parents' cars and
golfers being struck by lightning and some guy who'd managed to
survive having a railroad spike rammed through the front of his
skull and out the back. Their usual sensational garbage, in other
words. The woman at the news desk did mention that Harper Stone
the movie actor was still dead, over a colorful graphic that showed the
resurgence of his Amazon and Blockbuster numbers, but that was it.
Only when they cut to the local news, which in this case was an affiliate in Burlington with sputtering microphones and video production values that reminded Manny of something out of the early days
of color television, was there anything like actual coverage. That
should have been no surprise, really. The death of Harper Stone was
the biggest thing to have happened around here since the Lake Placid
Olympics, and that was thirty years ago.

Stacey finished buckling her boots, snugged a gaiter down over her
neck, and strapped on her helmet. She zipped up her coat, lowered
her goggles, and put her gloves on, then she took them off again so
she could tear the story out of the *Herald* to take it with her. Just
so she would remember to ask Brian about Stone's rental house
when she saw him. As if she could forget.

Frank Schmidt flipped right past the network morning shows and
found himself at Turner Classic Movies, where a Harper Stone film
festival was under way. The guy's big mug filled the screen in a
close-up from twenty years back at least. Maybe thirty. Frank fig-

ured it was better for people to remember him that way than as a frozen corpse, and he hollered something to that effect into the kitchen. No answer.

Manny Seville lay in bed until nine, reaching over to the bedside table now and then to run his finger into a little plastic bag and scrape some white powder out of it, then bringing it back and massaging it into his gums. Not even the powder could make Regis and What's-Her-Name tolerable, so he found the remote and switched the television off. He licked his finger and guessed he might not mind staying around this hick town for a few days more. He kind of liked it here. It was restful. That whole mountain village thing. As hard as he'd been working, wasn't it about time he took a vacation?

Stacey was on a chair all by herself, fiddling with her iPod to get the volume just right in the headphones built into her helmet—not so soft that she couldn't make out the music, but not so loud that she couldn't hear somebody coming up behind her—when she soared over a huddle of patrollers running some kind of first-aid drill. An older guy she recognized but didn't know was strapped onto a toboggan, and Chip was gearing up to take him down the treacherous mogul field on Devil May Care. He saw her at the same instant she saw him, and judging by the way he waved and pointed she figured he was planning to meet her at the bottom. The guy strapped to the toboggan grinned at her and tried to wave, too, but it was hopeless. All he could do was wiggle his fingers, which in his big black gloves made his hands waggle like flippers.

She got off at the top and came straight down without a break, skirting around the back of the Peak Lodge to pick up Finesse, cutting over to The Falls, and winding up at the bottom of the lift long before Chip got there. She didn't take any pride in it. Hauling a loaded toboggan down any ski trail had to be tough, but taking

one down a bump run must have been murder. Plus she figured
he'd have to untie the other patroller once they got to the shack.
Sure enough it was a few minutes before Chip and the other patroller skied up to her at the margin of the lift line, Chip pulling
the toboggan and the other guy flexing his shoulders and neck
from where he'd been strapped down. Chip was still red-faced from
the effort.

"Nice job," Stacey said.

"Ask *me* how nice it was," said the other patroller, pushing at a
sore spot in his neck with the heel of his hand.

"If I'd pulled those lines any less tight, you would have rolled
right off," said Chip.

"Right. Sure. Just wait till it's *your* turn to go for a ride."

Stacey looked at Chip. "Are you up next?"

"I wish," said the other guy, still rubbing at his neck. "I wish he
was."

"Nah," said Chip. "We're done for now." The chair came and they
all got on it together, with the toboggan dangling between the two
patrollers. "We get this thing back and I'm headed over to the Northside chair for a while," he said once it had stopped rocking. "You
want to come?"

Of course she did.

At the top she skied down to a flat spot just below the Peak
Lodge and waited while Chip put the toboggan away. The other guy
went off somewhere else, leaving the two of them alone to head for
the Northside. It was even colder over there than usual, windy as
anything, and pretty empty, too. They had nearly every run all to
themselves, and there was never anybody else within seven or eight
chairs of them on the way up. The wind cut through them once they
were airborne on the chair, though, and they had to huddle together
to stay warm. Neither of them minded.

"You know what you were saying about Buddy Frommer being a dealer?" she said.

"Yep."

"It's true. No question."

"Right." He gritted his teeth against the cold. "How do you know?"

"Something Guy said."

"He came right out and—"

"Not exactly, but he let me know that he's pretty sure." They rode along in silence, battered by the wind, and then she said, "So why doesn't he seem to care?"

"I don't know." A gust came up and they strained against it. "Could be Buddy's *already* under investigation, right? Maybe they've got a big sting under way or something."

"Maybe."

"It might have been going on for years. With the state troopers, the FBI, the DEA, the whole nine yards. Maybe he doesn't want to blow it."

"I guess you could be right."

The wind picked up again and they leaned forward against it.

"You've got to give him the benefit of the doubt."

They got off the lift, hit the trail, and got down into the trees as fast as they could. It was warmer there and they stopped.

"One more thing," she said. "Guy said I should ask Brian about something he'd seen on the coffee table in Stone's rental. Back when he was looking for him the first time."

"He say what it was?"

"Just something on the coffee table."

Chip adjusted his goggles and looked out at the horizon. Mountains all the way to New Hampshire, under a low sky. "Drugs," he said.

"That's what I thought."

"Drugs for sure. Oh, yeah. It's got to be drugs. Coke, I'll bet."

"But why would he want me to ask Brian?"

"Maybe he didn't want to tell you himself, on account of confidentiality and all. But he wanted to let you know that he knows."

Stacey thought for a minute. "So maybe there *is* something under way. A bust. Like you said."

Chip shrugged and took off. She followed him, taking a straighter line, and zoomed past him in about three seconds, no problem.

THIRTY

Doc's, the seedy bar that sat alongside one of Spruce Peak's remote parking lots, had given up any hint of ski-town sophistication a long time ago. The truth was, it had never had any. A squat pile of crumbling bricks roofed over with tar paper, adorned with a clumsy but alarming two-story likeness of its animated Seven Dwarves namesake done in latex housepaint that had all but faded away with the years, Doc's had occupied the same little islet of land since long before the first rope tow was ever installed at Spruce Peak. It had begun as a private residence, a bootlegger's place in the deep woods, and when the bootlegger had passed away his widow had moved upstairs and kept on selling whiskey out of the kitchen. When every other landowner in the region had sold out to the Paxton family and moved south, that cantankerous widow had stayed put.

Her son, the original Doc, came of age under prohibition and was much benefited by it. To this day he sat in an alcove behind the bar, nursing a cirrhotic liver and inhaling bottled oxygen from a wheeled tank, remembering the old days when the front door had had a little sliding panel in it and a person had needed to know the password if he wanted to get inside. Nowadays, Doc liked to say, any damn idiot could get in. Idiots who didn't even know that skis came in pairs. *Snowboarders.* He watched them stream in with their baggy pants and their spiked-up hair, and he cursed them furiously under what little breath he had left.

Doc Junior, his son and namesake, worked the taps and ignored the old man. Doc Junior was a giant who rubbed against the bar in front and the cash register behind as he squeezed his way from customer to customer. Summer and winter he was forever damp with an oily sweat that soaked his clothes and probably did at least a little to lubricate his passage as he surged from tap to tap like some seagoing beast, ceaselessly weary, out of breath, and overwhelmingly anxious. It was this ongoing anxiety that had made him post a notice in the Ski Patrol shack at the base of the mountain, looking for a skilled professional to oversee Rail Jam Night. (God forbid he should pay for a want ad in the *Mountain Times*.) It was that posted notice that had caused his path to cross with that of Chip Walsh.

Rail Jam Night, which took place in the cramped little yard behind the tavern, was a one-ring circus of draft beer, testosterone, and lousy judgment. It consisted of thirty or forty underage college boys with fake IDs, riding their snowboards up and down a couple of homemade ramps just as recklessly as their blood alcohol levels would allow—all of it accompanied by thudding rap music or hip-hop or whatever it was that they called it. Doc Junior didn't know and didn't care. Rail Jam Night started as soon as the lifts on the mountain closed, and as a rule it wasn't over until an ambulance from the Rutland hospital showed up. This is why Doc Junior thought he could use a professional around—somebody who could keep a lid on things, and maybe take some of the liability hit if push came to shove.

So it was that Chip found himself freezing his butt off on a bar stool below a sizzling arc lamp, his back to a neon sign advertising Jenny Cream Ale, watching as a parade of tipsy college boys got loud and sloppy drunk in the great outdoors. He'd lifeguarded at Rehoboth Beach growing up in Washington, D.C., but it had done nothing to prepare him for this. There were rules on the beach. There were guidelines both posted and customary. Even though somebody out there always had a couple of beers hidden in a cooler, they were always stealthy about drinking them. Everything in moderation.

Not so at Rail Jam Night. Doc had a couple of kegs set up outdoors and he sat alongside them with a cashbox stuffed between his enormous thighs, taking in money and pouring out Long Trail in a pair of more or less coordinated streams. Some of the regulars from town were inside at the bar, coaxing boilermakers out of old Doc himself, who was up on his feet against his better judgment, dragging his oxygen tank like a penance, but everybody else was outdoors. Spilled beer had made the snow into a rusty yellowish slush under the arc lights. College boys tramped through it and slid over it and would soon enough be falling down into it. Chip watched them, wondering how low the thermometer had to sink before beer would freeze. The evening was getting colder and colder and he blew warm air down into his jacket, beginning to think that he might find out before too long.

Mainly, though, what he was thinking about was whether or not this discomfort and annoyance was worth the fifty bucks in cash that he was getting for it. Doc Junior had offered twenty-five on the sign he'd posted in the Patrol shack but there must not have been any other takers, because Chip had gotten him to double it. Chip felt the weight of that compromise every time he looked in the fat man's direction.

The music was terrifically loud, so loud that Chip signaled to Doc Junior and went inside to jam some toilet paper from the hideous men's room into his ears, then pulled his wool hat down over them and came outside again. He was only away from his post a minute or so, but the fat man gave him a threatening look, as if he meant to dock him a few bucks. Like a guy couldn't even use the bathroom during his shift. What job in the world held you to that kind of standard? None that he'd ever had. None that he'd ever have again, that was for sure.

And now the college kids wanted him to judge their antics. That was always a problem at Rail Jam Night. Doc Junior never set up any kind of protocol, so the drunk college kids would always end up fighting it out among themselves. Now a bunch of them began arguing over which one had done a better pop-tart or something, and they took their disagreement to the only credible authority in sight: Chip, the lifeguard. They came at him in a torrent of slurred language that he could barely understand, and not just on account of their blood alcohol level. Boarders had words for every little variation on every little trick: They rode fakie and goofy, they got backside air and Swiss cheese air, they did flips and grabs and seat belts and ho-hos. It was ridiculous. How was Chip supposed to judge anything, when he didn't know a Rippey flip from a roast beef?

Still, it was better than having to break up fights. So he said yes, he'd let his opinion be known, as long as everybody promised to abide by it and not give him any crap. Amazingly, they agreed and settled right down, then went back to their fun like a bunch of happy kindergartners. That kind of authority was enough to make Chip, all of twenty-seven, feel old.

The evening wore on and the music got louder and the boarding on display got worse. It was more daring, that was for sure, but it was also a whole lot less controlled. There were more mistakes and more crashes and more face-plants, which must have hurt like anything since the snow on the wooden ramps had been compressed until it was hard as rock. There was blood on the snow here and there, most of it left behind by scraped cheekbones and chins, but nobody much noticed. What everybody did notice was the arrival, a couple of hours into the festivities, of a certain undistinguished kid with a baggy jacket and pants in a kind of urban camo pattern that turned into skulls and crossbones when you looked at it up close, a dinky little black hat with a Grenade logo on it, and a pair of big Spy goggles levered down over his eyes in spite of the late hour. Everybody in the yard seemed to know him. They welcomed him like a king, with a roar that drowned out the rap music and nearly made Doc Junior drop his cashbox.

THIRTY-ONE

The kid's name was Anthony, apparently pronounced without the H. He had a Long Island accent you could saw wood with, and an attitude to match. Anthony leaned his board against the fence and strode into the crowded yard with both of his fists thrown skyward in what Chip figured were supposed to be devil horns, although the kid had on a pair of big mittens so you couldn't be sure. He might have been making peace signs. He might have been doing a Richard Nixon impersonation.

There were three reasons Anthony was a hero. First, he was clearly pretty well zonked on ganja. Second, he usually had plenty to go around. And third, a large percentage of the kids at the Rail Jam had spent a good chunk of the day thinking they'd never see him again. He was Lazarus with a backpack full of weed.

Anthony and his crowd hadn't arrived at the mountain until eleven or so in the morning, although they'd overnighted in Bennington after a fast trip north in somebody's dad's BMW. (They would have to drive all the way home with the windows open to get the smell out, but so what?) Sometime shortly after lunch, Anthony had slid under the rope on the Mountain Road trail where it skirted the boundary of the Spruce Peak property, way up at the top of the North Peak, and vanished down into the trees off-piste. The going was steep and the trees were dense and none of his pals had gone with him. They didn't think they were skilled enough, and they were right. The problem was, Anthony wasn't skilled enough either.

He wasn't at the bottom of the Northside lift when his friends got there. They waited for as long as college boys will, which wasn't very long, and when he didn't show up they took another run. He wasn't there when they got to the bottom a second time, either. Some of them said to hell with him then, and some of them said maybe he'd changed his mind and was going to meet them at the Peak Lift, and some of them said they ought to notify the Ski Patrol, but nobody did anything of the sort. They all just rode the lift again, missing Anthony a little bit and missing his stash a little bit more. There was nothing like smoking weed in the fresh mountain air. Now *that* was living.

As the afternoon wore on the word got around the riders on the mountain: Keep an eye peeled for a dude with skull-and-crossbones camo and Spy goggles and one of those cool Burton boards with the half-naked girl on it. He'd gone out of bounds and hadn't come back. Or maybe he had. Because as the rumor of his disappearance started picking up speed, a counter-rumor of his return got started. Somebody had seen him in the men's room in the base lodge. Somebody else had seen him toking up behind the Patrol shack at the top of the Peak Lift. He'd hit on somebody's girlfriend on the Northside lift. Like Bigfoot, Anthony was everywhere and nowhere.

It was only when he didn't show up at Doc's Rail Jam that the truth began to sink in. Then the beer started flowing, which smeared the details of any concern that anybody might have still had. So in the end, when Anthony actually showed up in the flesh, the welcome was huge and sodden and overwhelming.

A handful of guys lifted him up onto their shoulders and carried him to the center of the yard, where the two ramps came together under the lights. They stumbled some on the ice and the beer slush, but nobody went down. From his kingly perch on their shoulders, Anthony calmed the crowd, threw back his head, and told his story.

He said that the riding over there was awesome, although not for everybody.

He confessed to having gotten a little bit turned around when he came to a flat spot, and had to pull his left foot out of the binding and skid along on one leg for a while. He confessed further to having gotten tired from the slog (he blamed it on the altitude, and nobody challenged him on it, even though Spruce Peak had a total vertical drop of just under 2,000 feet, which made it no Everest). He also confessed to having sat down on an exposed ledge after a while and fired up some weed and maybe kind of forgotten which way he was supposed to be going by the time he was through. This produced a great cheer from the crowd.

Somebody brought him a beer. He drank it fast, sloshing only a little of it on the shoulders of the guys who were keeping him aloft. They cursed and howled and shook their fists but he kept on with his story.

He said he'd finished his smoke and set off down a little ravine at the end of the flat spot, trying to keep himself oriented toward the front side of the mountain, but what must have happened is that the ravine twisted one way and another until he was facing the back side and didn't even know it. So down he went. He said he didn't see any signs of a familiar trail or even so much as a lift pylon, but he wasn't worried. He traversed a lot, though, trying not to put too much vertical behind him before he ran into the safety of a groomed trail. The longest time went by. Nothing. He tried his cell phone. Nothing. Rather than keep going down he unclipped one boot and skated for a while across the face of the mountain just as straight as he could, looking downward for signs of the familiar. After a while he unclipped the other boot, put the board over his shoulder, and headed up, even though he knew he couldn't keep climbing in the deep snow for long.

At the suggestion of such hard labor somebody asked if he could use another beer, and he didn't deny it. The other guys put him down before it could be delivered, rather than risk being spilled on again.

Anthony's salvation arrived just as the beer did. He told about coming to a clearing from where he could see something he'd never noticed from the mountain: the top of a little wobbly metal windmill, maybe a couple hundred yards below where he stood and off to the left. Wind power meant civilization, he figured, so he calculated its location and set out for it. It disappeared as soon as he got back down into the trees but he kept his wits about him and kept going. Soon something materialized out of the woods. Not the windmill— it turned out he'd overshot that—but a cabin. A little house, with a plowed road up to it and everything. A light on in one of the windows and the television going and smoke coming out of the chimney. He was definitely not on the front side anymore—any moron could see that—but he was saved.

He told how he whooped and shot down the rest of the way, zooming under low-hanging tree limbs and jumping over big holes in the snow that would have eaten a lesser man alive—most of the people in the crowd laughed at this, knowing Anthony's abilities— and he told of how he flew over the bank that the snowplow had built up and sailed out over the lane, then skimmed the top of the bank on the opposite side and pulled a one-eighty with a Miller flip and landed practically on the guy's doorstep.

The applause in the yard behind Doc's was deafening.

Anthony told how the old guy in the cabin sure took his own sweet time coming to the door. The television was on inside like he said and the volume was cranked all the way up and he figured maybe whoever was in there couldn't hear him over the noise of it. So he knocked louder. There was a button for a bell but it didn't make any sound that he could hear so he just kept hammering on the door. He hollered a couple of times, too. *Hello,* like you'll say. *Anybody home?* like you'll say, even though you know somebody's home on account of the television's on.

When nobody came he thought about giving up and walking down the plowed road to the bottom of the mountain and just getting it over with, but he didn't because who knew where he'd end up? Some back road somewhere on the far side of the mountain, ten or fifteen miles away from civilization. No cars on it and no chance of thumbing a ride anywhere. He sure as hell wasn't climbing back up to the peak and trying again. Not with this television on right here and the smoke coming out of the chimney. Not with civilization right at his fingertips.

He told of how he kicked at the door a couple of times and how that knocked the snow off his boots in clumps. He described, complete with elaborate body language, how he nearly lost his footing a couple of times on the slick floorboards, and how the old guy finally got off his ass and turned down the television and came creeping over to the door. He took his own sweet time and came slow, and he acted all suspicious when he got there. There was a curtain over the glass and he slid it open just the slightest bit like whoever was knocking was some kind of burglar or serial killer or whatever. Like it was the secret police come to haul him away. Like it was a freaking grizzly bear on the loose. Did they have grizzly bears around here? Anthony guessed they did. No wonder the old guy was spooked. He didn't get a lot of visitors up there, that was for sure.

The crowd at Rail Jam Night was starting to lose interest on account of the long subplot about the old guy, and a couple of boarders had begun climbing the backside of the ramps to get on with their runs, so Anthony cut to the good part. How the old dude let him in and smelled grass on him and asked if he had any to spare. Anthony said sure he did, sure as hell he had some, but he wasn't giving it away. He'd swap some, though, for a ride back to town. That's what he'd do. No prob with that. At which the dude bounced his old head up and down and said sure, sure, he could arrange a ride. There was a snowmobile in the shed out back and they'd take that. Now where was the reefer? That's what he called it. *Reefer.*

Anthony's cell phone didn't work in the cabin and the old guy didn't want him using the phone for whatever reason so he didn't call anybody to let them know he was safe. Plus there was the reefer, which was distracting, and a little something else that the old guy had tucked away somewhere. Anthony didn't want to say exactly what that little something else was, but he sniffed and ran his mitten across his upper lip enough to give people the idea. It was either that or his nose was running thanks to the cold, but it was probably what everybody figured it was.

Anyhow they blew away most of the afternoon watching television and eventually they went out the back door, fired up the snowmobile, and took it down the mountain to the main road. There were tracks in the fields parallel to the road and they stayed in those. The old guy had a big heavy jacket with a hood snugged tight around his face and Anthony pulled his goggles down because the cold wind made his eyes water. They didn't go all the way to the mountain base but they got close enough. The old dude left him in the field across from the parking lot at Judge Roy Beans. He wouldn't go any closer. It was like he was a vampire or something. The old guy said he was in a hurry to get home before the light died and he'd have trouble finding his way. He was fumbling with the switch for the headlight on the snowmobile while Anthony got off and freed up his board, and before Anthony got a chance to thank him for the lift, he got it working and roared off. Anthony had to walk all the way back up here and boy oh boy he'd worked up a thirst. He sure could use another beer if nobody minded—and nobody did.

THIRTY-TWO

According to conventional wisdom, if you wanted to go to the movies in Vermont, you had to go to New Hampshire.

Although that may not have been entirely true, it wasn't far off. There was a movie theater forty-five minutes away in Rutland, after all. But Stacey had gone there once and it was shabby and smelly and her feet kept getting stuck to the floor. The whole experience felt like movie night in prison. They might as well have tacked a bedsheet to the wall and made everybody sit on wooden benches. Rumor had it that there was a theater in Bennington (an hour away) and another in Springfield (an hour away in a different direction), but the odds of their being any better didn't strike Stacey as all that great.

She hadn't been a huge moviegoer when she'd lived in Boston, but it was nice to go sometimes and she missed it a little, especially since she didn't have a television of her own and had to watch with the whole Ramsey family. Which wasn't that bad or anything, they made her feel perfectly welcome and all, but still. So when Chip invited her to the movies, she didn't quite know what to think. It turned out to be a Harper Stone film festival, which was an even bigger throwback to the old days before multiplexes and stadium seating. "Where is it?" she asked him, expecting the worst.

"Up in Woodstock," he said, "at the town hall. They show movies on the weekends, since there's nowhere else to go."

Stacey brightened. "As a public service," she said. She hadn't yet made it up to Woodstock, but everyone said it was a lovely little classic Vermont village—nothing at all like this grim old has-been mill town where she'd found herself, a place that sidled up to Spruce Peak as if it were tugging on its coatsleeve, looking for a handout.

"I guess that's the general idea," Chip said. "There's a lot of money in Woodstock. Permanent money and tourist money both. They've got a farmers' market up there that's never had a farmer anywhere near it, I'll tell you that. All this imported stuff from Europe and places. Everything costs an arm and a leg."

"You know how it is with some people. The more they spend the better they feel." She was thinking of Brian.

"Tell me about it." He was thinking of his parents.

They went up early and ate good burgers at a little place on the corner, and when that didn't take up much time and there was still an hour or so before the movie started they walked the streets of the village. The sidewalks were busy and the stores were all open late, and the trees were lit with white lights that twinkled through thin branches. It felt to Stacey like the kind of moment where people in their situation might be walking arm in arm or hand in hand—but they didn't, and that was all right, too.

Chip was correct: There was definitely money in Woodstock, big-time. The houses and storefronts were immaculate, for one thing. But there was more to it than that. It was as if the village fathers had long ago passed an ordinance that said you had to keep your place not just perfectly maintained—the paint fresh, the brickwork pointed, and the brass on every metal surface polished to a high sheen that glowed even in the faint light of those tiny twinkling Christmas bulbs—but that you actually had to strive for and achieve a certain measurable level of *charm*. How was that possible? What was it that caused a town like this to turn itself into something that Walt Disney might have billed as Vermontland?

Competition, Stacey figured. Competition and pride, if you kept in mind that pride was one of the seven deadly sins. The more they walked down the streets and lanes of Woodstock, the more she was sure of it. The library was a showplace. The covered bridge that spanned the river, lit with a pale white disk of a moon, looked like a painting Norman Rockwell had rejected for being too cute. The tourist places—a couple of inns and a handful of B and Bs and one little motel—were all lovely, but they paled in comparison to the places where regular people lived, at least in tiny ways. A wooden doorstep with scuffed paint. The hinge of a shutter that had somehow dripped a little rust. In other words, it looked like the people in this town who didn't *need* to make their places gleam were spending more time and money on it than the people who *did*. It was pride and competition, all right. Pride and competition and out-of-town money.

She didn't know what to expect from the movies at the town hall. Would it be the real thing, just a little village up here in the woods making its best effort to bring in a little bit of culture? Or might it go the other way, and be just a bunch of rich people from New York amusing themselves? She floated both of these ideas to Chip. He thought for a minute and then laughed. "You've got me," he said. "My guess is it's a bunch of rich people from New York, doing such a good job of pretending to be the real thing that we won't be able to tell the difference."

"Oh, great," said Stacey.

"Or else a little of both, and we'll have to figure out who's on which side."

"No problem," she said.

There was a line of people waiting outside the town hall, and once they got inside there was hardly a seat left. Some folks seemed to have programs, just single sheets of paper folded in half the short way, but Stacey couldn't manage to get her hands on one. She was curious, though. By the look of the technology, there was grant money somewhere behind this operation. She thought she'd like to see who was supporting it.

The room echoed with a murmur of hushed voices and a low rumble of boots on hardwood, all of which came to a stop when a tiny white-haired woman approached a podium alongside the screen. She was no taller than a fourth-grader, thin verging on disappearance, and dressed in an elevated version of the Vermont sweater-and-corduroy aesthetic.

Stacey leaned toward Chip. "Imported money."

"I'm withholding judgment."

"My bet's on the table. You know what I think."

The tiny old woman climbed to the podium, took the microphone in both hands, and tipped it downward, aiming it toward her upturned face.

"I don't know," said Chip, shaking his head and narrowing his eyes. "I'm starting to settle on local. Local for a couple of generations anyhow."

"No way."

"Way. You'll see."

The old woman tapped on the microphone with one manicured nail, making a hard sound that startled everyone, including herself, into rapt attention.

Stacey looked around at the crowd, almost every face smiling up expectantly at the white-haired woman. She tilted her head toward Chip and lowered her voice to a whisper. "I'm having second thoughts," she said.

"Too late."

"How many generations does it take to make a local?"

The woman smiled, took a folded piece of paper from her pocket, and painstakingly flattened it on the surface before her.

"Around here?" Chip shrugged, and the white-haired woman at the podium began to speak. Her voice was low and large, doubly surprisingly for coming from such a small figure, and it had the most astonishing down-east accent imaginable. She sounded like a lobsterman. Chip gave Stacey the point of his elbow. "I'm thinking all the way back to the *Mayflower*," he said.

It was a double feature: *Murder Town*, followed by *Lights Out*.

The *Mayflower* lady, whose name was Druscilla Peru and whose people had come south to Vermont from a saltwater farm on the coast of Maine a hundred years back, and whose inheritance had funded not the film series itself but a lobbying effort to persuade the NEA to back it over the long term, apologized for the similarity of the two pictures but said that these were all the library could get on such short notice. They had hoped to contrast one of Stone's classic crime movies with something different—*The Ne'er-Do-Wells*, maybe, or *Last Stand at Appomattox*—but facts were facts and they'd just have to make do.

Stacey looked around the crowd as the lights went down, and figured that about half of the people in the town hall looked as if they had plenty of experience making do. The rest, not so much. So she guessed Chip had been right. It was a little of both.

Murder Town, first on the double bill, was the movie that established all the great themes of Harper Stone's work. The alienated outsider. The corrupt society that requires his heroism but ultimately rejects him. And the outcast dame who wins his icy heart, if only for a while.

But if *Murder Town* set the tone for his career, *Lights Out* was his bare-knuckled masterpiece. The hero, a certain Harry Smith—for every one of Stone's characters shared the actor's initials and the three doomlike beats of his name—was jut-jawed and narrow-eyed and independent as a hog on ice. He was a private investigator, fifty bucks a day plus expenses, and if he felt a shred of compassion for the industrialist whose empire was saved by his quick wits or for the blackmailer who plummeted down that famous elevator shaft, he wasn't letting on. Likewise for the industrialist's daughter, played by some starlet whose career arc had peaked here and then plummeted. Steer clear, baby. Harry Smith was just doing his job. There'd be time for romance after the credits rolled.

"Ooh, I love this one," Chip said when the titles came up over an animated graphic of a yellow flashlight beam prowling the cut-paper streets of a city straight out of some German expressionist's nightmare. Lurking criminals ducked into alleyways at its sudden and illuminating touch. Cats scattered from high fences. "It's my dad's fave, too."

"I thought you said he liked *Afraid of the Dark* best."

"Did I say that?"

"You did. That's what you told Stone. That day on the mountain?"

Somebody shushed the two of them from behind.

"Wow, good memory," Chip whispered. "I think you're right. I think he did like *Afraid of the Dark* best. But that was pretty much a remake of this one, wasn't it? Only with a bigger budget? And Anne Bancroft, I think?"

"Maybe your dad goes for Anne Bancroft."

"You could be on to something."

The flashlight beam passed down an alley, slipped through an open door, and then disappeared, the whole scene going black on black for a few seconds to the accompaniment of a screeching trumpet. A few more beats and the trumpet stuttered out and a bass picked up the rhythm. The light appeared again from behind the

windows of an upstairs room. Two windows, each framing the silhouette of one man. The men leveling pistols at each other. The
bass thumped, steady and urgent. The flashlight beam flicked from
one man to another and back again, and at last the guns fired in
a coordinated explosion that washed out the black city and lit the
upturned faces of a hundred or more spellbound Vermonters seated
row upon row in folding chairs. One last blast of horns. Then,
Lights Out.

THIRTY-THREE

For certain people gathered in the town hall—the under-forty crowd, mainly, raised as they were on MTV—the movie was surprising talky and molasses-paced. How on earth Harper Stone ever got a reputation as a man of few words was anybody's guess. It seemed to Stacey as if he were always explaining things: the plot, his motivations, the workings of a Ford Thunderbird Coupe or a Smith & Wesson .38 Special. There was no end to it.

The elevator scene, on the other hand, did not disappoint. To begin with, the angles were flat-out dizzying. The camera flicked up toward the gaping doorway on the top floor, down toward the filthy black roof of the cab, and over the edge to the dizzying drop below, exactly the way a panicked person would. Wobbling and shimmying. Pure cinematic vertigo. It made you feel as if you were right there in the shaft, hanging on to those greasy cables and breathing hard and clinging for your life. The editing was something special, too. This was where those long, lazy shots that drove the younger members of the audience crazy during the rest of the movie paid off. A single shot could last for half a minute, a minute, maybe more. The camera bobbed and swayed and tracked and never lost focus while Harper Stone and the soulless extortionist—Joseph Cotton, in a last-minute return to form after the years he'd wasted guesting on *The Rockford Files* and *Fantasy Island*—duked it out. Each endless shot was like a bad dream from which no escape was possible, and when it finally cut away things only got worse.

The whole crowd held its breath, although by now everybody on the planet knew that Harper Stone would come out smiling in the end. (Not smiling, really. The expression fixed on his face would be more in the line of a grimace. Still, whatever you called it, it was better than what was going to become of poor old Joseph Cotton.) The movie ended only a minute or two after Stone lost his grip and Cotton took his long and twisting fall, as if everybody involved in the making of it knew that it had nowhere to go from there but down. The critics said that Stone's career should have ended there, too, right there on that unforgettable high point. But who in the world ever took that kind of advice?

When the lights came up and the applause died down—that was the power of an old picture like this one, it could still draw an audience to its feet just on general principles—Druscilla Peru approached the microphone again. But instead of thanking everyone for coming, talking up next week's movie, and advising one and all to drive safely going home on these treacherous roads, she held up her index finger like a schoolmarm and said that she had a wonderful surprise for everyone. The crowd murmured, boots shifted on the hard floor, and without further ado she introduced an individual who had sat in the back all this time, admiring the movie from a certain very personal point of view and swelling with a little bit of unexpected pride when the crowd burst into applause at the end.

Manny Seville. She called him *Manfred*, the way his name read in the credits. Manfred R. Seville, technical director on the movie they'd just seen. Up from New York for a few days and generous enough to share his insights on the making of *Lights Out* with this roomful of poor unsophisticated country people. He rose to his feet amid a spontaneous roar of applause, and came to the podium beaming in spite of himself.

The first question came from an old-timer in khakis, a plaid shirt, and a fly-fishing vest, a self-professed film buff retired up here from New York, whose chief objective was to show off every single thing he knew or thought he knew about movies. He stood up, cleared his throat, and spoke in a high, wavering voice, starting with film grain and shutter speeds and low-light shooting, concluding eight or ten minutes later with his personal readings of the major films of Sergei Eisenstein. At no point along the way did he give any indication of what his question might have been, or even trouble himself to suggest that he actually might have one. Manny thanked him for his insights, calling him a shrewd observer of filmmaking technique, and the old man sat back down satisfied.

The next question was about Harper Stone. In fact, all of the remaining questions were about Harper Stone.

How well did Manny know him?

Very well indeed. They'd come up through the ranks side by side. They'd been kids together on the Warner's lot, for Christ's sake—if you could say "for Christ's sake" in a nice place like this.

What about the real Harper Stone? What was he like?

He was a cast-iron sonofabitch, if they'd pardon his French. Hah hah hah. No, really, he was a gentleman. A true gentleman of the old school. No kidding. An absolute sweetheart.

Did Manny have an inside scoop on his death?

No. They'd been up here in the mountains working on a commercial, but they hadn't had all that much to do with each other. Hadn't even seen each other off the set.

Where did Harper Stone get that tattoo on his forearm? The one you could see just for a second or two during the elevator scene?

Frankly, he didn't know. He didn't even remember that the guy had
had a tattoo, come to that. Maybe . . . oh, never mind.

Maybe what?

Maybe if the librarian hadn't made off with the reels they could
take another look at the film and he'd remember, but it was too late.
What did it look like?

A heart, an anchor, chains.

Not a kitty in a sailor hat? Hah hah hah. Not Woody Wood-
pecker with a cigar? Was she positive?

*No. It was a heart and an anchor, with chains wrapped around
them. And it was there on the screen for just a second. Just a flash.*

He scratched his head and said maybe it was makeup. Maybe
since Stone was such a stickler about getting into his characters,
he'd had somebody in the makeup department paint the thing on
his arm just for that one shot.

Stacey didn't think that sounded likely, but she thanked him
and let it go.

"Pretty sharp eye there, Stacey." Chip whacked the ice scraper
against his pantleg, tossed it behind the driver's seat, and slid back
inside the Wrangler.

"The thing is," she said as he slammed the door, "I've seen that
tattoo before." She rubbed the inside of the windshield with the
back of her glove, sending down a little shower of ice crystals. They
were going to have to sit in the car for a while and let it warm up
before it was safe to move, especially given the pitch darkness of the
roads between Woodstock and home. "And not just on Harper
Stone, either. I'm sure of it."

Chip blew on his window and rubbed at it with his forearm.
"Where?"

"On Mr. Wonderful, over at the Slippery Slope."

"Buddy."

"Yeah. Buddy."

"It's a small world, I guess," said Chip.

"I'll say." She sat shaking her head just a little.

"Then that's that."

"I don't know. I don't know if the world is really *that* small."

"Meaning what, exactly?" He goosed the accelerator a bit and the heater fan speeded up. Little patches of transparency were just beginning to melt through the fog at the bottom of the windshield.

"Meaning I think there's a connection between the two of them. And not just the drug deal, either. I think that if Harper Stone's history goes back with that Manny Seville, then it goes back even farther with Buddy Frommer."

"All the way back to what? To some tattoo parlor in Singapore? Some fraternity prank?"

"It's anybody's guess." She tried upping the knob on the fan but it was at the top already.

"I could see a hazing ritual, maybe. Although getting a tattoo seems like a big commitment."

She nodded a few times, sitting there under the streetlamp, the outside world growing less and less vague as the windows defogged. Finally she turned to Chip and said, "Does either of them seem like a real joiner to you?"

"That's hard to say. Were fraternities all that big back then, anyhow?"

"Huge. They were *huge*."

"That's a start."

"And how long ago exactly is *back then*? I'd think Buddy's maybe fifteen years younger than Stone."

"Brothers don't have to be in the fraternity at the same time."

"I don't know." She still had him fixed in her gaze. "Neither of them looks like the kind of person who'd want to prop up a weak ego by joining a fraternity. Do you think?"

"You've got a point." He goosed the engine again, keeping his foot down while the engine revved, and soon the windshield was nearly clear enough to drive. "Besides," he said, "what fraternity would have Buddy Frommer?"

THIRTY-FOUR

Come morning, Stacey got a late start. She hadn't even set her alarm. There wasn't any rush. No significant snow had fallen since the big blizzard, and although conditions on the mountain were pretty good they weren't great. On top of that it was the weekend, which meant that all of the flatlanders who'd put off coming when the snow was deep would be up now in droves.

Guy was pulling on his coat in the front hall when she came out into the kitchen. "Glad you're up," he said. "I thought you'd be interested to hear what the medical examiner had to say."

She pulled her hair back and looped it loosely over itself, then stood alongside the coffeemaker, waiting. "You bet I'm interested."

"Heart attack," he said.

"Heart attack," she repeated, a little crestfallen. "So it wasn't drugs."

Guy took his flat-brimmed hat down from its peg. "Nope, it wasn't drugs." He held the hat in his hand and permitted himself a little smile. "Not unless you count the cocaine that brought on the heart attack."

She jumped, grinning. "What'd I tell you, Guy?"

"I know, I know. Good call."

"So, are the troopers going to talk to Buddy Frommer? Are *you* going to talk to Buddy Frommer? Is *somebody* going to talk to Buddy Frommer? Huh?"

"Somebody is, no question about it."

"Good."

"Somebody's going to talk pretty seriously with him."

"Good."

"I don't want to tell tales out of school," he said, "but it turns out that people have had their eye on Buddy for a while now."

"I thought maybe."

"I'm thinking this Harper Stone deal might shake a few things loose."

"You think it might?"

"I think it *should*."

"Me, too."

"I think it will."

"I hope so."

He settled his hat on his head and put one hand on the door-knob. "Thing is, Buddy's still kind of incidental if you look at the whole picture. See: Let's say you're right, and Stone bought some coke from him."

"Of course I'm right. It's not like, 'Let's say maybe I'm right.' I *am* right."

"Fine. So Stone bought coke from him. Take that as a given. We've still got to explain how the guy ended up three-quarters of a mile away from that nice warm house he'd rented, out there on the undeveloped side of the mountain, in the middle of a blizzard."

"Right."

"Stoned to the gills."

"Roger. And in the middle of the night."

"Now, we don't know that. We don't know when it happened, exactly."

"Oh, right. Of course."

"He could have ended up out there any time during the day of the blizzard, or even the night before or the night after. As low as the temperatures have been, the medical examiner's office is keeping the timing pretty loose right now. Plus the snow over him was well enough drifted that it's no help at all. The poor guy's clothing was frozen solid, like he'd been wrapped in wet sheets and put in the freezer, on account of what was probably hyperthermia caused either by the effort of getting out there or by the cocaine or both. He had a workout before he went down, one way or another."

"Somebody asked me if he'd had snowshoes or whatever, but I couldn't remember."

"There's a pair missing from the house, but they haven't turned up." He turned a little and tightened his grip on the doorknob. "Did the state boys ever get your skis back to you?"

"No."

"I'll ask if you want me to. But don't hold your breath."

"That'd be good. I'd appreciate it."

"No problem."

While Guy was offering information, she thought she'd ask: "Other than the snowshoes, anything else in the house?"

"Nothing useful, except . . . well. You know."

"I know."

"It's pretty well trashed, but the guy was probably a slob. Overgrown frat boy."

"He had people to clean up after him."

"My thinking exactly." He turned the knob and cold air began to sneak in through the front door. Stacey put her arms around herself. "Of course the place is wall to wall fingerprints," he said, "but it's a rental. If the guy had visitors, so did lots of other people."

• • •

Stacey had a question for Buddy Frommer. It was a little personal, but then again Buddy seemed to take everything personally, so she figured there wasn't much difference between asking him where he got that tattoo and asking him to sell her a pair of mittens or whatever. It was all an intrusion into the wonderful private world of Buddy Frommer, and it was all a pain in his butt. She'd have to risk it and take the consequences.

First, though, she had to wait for the store to empty. When she pulled up the lot was half full of people who clearly didn't know any better, out-of-towners after a pair of glove liners or a gaitor, flatlanders who'd left their skis here last week for a tune and now wanted to get out on them pronto. One thing you had to give Buddy Frommer: By putting up this building on the main route in from Connecticut, he'd guaranteed himself a constant supply of fresh victims. She pictured him plotting the whole thing out, setting himself up like one of those anglerfish you saw on Animal Planet.

She pulled into a parking slot and kept the engine going rather than give the windows a chance to fog over. People came and went, entering the Slope prepped for a great day on the mountain and leaving with a hundred different varieties of disgust on their faces. She watched them come and go, and she switched back and forth between the only two radio stations you could get around here. It was always either Vermont Public Radio or the world's worst classic rock. Morning Edition or some hair band from the eighties. Garrison Keillor or Foghat.

It pained her to wait, but she kept her attention on all of the little kids bouncing in the cars and consoled herself that their parents had to get every one of them into Ski School, or at least into their snowsuits and helmets and rented equipment before any of them got out on the hill. That helped a little, and it made the wait a bit less aggravating. Finally, once the crowds thinned out, she switched off the engine and got out.

Inside the Slippery Slope, Buddy was ensconced behind the elevated counter as usual. He stood facing the door but he didn't seem to see her come in. A least he didn't seem to be in any hurry to register her presence. His head was tilted back and his reading glasses were down at the tip of his nose. He was studying a long loop of register tape that he ratcheted inch by inch through his fingers. Written upon his face was a rare smile.

It vanished when Stacey said hello.

In any other ski shop in the known universe, Stacey would have been greeted with a smile and a genuinely curious look and an inquiry as to how those new Heads were working out for her. A great number of the people who worked in ski shops were skiers themselves, and skiers wanted to know what was up with the latest gear. Part of it was the plain fact of being an avid and helpless aficionado—the kind of person who simply had to file away every bit of sport-related info he could—and part of it was just job-related research. One person could only demo so many different kinds of equipment every season, and you were always limited—in terms of physique and gender and ability level—to a certain cross-section of available stuff. So a big meaty guy like Buddy Frommer wouldn't know anything firsthand about the performance of a pair of skis that suited a small woman like Stacey Curtis. He'd have only three ways of knowing: the ski magazines, which you couldn't trust; the manufacturer's reps, whom you couldn't trust either; and customer experience, which was untrustworthy, too, given how unsophisticated most customers were, and the way that 90 percent of them overestimated their ability anyhow. Yet an alert and engaged ski shop employee would have known Stacey for one of the good ones. A person who skied a ton and knew what she wanted in the way of performance.

Buddy, on the other hand, could not have cared less. He didn't even remember that she'd bought skis from him a week or so back, except in a kind of general way. The way a person could still recall a painful rash he'd had last summer.

Stacey forged ahead anyhow, just as if he'd asked. "Those Heads I got last week?" she said. "I never got out on them much, but it was fun while it lasted."

"That's nice." He didn't even look away from the register tape.

"It wasn't like the snow was exactly perfect for them anyhow," she sighed, "once all that fresh powder got groomed down."

"I wouldn't know."

"Sure you would. They're too fat."

"Whatever."

She pulled her wallet out of her jacket pocket and thumped it down on the counter, the change purse on the face of it jingling, with a vague hope that the sound of money might get his attention. It didn't. So she tried something different. "Anyway," she said, "now that the state police impounded the skis as evidence in the Harper Stone case, I don't guess I'll ever get them back."

She was expecting at least a *"What?"* Or maybe an adjustment of the reading glasses on his nose. At the bare minimum a reflexive impulse to set aside the paper tape for half a second, but Buddy was Buddy, and he didn't give an inch.

"Not like they thought they're a murder weapon or anything."

Nothing from Buddy.

"But they *were* kind of instrumental in finding his body. Rolling right over him like that."

Buddy put down the tape at last. "You got problems with your skis, you've come to the wrong place. I don't do refunds and I don't do replacements. Take it up with your homeowner's insurance."

"No, no," said Stacey. "I don't want a refund."

"Then you want to buy something, or what? I'm kind of busy."

"Yeah," she said, reaching into the basket alongside the register. "A ChapStick, is all."

He growled.

"Maybe a couple." She grabbed two and put them down on the counter. "Here."

Buddy reached over to pick up one of them, and his sleeve rode up on his arm just enough that Stacey could point to the heart and anchor.

"Where'd you get that?" she said.

"No place around here."

"I'll bet. But really, where'd you get it?"

"That kind of information," he said as the register beeped once, "would cost a whole lot more than a couple of damn ChapSticks."

"Hey, those Heads you sold me weren't cheap. And I only had the use of them for a day."

"That's no fault of mine." He passed the bar code under the scanner a second time and the register beeped again.

"Come on," she said. "My dad has a tattoo just like that one." She was surprised how easily the lie had popped out. It had taken no effort at all.

"Ask *him*, then, why don't you?"

"I did," she said. "He told me Singapore." She was thinking of what Chip had said, when they were sitting in the car in Woodstock after the movie. Who ever thought of Singapore?

"Wrong," said Buddy, slapping the ChapStick down onto the counter. "It wasn't Singapore. It was Copenhagen."

"Copenhagen? Really?"

"Really." He showed her his empty palm. "That's four and a quarter. You don't need a bag, do you?"

"No. No, thanks." She dug in her wallet. While she had him engaged, she went for it. "Did your friend get his there, too?"

"What friend?"

"You know." She slid change onto the counter little by little, keeping him interested. "Stone."

"Stone who?"

"Harper Stone."

"Never met him. All I can think of is maybe he was in the Merchant Marine, too." Buddy scooped up the change and slid it into the drawer. "Anything else you need, or can I get back to work?" He slammed the cash drawer shut with his belly, and that was clearly the end of that.

THIRTY-FIVE

She didn't even go to the mountain. She went to the township building instead, where Mildred Furlong held sway over access to the sheriff's office. There was a line, half a dozen people sitting in plastic chairs out along a partition in the assembly hall, but all of them weren't there to see Guy. That didn't make any difference to Mildred, though. She could only concentrate on one thing at a time. She was adamant about that. A couple of the people wanted to file complaints about a recent property assessment, somebody else was hoping to get information about flu shots, and the rest needed to have some kind of paperwork notarized. The property complaint people looked furious, their faces set in stone. The woman about the flu shots looked confused—as well she might have been, given that flu season was already at least half over—and she kept nervously tap-tap-tapping a yellow pamphlet on her leg. The people who'd come about getting something notarized just looked fed up. Mildred, however, was in her glory, especially with the notary business. It was her favorite part of the job—particularly using the embosser to make that all-important official imprint— and the joy of it was written large on her face.

"Excuse me," said Stacey, approaching the desk.

Mildred put down the papers she was working on, took the glasses from her nose, and dropped them to let them dangle from the chain around her neck. Slowly, she looked up at Stacey. "You'll have to wait your turn, my dear." She said it so politely and patiently that anyone would have thought she had a good reason.

"I'm just here to see the sheriff."

"Unless it's an emergency, dear, you're just going to have to wait your turn like everyone else." Mildred slowly picked up her dangling glasses and positioned them carefully on her nose again. Through them she could focus only on the paperwork that lay on the desk, not on Stacey. She was very clear about that. "As you can see," she said, "I'm quite occupied."

"But . . ." Through the records room behind Mildred's desk and out the other side, Stacey could see a brightly lit hallway and about three-quarters of a door with an engraved plaque that read SHERIFF GUY RAMSEY. Judging by the angle she was pretty sure that the door was open a few inches, which meant he probably was in there alone—or at least not up to something top secret. Was Guy ever up to something top secret? Maybe. Probably. Not now, she didn't think. "But," she said, "I . . ."

"If I make a mistake on these documents," Mildred said, "they'll take away my commission. And then where would the township be, hmm? We'd be without a notary, that's where." She reached into her drawer, drew out the embossing stamp, and lined it up over the corner of the paper she was working on.

Before she could get it squared to her liking, Guy Ramsey's door creaked open the rest of the way and he emerged, coffee cup in hand, heading for the kitchen. Stacey didn't know what to call him here at his place of business—Guy or Sheriff or what—so she just said, "Hey!" That was enough. He turned his head at the sound of her voice, smiled, and raised his coffee mug, then motioned to her to come on back.

"That's the records room," said Mildred, hammering the embosser with her fist as Stacey slid past the desk. "Don't touch anything."

"You didn't tell me that Buddy Frommer was in the Merchant Marine," she said when she sat down across from his desk with a mug of her own.

"Jeez," Guy said, looking amazed. "He *was*, come to think of it."

"So he says."

"I'd forgotten. I was thinking he'd gone straight to college. My brother went off to UVM and I had this picture of Buddy going at the same time. I was little, remember."

"So why would the rich kid go into the Merchant Marine, instead of heading straight to school?"

"I'm thinking it had something to do with his father." He sipped his coffee and squinted at the wall behind Stacey, remembering. "He was a tough one. A veteran of World War II, like the rest of our dads, even though he was a good bit older. Maybe he was one of those guys who never got over being in the army. It could be that he thought some kind of service would do Buddy good."

"He thought it would build character."

"Right," said Guy, laughing. "Although I've never imagined I'd hear the words 'Buddy Frommer' and 'building character' in the same sentence."

"Anything's possible."

"Not really. But you can't blame the old man for trying."

"Old," said Stacey, "might be the word for it. You said Buddy's father was older than the rest of your dads."

"Right. Yeah."

"Old enough to make Buddy as old as Harper Stone?"

Guy nearly spat out a mouthful of coffee. "Come on, Stacey," he said. "I know you're young, but jeez, give me a break. Stone must be my own dad's age, or thereabouts."

Stacey nodded.

"I mean, other than being dead and everything."

"Right," she said. "Other than that."

"It's enough that you've got Buddy selling dope to Stone. They don't have to be . . . I don't know, they don't have to be, like, college roommates or something."

"Not now, I guess they don't. Not if they're that many years apart."

Guy shook his head, still a little blindsided. "Wow. You must think I'm about a hundred."

"No." Stacey sat and chewed at her lip for a second and looked at nothing. "I *thought* there was too big a gap. That's why I was asking."

He leaned forward just a little. "Too big a gap for what?"

"For—" She shook her head. "I don't know. It's probably stupid."

"Nothing's stupid," Guy said. "Well, I take that back. Lots of things are stupid. Nonetheless . . ."

Stacey put both hands around her coffee cup and squared it on the desk in front of her. She looked like she was testifying. "They both have the same tattoo. I saw it first on Stone, down in the basement; then later on I saw it on Buddy. Twice. They looked exactly the same. Same age and everything. Pretty well faded. Kind of smeary."

"Hmm," said Guy. "That would be interesting, if it weren't just a coincidence."

"Pretty big coincidence."

"What'd it look like, anyhow? I mean, what was it a picture of?"

"A heart and an anchor. With chains around it."

"That's a pretty ordinary design, don't you think? Pretty common?"

"Sure, but—"

"And anyhow, those guys are fifteen years apart. No way they could have gotten tattooed at the same time."

"I know."

"Probably Stone was in the Merchant Marine, too. I mean, that's possible. And they got the same tattoo fifteen years apart. We could Google him and find out."

"Or you could ask his old friend, Manny What's-His-Name."

Guy leaned back and folded his hands behind his head. "I could," he said, brightening. "I will."

"Do it."

"So how come you're thinking like law enforcement now?" he asked. "One murder solved and you've got a new career?"

She picked up her coffee and drained what was left of it. "The better question is how come you're thinking like a high school kid, with your Google and everything."

THIRTY-SIX

Chip was in the Patrol shack near the base lodge when Stacey finally made it to the mountain. She stuck her head in the door just to see, her boot bag still slung over her shoulders, and there he was, shivering a little and stirring the fire with a poker. "You just come in?" she said, getting his attention.

"Yeah, yeah. Just now." He left off with the fire, leaned the poker up against the bricks, and sat down on a bench. "Twenty minutes till I've got to be back out there. I've got a PB and J in my locker. What're you doing for lunch?"

It was early, even earlier than usual, but it was either eat now with him or eat later without him. No choice, really. "The usual," she said, stepping inside and pulling the door tight behind her. On a shelf above Chip's head there was a battered old copper teapot on a hotplate, switched on since sometime back in the sixties and usually boiled dry. She put some fresh water into it and dug in her backpack for energy bars and a tea bag. Chip leaned over and stretched out his arm to grab a couple of foam cups from a stack on the table.

"I hate using those."

"I know, but consider the alternative." He nodded toward a jumble of filthy mugs in the sink. "No amount of scrubbing is going to decontaminate one of them."

"I guess," said Stacey. She looked at the teapot and decided that the old saying about a watched pot was probably right. "So," she said after a minute, "you never told me how Rail Jam Night went. You going back this weekend?"

"No way."

She lifted her eyebrows.

"It's just not worth it. Somebody's going to get killed there one of these days, and I don't want it on my head."

"Smart man."

"Plus . . . I don't know. It's just that the whole thing's so completely annoying and juvenile. I guess there was a time I would have thought it was pretty cool—you know, the beer and the tricks and everything—but that time's long gone."

She just nodded slowly, listening and waiting for the water to boil.

"I thought it would be an easy fifty bucks, but I was wrong. It'd take a lot more than fifty bucks to make me want to spend another evening around that crowd."

"Really obnoxious, eh?"

"Like the worst of the dopey college kids I have to holler at from the lift, the ones that make me embarrassed that I'm only a few years older than they are. Like them, plus beer." He went on to describe Anthony-without-an-H from Long Island, the unruly king of them all, who'd gotten himself lost out of bounds and was welcomed back like some kind of hero on account of it. About how Anthony was lucky he hadn't killed himself. About how much trouble it would have been had the Patrol learned of Anthony's Adventure and been called on to go rescue him from the clutches of his own bad judgment. "And you know what would have happened if we'd spent the whole day risking our necks for him? It wouldn't have cost

him a dime and he'd have been ungracious about it, and at the end
of the day he would still have shown up at Doc's Rail Jam like
Rocky Balboa or something."

The teakettle shrieked and Chip jumped.

"So how did he find his way home?" Stacey asked as he poured
hot water into the two foam cups.

"Remember that guy at the cabin on the backside?"

"I do. He showed up there? Anthony-without-an-H?"

"Funny," said Chip. "I remember that guy bellyaching about
how lost skiers were knocking on his door all the time, but I don't
think I ever heard about one until now."

"I guess you wouldn't, necessarily."

"I guess not. That Anthony sure got lucky, though. I mean he
got lucky that the guy was even home in the afternoon. He said he
drove him back to town on a snowmobile."

"Why not take the truck?"

"I don't know. What of it?"

"Maybe the truck wasn't there," Stacey said. "It being the afternoon and all."

Chip ran his hand through his hair. "I don't get it. If he was
home, the truck was there."

"What if he wasn't?"

"But he was, simple as that. Anthony said the TV was on loud
and this old guy came to the door and they rode down the mountain on a snowmobile."

"He called him an *old guy*."

"Yeah. Why not?"

"Not a *tall guy*."

"No."

"How big was Anthony from Long Island?"

"Not big. Not very." He put down his cup and stood up and lifted
his hand to about eye level. "About like that."

"Never mind," said Stacey, and she paused to tear open an energy bar with her teeth. "It's probably nothing."

"Probably. You know how it is. To a kid like that, everybody's an old guy. Even me."

They sat for a while, sipping their tea. Chip's sandwich was squashed flat and looked horrible, with the jelly soaking through on one side and smearing on the wax paper. By comparison, Stacey's energy bar was Thanksgiving dinner. She offered to trade halves but he said no. He just kept looking at the clock on the wall, watching his break time run out.

"Hey," he said after a while, his voice sticky with peanut butter. "Did I tell you Amazon's got *Lights Out* now? I got a copy for my dad."

"Things are looking up for Harper Stone, don't you think?"

"You know it. Dying was one smart career move. It's this really cool commemorative version and all. Remastered, I guess you'd call it."

"Do they remaster movies, or is that just records?"

"I don't know." He crumpled the wax paper and threw it into the fire. "Nice packaging, too. A little souvenir booklet and everything. All embossed and all."

"And you've got it? I mean you've got it at home?"

"Oh, yeah. It came yesterday. His birthday's not until March." He rose slowly to his feet and stretched, making the most of his last minute or two in front of the fire.

"Then how about we watch it tonight?" she asked. "I'm off."

"You mean like a date?"

"Sure," Stacey said. "Like a date. I'll even bring a bottle of wine."

"You sure you want to see it again? I mean, we just saw it."

"No. I want to see it again."

"I could get us something else at the VideoDrome. You like Monty Python?"

"No, thanks. Really, I'd like to see *Lights Out* one more time."

"How about Mexican food?" he asked. "You like Mexican food?" He was nervous all of a sudden, and she thought that that was kind of nice. "If you do, I could stop at Cinco de Taco and pick us up something."

She said that would be good, that she liked Mexican just fine, and that she'd be over around seven or seven thirty.

She didn't really have the night off, which made that the second lie that had spilled effortlessly out of her in the last twelve hours. Now she was looking at a third. She needed to call the Binding and tell Jack or Pete or whoever answered the phone that she wasn't feeling all that great and couldn't make it in. So she sat in her car at the one light in town, turning her cell phone on while she still had service. This lie was going to be a million times harder than the others, probably because she was thinking about it. She dialed and the phone began to ring at the other end, and she wondered if she should cough or sniff audibly or something, but she decided against it. A stomach bug would be better. Just a twenty-four-hour thing that would be done tomorrow, no questions asked.

"Think it was something you ate?" Jack said when she got him. "If it was the buffalo wings, you wouldn't be the first."

"I wouldn't say that," she said.

"I would. I've been around a lot longer than you. I've seen those wings take a lot of good men down."

"Well, either way, I'm sure I'll be in tomorrow night."

Jack wasn't giving up. "Maybe you ought to start taking better care of yourself. You know you can get anything you want off the menu, half price. Go with the broiled fish. Squeeze a little lemon on it. That's nice and light. Easy on the digestion."

Stacey swallowed. "Please, can we talk about this some other time?"

"Right. Sure. Sorry."

"That's OK."

"I wasn't thinking."

"That's fine."

"I mean I was only thinking of you."

"Thanks, Jack," she said. "But hey, I've got to go." She tried her best to make herself sound desperate, but she wasn't sure she did.

She was on the porch at Chip's place, one finger on the doorbell by a strip of adhesive tape with his apartment number scrawled onto it, when his Wrangler came careening into the driveway. The gravel was ankle-deep in slush and his wheels spun in it, sending up a shower of spray that doused the snowdrifts. By the gleam of the streetlamp it looked kind of pretty, although once daylight came it would be nothing but a speckling of grit and frozen mud. Things had a way of changing, the more closely you looked at them.

Which is exactly what Stacey had in mind relative to *Lights Out*.

She put down the wine bottle and left the porch and met Chip at the car. He had the back of it stuffed—*stuffed*—with Mexican food. Sack after sack of it, arranged in cardboard trays. Tonight must have been Cinco de Taco's biggest night in a month. The spectacle of it was overwhelming and a bit ridiculous, but Stacey had to admit that the aroma rising from the open back of the Wrangler was beyond fantastic. Her mouth began to water. "Are we expecting Pancho Villa's army, or what?" she said as she picked up the nearest tray, and Chip laughed. "Because there's not going to be enough once I get through."

"I didn't know what you liked best," Chip said, "so I got a little of everything."

"You call this *a little?*"

Ten minutes later they had all of it in the apartment, spread out over the kitchen table, the countertops, the coffee table, and anything else that was more or less horizontal. Stacey thought the apartment was pretty nice. There was nothing of the dorm room or bachelor pad about it whatsoever, which meant either that Chip had cleaned up on her behalf or that he was by nature pretty neat. She figured the latter. She thanked God that the place was clean, since there was now Mexican food arrayed on almost every surface. Chip got some plates and opened the wine, then took a roll of paper towels off the hanger on the wall to use by way of napkins, and they made their first pass through the food.

"When this cools off," he said, motioning with a tilt of his head, "we've got the microwave."

Stacey laughed. "Who's going to give it a chance to cool off?"

They cleared a space on the coffee table and set their plates and glasses down. Chip had the movie in the player already. Stacey scooped up salsa on chips with one hand and located the DVD packaging with the other. "Fancy," she said, putting the accent on the second syllable, talking through a mouthful of crunchy goodness.

"And not cheap, either."

"Hey, it's for your dad. He's a fan, right?"

"He is. But somebody's making a killing on this stuff. And Stone didn't even leave any next of kin, did he?"

"That's right. Or so they say."

"Too bad. To see all this go to the government or whatever." He bit into a chimichanga, making a reflexive kind of happy carnivore sound somewhere deep in his throat. "Then again," he said, "I guess he's not seeing much of anything anymore."

"True," she said. "Maybe he had a foundation set up or something. Something charitable."

Chip wasn't buying. "Did he look like a charitable type to you?"

"You never know." But she knew that you do know. You always know. And what she knew was that Harper Stone was anything but Mother Theresa.

THIRTY-SEVEN

f either Stacey or Chip had had the idea that something might happen between the two of them that night—if either of them had thought that this "date" might amount to the beginning of something, or the turning of some page or other—Harper Stone and a Jeep Wrangler full of Mexican food had different ideas. By halfway through the movie, around the part where Stone's character gets whacked over the head and dragged unconscious into a mental hospital only to wake up under the care of a suspiciously Teutonic doctor with a little black mustache, a white lab coat, a pocket full of scalpels, and a syringe full of God knows what, they had crawled off to different ends of the couch and lay there groaning. Every now and then their stocking feet touched, but that was the extent of the romance. Around them lay the wreckage of the Mexican food, bags and trays and plastic containers and a pile of those little waxed cardboard boxes that usually hold either chow mein or live goldfish, half emptied and shoved inside one another like Russian dolls. The wine bottle was empty and Chip kept promising to go to the kitchen and find another one, but he couldn't exactly move. That was all right with Stacey. She was half asleep already, struggling to keep her eyes open, and they had another hour or so of the movie to get through.

She drew her knees up, shifted her weight, and put her feet down flat on the floor, hauling herself up straight with a great effort. Chip looked at her over his toes and groaned. "If I don't sit up," she said, "I'll never make it through."

"How about I go put up some coffee?"

"Go ahead," she said, knowing that he'd never manage it.

The hall light was on, and in the kitchen there was another little lamp glowing beside the microwave, but otherwise the apartment was dark. Chip's television was old and small, and in the dim light of the screen she had trouble finding the remote for the DVD player. There wasn't a whole lot of light in *Lights Out*. Still, when Harper Stone/Harry Smith fought his way out of the sinister hospital and the scene shifted to an external shot, that big hospital towering white and the sky a vivid California blue that glowed even on that dinky little screen, she located the remote under a pile of greasy napkins. She leaned back and groaned and pointed it at the screen. "You mind if I skip ahead?"

"Be my guest."

She zipped forward to the elevator scene: Harper Stone and Joseph Cotton going head-to-head and fist-to-fist in a space that seemed both claustrophobic and infinite.

"Does this thing have some kind of zoom on it?"

"I don't know."

She pressed the pause key and held the remote aloft, tilting it away from the television to catch what light there was, turning her head away from the screen, and squinting at it until she thought she had it figured out.

Chip lifted his head. "I could turn on a light," he said, but she knew she had about as much chance of his doing that as she had of his making a pot of coffee, which was still roughly zero.

"That's OK. I've got it."

"Good." He let his head fall back to the pillow with a thump.

On the screen, Stone and Cotton were locked in struggle. The camera veered and swiveled and swooped. Stacey leaned forward, one hand holding her stomach and the other aiming the remote. Bars of light and dark swept across the screen as Cotton's character lost his footing—and the camera, keeping pace with his movement, plummeted alongside him for what felt like an eternity but couldn't have been more than two seconds. Stacey clutched her stomach tighter and paused the DVD and waited, breathing slowly, until she got her equilibrium back. She looked over at Chip and saw that his eyes were shut. Lucky boy.

She checked the remote again, found the correct button, and zoomed the picture in a notch, panned it side to side. So far so good. She pulled back out and pressed PLAY.

The camera righted itself and looked up from Cotton's perspective to find Stone's face peering over the black edge of the elevator roof. His eyes lit up with panic and potential. Then he thrust a hand over the edge to help the bad guy. The hand was blackened in streaks, greasy, and it thrust over the edge and down the side like some kind of purposeful snake. Even as she watched, Stacey realized that the geometry of the scene didn't quite make sense, that there surely wasn't enough room between the side of the cab and the wall of the shaft to let a person of Joseph Cotton's size—a person of any size, come to that—slide down between them. Yet there it was, and in the heat of the moment it was convincing. It had been convincing audiences for years and years, no questions asked.

The camera—another camera, she realized, or probably an entirely different setup taken later or earlier or God knew when—shifted to an alternate perspective where it caught the fingertips of one of Cotton's hands gripping a metal bar on the side of the cab. Gasping overwhelmed the sound track. Another set of fingertips came into view from below and they gripped the metal bar, too. Cotton exhaled (somebody exhaled, anyhow; she realized that the audio didn't necessarily originate with the shot), and then the shoulder of Cotton's gray pin-striped suit blocked the angle as he lifted himself up.

The shot switched again, this time to a position from somewhere above Stone's spot on top of the cab, the back of his head to the camera. He was flattened on the greasy panel, his sportcoat split up the back and torn mostly free, his left hand seeking purchase on a rigid cable, his right arm reaching down for Cotton, whose own hand shot up to take it.

Freeze.

There it was, on the back of the rescuing arm.

The tattoo.

Stacey zoomed in to make sure that it wasn't just a grease smear, and it most definitely was anything but. The details of it were a little vague in the dim light of the elevator shaft, but it was definitely the tattoo she'd been expecting. A heart and an anchor and chains.

The tattoo that Manny Seville didn't remember Stone ever having.

The tattoo that she'd seen with her own eyes, both on Buddy Frommer and on somebody who looked an awful lot like Harper Stone.

"There it is," she said, whacking Chip's stocking foot with the remote.

He roused up, but only a little. "You've got a good eye."

"I told you."

"But what do you make of it?"

She didn't answer. She just pressed the play button and let the movie continue. The shot changed again—who thought there'd be so many? Watching it this way was an education—taking Cotton's perspective once more and watching while Stone inched over the edge of the cab to extend his reach. That face. That movie-star face. It was exactly as she remembered seeing it in the basement of the Slippery Slope. Then Stone's hand came down, the camera moved in, and she saw his face and his forearm in one shot and knew what was wrong. She knew what it was that had been bothering her from the beginning.

Click. She froze the shot.

Click. She zoomed in.

Whack. She gave Chip's foot a slap. "See that?" she said.

"See what? I don't see anything."

"Exactly," she said.

"So?"

"So a stuntman would be younger than the guy he doubles for, don't you think?"

"Maybe. What stuntman?"

"Never mind that," said Stacey. "Let's go for a drive."

THIRTY-EIGHT

They took the Subaru. Her skis were still in the back and she'd need them for what she had in mind. She'd need boots, too, but hers were home drying out in a corner of Megan Ramsey's kitchen. That fact alone was a huge improvement from the old days when she'd lived out of the car behind the pizza joint next to Bud's Suds, and Stacey appreciated it every day. If she'd had to put her finger on it, the act of sleeping curled around her ski boots in order to keep them from turning into complete icicles by morning was probably the worst part of the hard-core ski bum lifestyle. That and how that awful Danny Bowman had tormented her night after night, scraping little lines in her frozen windows with a stick or a bottle or God knew what, making her think that she was being hunted by the Claw or something. Even now that she knew it had been just Danny, she still shivered to think about it.

Anyhow, there was no way they were going back to the Ramseys' to pick up her boots now. She'd need a pair if she was going to pull off the lost skier act, though, but it occurred to her that there was no reason they needed to fit. They didn't even have to fit her skis. So they grabbed Chip's from the hall and tossed them in the back of the Subie.

"You cold?" said Chip from the passenger seat as Stacey backed out of the driveway. "I am."

"Me, too." She turned up the heat and jacked the fan up all the way even though the engine was cold, as if just getting a little more air moving might help things.

Chip bent forward, groaning again over his bellyful of Mexican, and poked at a dial on the console. "You lucky dog," he said. "I only wish *my* car had heated seats."

Stacey didn't even look over. "Don't get your hopes up."

When the dial spun and the light behind it didn't come on, Chip slumped back in the seat and shivered. "So where're we going, anyhow?" he said from somewhere down inside his coat.

"The cabin. The one with the tall guy?"

"How come?"

"Because I'm a lost skier, and I'm going to be knocking at his door."

"Oh. That explains everything." The words emerged from his coat on a pale cloud.

"It'll be a start."

They drove through the silent town, past the dark barracks of the library with its one searing arc light out front, through the single blinking traffic light, past the last few stragglers leaving Vinnie's Steak-Out and Maison Maurice and firing up their engines and setting off for home. They passed the access road to the ski mountain and kept on going until they left the town limits behind and entered the truly dark Vermont night. Not a star in the sky and no visible moonlight through the low clouds, this was the hour when the Green Mountains turned solid black. The turnoff to the lane up the backside of the mountain nearly slipped past in the shadows, but Stacey caught sight of it just in time and swung the Subaru off the open road into even greater darkness.

That's when she switched off the lights.

"Are you crazy?" Chip asked.

"I'll go slow. If I'm going to knock on their door like a lost skier, I can't show up with the headlights on."

"And what do you hope to gain by this, anyhow?" Chip pressed his face to the glass and watched the drifts creep by. "The state troopers have already talked with the guy. The sheriff has already talked with him. Heck, *we've* talked to him a little."

"Correction: *You've* talked to him a little. I don't think he'll recognize me."

"So what?"

"So I think he's been keeping a big secret up there. And I don't think he can keep it forever."

"How big a secret?"

"About six feet."

"Whoa." Chip sat up straighter. "You think whoever got Stone is up there with him?"

"Sort of. Remember what that little Anthony said about an old guy?"

Chip's window was beginning to fog so he rolled it down. The cold night air blew in on them as he asked, "So how come you think you can get at this big secret, when Guy and the state troopers couldn't?"

"That's easy," she said. "I'm a girl."

All the lights were on in Frank Schmidt's cabin. Between the windmill and the solar panels and an emergency generator back by the storage shed, he was apparently self-sufficient beyond all reason. Chip saw the glow in the cabin windows first, since Stacey was too busy concentrating on the twists and turns of the road ahead. They came around a curve and he looked right to watch something sweep past the window—a branch or an owl—and there it was, that yellow gleaming in the black distance, flickering through the dense forest.

"Land ho," he said, pointing, and Stacey pumped the brakes. The car came to a stop right in the middle of the lane, and she tapped the gas again to slide it over to the right side, hard up against the drifts. "Hey," said Chip, "How'm I supposed to get out?"

"My side," she said, yanking the key and tugging at the door handle. She gasped when the dome light came on, fearing that its dim glow might give their presence away, but Chip reached up fast and switched it off. She climbed out and he followed, complaining his way over the gearshift. She already had the rear liftgate open by the time he got one foot down on the snow, and she whispered fiercely to him that he should go easy closing the car door. He did.

Stacey had her helmet on and her skis leaning up against the car when he caught up with her. She sat on the tailgate and swapped her snow boots for his ski boots and buckled them as tight as they'd go. Close enough. They'd do. She stood up and had him shut the hatch lid, *easy does it*. Then she dug in her pocket for her cell phone, switched it on, and handed it over before it was even done starting up. It sang its little startup song and she snatched it back and set it to vibrate, then handed it to Chip again. "Wait ten minutes," she said, "and then call Guy. His number's in there."

He flipped it open. "No signal."

"Walk down till you get one. *Ten minutes*."

"This doesn't seem like a good idea."

She hoisted the skis over her shoulder and fixed him with a hard look. "Go."

Chip started uphill but she grabbed him by the shoulder and said no, she was going that way and kind of needed to be alone, and he turned around and started back down, his face lit just the slightest by the phone's screen. She hissed at him to keep that little bit of light pointed downhill and he did.

She hurried up the hill and was winded when she reached the cabin, which was fine. The whole idea was that she'd been slogging through the woods half the night. She tromped trough some loose snow to get plenty of the white stuff on Chip's boots, just in case anybody looked down and chanced to see how oversized they were. As if anybody would notice. As if anybody would care. She didn't have proper pants on, but the kind of person who'd get lost on the backside of Spruce Peak might wear anything. So be it.

The cabin made its own bright spot in the woods, its windows glowing yellow and lighting the underside of the trees and painting the snowdrifts like some kind of supernatural thing. She squinted as she looked at it from the cover of a snowdrift. Then she adjusted the skis on her shoulder, walked on past the cabin, and ducked into the drifts separating it from the shed behind. The snow was cold on her legs and she pushed through it and out the other side, onto a shoveled path between the cabin and the shed. She stamped her feet a little to shake the snow from her jeans without making any appreciable noise. There was light back here, too, but not as much as in front. The only windows were a small dark one that she took for a bathroom, a single broad pane with curtains behind it that was probably the kitchen, and a pair side by side that must have been the bedroom. She crouched down and moved closer to the house. In the bedroom a television was going, and there was a dim lamp switched on at the head of the bed. The television was showing the Food Network, a bunch of people baking cakes that looked like Muppets or something. The tall man was sitting on the bed with his back to her, beneath the light of the lamp, bent over, taking off his shoes. The bedroom door was shut.

She backed away and moved toward the kitchen, which was lit only by a single bulb over the sink. The walls danced with other light, though, light and color and movement reflected from what was apparently a bigger television in the front room. She tried to see it through the door but the angle was wrong. She kept low and moved around the backside of the cabin to another set of windows, these shielded by a couple of big arbor vitae that spilled snow all over her, and tried again. Just as she imagined. A movie was showing on the big TV. Some outer space thing. Any money said it was *Mission to Antares*.

There was a silver head watching the space movie. All she could see was the very top of it above the back of the recliner. She told herself it still could be the woman, the farm wife she'd imagined silhouetted in the front window when she and Chip had been up here on the night they'd found Harper Stone's body. While her face was still flecked with snow from the arbor vitae, Stacey plunged through the drifts to the front of the cabin and stepped up onto the porch to find out for herself. Once and for all.

THIRTY-NINE

She had been greeted more warmly at other times in her life, that was for sure.

Her innocent knock at the cabin door produced a torrent of profanity and recrimination and bile from one of the two individuals inside, some of it directed at whoever dared to knock at this time of night and the remainder directed at the other individual, who was apparently refusing to *answer the goddamned door for a change why don't you and tell 'em to get lost.*

A second voice arose, this one belonging no more to the farm wife than the first one did. This one was lower than the first, more measured, verging on musical. *Mellifluous* is the word Stacey would have used, if she hadn't been standing all by herself in the middle of a snowy woods with Chip gone gone gone, wondering if her idea as to who was behind the door was correct, asking herself if ten minutes had passed and Sheriff Guy Ramsey might be on his way by now, provided Chip had found cell service at all.

Mellifluous, that was it.

Like the highly trained speaking voice of an old-time movie actor.

Like the familiar and well-known voice of Harper Stone, whose face appeared now in the opened door. She was sure of it. When something behind his eyes responded reflexively to the sight of Stacey's face—as if he'd seen her before and recognized her, as if he desired nothing more, right then, than to engage with her in long and intimate conversation, and above all as if he had been deprived of all proper feminine companionship for a week or more—she knew it all the more completely.

"By golly," she said to him, falling somehow into a vernacular that an old-timer like him could understand, "you must be Harper Stone's double!"

Delight burst across the old man's craggy face, and he invited her in.

FORTY

I am, you see," is what he said. "I *am* Harper Stone's double."

"What're the odds of that?" said Stacey, hugging herself, stepping inside, hoping that Chip had found some cell service.

The old silver-haired man went on. "I worked for that troublemaker ever since *The Ne'er-Do-Wells*. That scene where I charged the foxhole? Where *he* charged the foxhole?"

Stacey was clueless but she nodded vaguely, shivering.

"Jeez," he said, "everybody remembers that scene. But it wasn't Stone. It was me. Yours truly. From that moment on."

"Honest?"

"Honest. Old Harper Stone was a sissy. A pretty boy, always afraid of messing his hair. I did all the heavy lifting." He pushed back his sleeve and made a muscle. At his age it wasn't pretty, but it actually wasn't terrible, either. For Stacey, though, the main thing wasn't what it revealed about his fitness, but what it revealed about his utter lack of any kind of heart-and-anchor tattoo. The man standing before her had the face—and the forearm—she'd just frozen in time on Chip's television. It was Harper Stone in the flesh.

As for who the body in the Rutland hospital morgue belonged to, she thought she knew how to find out.

"So what's your name, anyhow?" she asked.

He stuck out his hand. "Enzo DiNapoli, at your service."

Chip was almost back to the highway before he got a signal. How much time had passed, he couldn't say. At least ten minutes, right? More like fifteen. Maybe more. However long it had been, as soon as the bars lit up he called Guy's number.

"Stacey?" It was Megan's voice on the other end, sounding sleepy.

"Uh, no. Sorry. It's Chip. Chip Walsh? I'm using her phone."

"Ah." There was a little bit of suspicion in her voice, though, and a little worry. "So what's up? Is Stacey all right?"

"Oh, she's fine," said Chip, not entirely sure that he meant it. "But can I talk with Guy? Please? It's kind of—" Before he could get it out, Megan had handed over the phone.

There were some glasses and a bottle of brandy on the table against the wall—not a table, really, but an industrial spool that served as one—and Harper Stone was fixing to pour a couple of drinks when the tall guy threw open the bedroom door and came charging out. He slid on his stocking feet, zipping up his trousers as he came, giving Stacey a look that would have killed somebody less determined. He paused, checked his fly, and then gave Stone a look that was at least twice as lethal. Although he gave the impression of not knowing which of them to assail first, in the end he settled on Stacey.

"What is it with you people?" he said. "This ain't a ranger station. It ain't some goddamn rescue mission. I'm trying to live a peaceful life, and every time the snow falls around here my front porch turns into Grand Central." He cocked an eye at her that made Stacey think he might actually have recognized her from the night they'd skied the power-line right-of-way, but she shook it off.

"Sorry," she said, half pleading and half apologizing. "If there'd been any other place to go, I'd have—"

The truth, however, was that he'd lost interest in Stacey already. "And *you*," he said, turning his attention to Harper Stone. "I thought you wanted a little peace and quiet, too. You don't get peace and quiet by playing St. Bernard the minute somebody knocks on the door."

Stone kept at his work, pouring two small glasses of brandy, imperturbable. "In case you can't tell," he said to the tall guy, cocking his head in Stacey's direction, "this lovely young lady is not just *anybody*. And besides, my dear sainted mother, *may she rest in peace*, would spin in her grave if I failed to do right by a poor frozen creature like her." He put down the bottle and handed one glass to Stacey and raised the other in a toast. "To my late mother," he said to the tall guy, with a barely concealed conspiratorial look. "To Isabella DiNapoli!"

Stacey raised her glass and drank a little. "How about Isabella *Stone?*" she said, fixing him like a bug on a board.

He wasn't through trying to wriggle free, though; wasn't through playing the part of the late Enzo DiNapoli for the benefit of anybody who'd listen, himself included. He tossed off his brandy in one swallow and showed her his pearly white teeth. "Stone this, Stone that," he said. "See what I get for playing second fiddle my whole life long? Even my own mother can't receive her due." He did everything but hold the back of his hand to his forehead in distress. No question. The guy was a thespian, all right.

Stacey smiled softly at him, just to let him know that she was in on the joke. "Are you sure we're not talking about Mrs. Stone?"

"Mrs. Stone? I don't think so. To begin with, the guy's real name was Schwartzmann." He substituted a V for the W, pronouncing his old surname with the derision and disdain of a Nazi underling in some low-budget melodrama.

"Really?" She'd decided that the guy was harmless, kind of amusing.

"Really!" he said. "Schwartzmann!"

"That's funny," said Stacey. "To me, you look more like a Schwartz-mann than a DiNapoli."

The tall guy was finally beginning to see that Stacey had figured things out, and he shot Stone a look meant to indicate that he could produce a chain saw and a rope on short notice. It just looked silly to Stone, who was accustomed to dealing with acting of a much more professional caliber.

"I'll prove it to you," Stone said. He put down his glass, moved to the coffee table, and picked up the remote. He pointed it and froze for just a second as he caught up with the image showing on the television screen—himself, bloodied but not beaten, staggering through the jungle, handsome as ever—and skipped ahead to the final reel. Rousing music accompanied the rolling of the credits across a black screen. He pressed fast-forward and squinted as the names rolled past and froze it just in time to catch MR. STONE'S STUNT DOUBLE AND PERSONAL ASSISTANT: ENZO DINAPOLI.

"See?" he said. "See that? There I am!" He poked at the big flat screen with his finger. "Mama DiNapoli's baby boy, in his recurring role."

"Wowee," Stacey said. "'Stunt Double and Personal Assistant.' *Personal.* You weren't kidding. I'll bet you went everywhere with him."

"I did, for a great many years." He gave her his cracked smile, which was kind of like the one that Stacey had seen in the basement of the Slippery Slope but not entirely. This was the genuine article. Pure Harper Stone. "I have been, as they say, around the block a few times." He probably didn't mean it the way it sounded.

"I'll bet you have been."

"To the finest of places. In the best of company."

"I'm sure."

"We were inseparable."

"So you were up here with him for that commercial, huh?" She moved toward the couch and slowly lowered herself onto the cushions.

"I was." He set down the remote.

"Until."

Stone pulled his mouth down into a pathetic little moue, and sat down alongside her. "Yes," he said. "Until."

She was pretty certain that he was on the verge of producing tears, whether by secretly yanking out a nose hair or by contemplating his own death, but the arrival of headlights outside threw a monkey wrench into his act.

FORTY-ONE

The tall guy who owned the place, Schmidt, ducked back into the hallway toward the bathroom and flattened himself against the wall as if he were the one with something to hide. For his part, Stone just sat there looking petrified.

"My boyfriend," Stacey said, wondering whether that was today's fourth lie or whether she meant it after all. Even a little.

Stone sat back, stunned. "There's a *boyfriend?*"

"I called his house when I saw the cabin and left a message, but I had such a bad connection that I didn't think it recorded."

Stone wasn't interested. "There's a *boyfriend?*"

"Well," she said, "we're kind of—"

Before she figured out what to say—or how much Stone needed to know, if he was entitled to know anything, since the whole business had become a creepy pickup scene between her and this sixty- or seventy-something relic, a moment whose ugly weirdness she had a natural impulse to squelch as quickly as possible now that she was inside the cabin and pretty much had the goods on him—everything changed. Thanks to a single earsplitting whoop from a siren about twenty feet from the door. That and a sudden assault of colored lights through the curtains, red and yellow and blue beams spearing everything in sight. It was a barrage, like close-up fireworks, and it made everybody in the cabin wince.

"Great," said the tall man, trying to merge more tightly with the wall. "Her boyfriend's a cop."

Stone, though, recovered his composure in about a second and leapt to approach the door. The tall man watched him go, marveling at the reversal of Stone's attitude now that he'd decided he could masquerade as his own double.

The knock—three businesslike raps as hard and rhythmic as gunshots—came as Stone reached the door. He opened it up to reveal Guy standing foursquare on the porch with Chip just behind him, silhouetted against the spinning lights. Stone turned on his patented smile, letting it gleam in the light bursting from the roof of the patrol car. "The cavalry!" he said. "To the rescue! Thank God!"

Inside, Stacey stood and moved over toward the television, where they could see her.

"The cavalry," Guy said. "Right. May we come in?"

"Of course!" Then, without wasting a second, said, "Enzo Di-Napoli, at your service." He bowed and swept the door open.

Guy smiled and stepped forward. Once he had his boots over the threshold Stacey spoke up. "He's not DiNapoli," she said. "He's Harper Stone."

Stone tut-tutted. *Poor, deluded child.*

"Any money says DiNapoli's dead," she went on. "He's the one that Chip and I found, not Stone."

"This is ridiculous," Stone said. "How can I be dead?"

"He figured nobody'd look too closely. No next of kin, right?"

Chip pulled the door shut behind him and Guy stood ramrod-stiff, withholding judgment.

Stacey showed no sign of slowing down. "And the second that Harper Stone 'died,'"—she made little quotation marks in the air that Stone himself seemed not to appreciate in the least—"his career went crazy again. Off the charts."

"I can vouch for that," Chip put in. "I bought my dad a reissued DVD. The commemorative edition of *Lights Out*? Forty-five bucks on Amazon."

Guy did not seem to be impressed.

Neither did Stone. "Perhaps the cold has gotten to her brain," he suggested to the sheriff, reaching out to take her arm. She shook him off. "In the morning," he went on, flustered but persistent, "things will look very different."

"You've seen it yourself," Stacey said. "The tributes on television. The film festivals. The re-releases."

Stone could barely suppress his delight, but he did his best.

"I've seen a whole lot," Guy confessed. Then he smiled and pointed toward the television. "If you'd watch something other than your own old movies," he said to Stone, "you might have seen it, too."

Frank Schmidt peeled himself from the wall. "Hey," he said, "I wasn't watching that old crap. I was watching the Food Network."

"Try the news," said Guy. He bent for the remote, took a second to figure it out, and then found CNN. He killed the sound. Larry King was on with some politician, sitting there with his giant misshapen head and his famous suspenders and his weirdly vampiric look, but the crawl at the bottom of the screen was all about Harper Stone. How the Vermont State Police had revealed that the body in their custody was not his at all. How Stone himself was at the moment not merely a missing person but a person of interest in the death of one Enzo DiNapoli, formerly his personal assistant and stunt double.

"Oh, shit," said Harper Stone.

"That would pretty well cover it," said Guy Ramsey.

Guy turned to Stacey. "I took you seriously about those tattoos," he said. "They showed up on the medical examiner's report, all right. But when it came to identifying the body, nobody even thought they might be important. I mean, it was Harper Stone, right? Anyhow, I gave the staties a buzz and they did some snooping around. Talked with their FBI contacts. Got some questions asked in California." He pointed toward the screen. "You see how it worked out."

Suddenly, Harper Stone looked every bit his age. He slumped onto the couch, his head in his hands.

Stacey, on the other hand, was grinning like mad—at Guy, at Chip, at Larry King, at the whole wide world. "So the guy I saw in the basement at the Slippery Slope—that was DiNapoli."

"No question."

She kicked Stone's foot. "He was younger than you, right? Your stunt double?"

Stone just nodded. He was either sobbing or pretending to sob, although whether it was for what he'd done or for what was about to be done to him was anybody's guess.

Guy picked up the thread. "Ten, fifteen years younger for sure. DiNapoli and Buddy Frommer were in the Merchant Marine together."

"I knew it," said Stacey.

"Buddy came clean about that, at least."

"I think he's got a lot to come clean about."

"Me, too. We'll get there, don't worry." He looked at Stone. "That coke in the rental house—it belonged to DiNapoli, right?"

Nothing from Stone.

"So he had a little too much, is all. Went for a walk. Got himself in trouble."

Stone brightened.

"Only problem is, his snowshoes never turned up."

"What did he know from snowshoes?"

"I can't say for sure," Guy said. "But somebody knew enough to take a pair down from the wall in the rental when he headed out into that blizzard." He let the idea hang there in the air for a minute, to see if Stone would respond.

He didn't.

"The boys from Rutland cleared the snow around the body right down to the grass for twenty-five feet in every direction. The closest anybody came to finding those snowshoes is that nice new pair right on the porch out front." Guy put down the remote and stepped toward Stone, one hand behind his back in case he needed to grab his cuffs. "Do I need to restrain you, Mr. Stone, or will you come right along?"

Stone nodded, rose, and took his coat from the peg by the door, where it hung alongside Schmidt's orange storm gear and hard hat.

"You too, Mr. Schmidt. You'll need to make a statement."

The tall man shrank back into the hallway. "I didn't know the first thing about this. I thought he was Enzo. He told me his name was Enzo."

"Sure." He reached beneath his jacket and unclipped the cuffs. "There are some fellows in Rutland who'll like that story as much as I do."

"Let me get my shoes at least," Schmidt said, and Guy let him.

Stone shrugged into his coat and frowned at the television, where Larry King had given way to a scene outside the Los Angeles County Courthouse. Stone's manager, identified in big red and white text, stood before a bobbing crowd of handheld microphones. He seemed to be making a statement. There were cops around.

"I'll bet he's turned on me, too," said Stone.

Guy just shook his head, turning to watch Schmidt emerge from the bedroom with his shoes in his hand. "Somebody had to handle all that brand-new money, right? That was the point, wasn't it?"

"*New money,*" Stone spat. "It'll be years before some of those checks get cut. You have no idea."

"How much does your manager get? Ten percent? Fifteen?"

"Fifteen. And that's fifteen percent too much."

"It wasn't enough to keep him quiet."

Stone just growled, glared at the television screen, and zipped up his coat.

FORTY-TWO

Guy walked them one by one to the patrol car, and when he
had them secured in the back he went into the cabin again,
turned off the lights, lowered the thermostat, and pulled the
door shut behind him. He put his gloves on, lifted the snowshoes
from the pile of junk on the porch, and knocked the snow off of
them before walking them over to the car. Stacey and Chip stood
to the side and watched.

"Hey," Guy said when he'd popped open the trunk and the light
inside came on, "I almost forgot."

The trunks of those big Lincolns are huge, and he bent over
into it to remove Stacey's brand-new, barely used Heads. "The guys
in Rutland thought you might like to have these back."

She shrieked and ran over, grabbed them and hoisted them over
her shoulder, thinking that this was the best development of the
whole day. Or maybe the second-best. Then, her with those brand-
new Heads and Chip with her old skis, they walked down the hill
behind the patrol car.